MY
ALMOST
FLAWLESS

TOKYO
DREAM
LIFE

MY ALMOST FLAWLESS

TOKYO DREAM LIFE

RACHEL COHN

HYPERION

LOS ANGELES   NEW YORK

First Edition, December 2018
10 9 8 7 6 5 4 3 2 1
FAC-020093-18306
Printed in the United States of America

Text is set in Palatino, Andale Mono, Avenir LT Pro,
Avenir/Monotype; Neutra Text/House Industries.
Designed by Jamie Alloy

Library of Congress Cataloging-in-Publication Data
Names: Cohn, Rachel, author.
Title: My almost flawless Tokyo dream life / Rachel Cohn.
Description: First edition. • Los Angeles ; New York : Hyperion, 2018.
• Summary: On her sixteenth birthday, Elle Zoellner leaves the foster
care system to live with the father she never knew in Tokyo, Japan.
Identifiers: LCCN 2017056536 (print) • LCCN 2018001485 (ebook) •
ISBN 9781368027014 (ebook) • ISBN 9781368008396 (hardcover : alk. paper)
Subjects: • CYAC: Fathers and daughters—Fiction. • Wealth—Fiction.
• Americans—Japan—Fiction. • Racially-mixed people—Fiction. •
Family problems—Fiction. • Dating (Social customs)—Fiction. • Foster
children—Fiction. • Tokyo (Japan)—Fiction. • Japan—Fiction.
Classification: LCC PZ7.C6665 (ebook) • LCC PZ7.C6665
My 2018 (print) • DDC [Fic]—dc23
LC record available at https://lccn.loc.gov/2017056536

Reinforced binding

Visit www.hyperionteens.com

SUSTAINABLE FORESTRY INITIATIVE Certified Sourcing
www.sfiprogram.org
SFI-00993

THIS LABEL APPLIES TO TEXT STOCK

To Zenobia and McLovin

---

chapter one

Keep your head down. Stay quiet. In ten minutes, it will be over.

"EZ! EZ! EZ!" The boys at the back of the bus chanted.

My bad luck that the initials in my name—Elle Zoellner—made me too "EZ" a target for unoriginal bullies.

A sharp pencil hit my neck and then fell to the floor behind me. I heard Redmond's voice say, "Damn, I was hoping it would catch inside her spiderweb of frizz hair." Hah, the joke was on him. My hair was indeed frizzy, but it was so dirty that anything thrown into it would have no scientific option other than to slide down, the result of that one-shower-a-week rule.

Today was my sixteenth birthday. While other girls probably wished for a driver's license or a new outfit or a later curfew, all I wanted was to be clean. Sucked for me that this year's birthday fell on a Tuesday. Wednesday was shower day.

Of course Foster Home #3 parents always denied to my social worker that the shower was off-limits to me except on Wednesdays. If I had a phone, I could secretly record them talking about it, but why bother? Then I'd probably be sent to an even worse home. Foster Homes #1 (lice) and #2 (bedbugs) had been bad enough, but #3 (overlords who were mean, and liars) was the worst. I didn't want to know what could happen at #4.

The devil you know is better than the one you don't, Mom always told me. Mom was raised in foster care; she would know. She tried for better for me, and until the car crash two years ago, she'd succeeded. She had a job. We had a nice, small house. There was laughter in our lives. A cat. Then, after the car accident, the Beast moved in and took over. He wasn't someone I could see or talk to; the Beast was addiction. And thanks to that Beast, my mom was now in prison.

Was Mom keeping track of time? Did she even remember today was my (Not So) Sweet Sixteen? If I had a phone, I knew I'd see a dozen emails/texts/GIFs from Reggie, my best friend from when we were both on the swim team at the Y, wishing me a happy birthday. But he also didn't have a phone and was stranded at a boys' home across the county, another foster care victim. Not victim—he'd hate that word. *I'm a survivor*, Reggie would say. His mother had also been an addict, but she never made it to prison. She died from a fentanyl overdose. Despite my miserable situation, I was still incredibly grateful that my mother was alive. I knew how lucky we were that Mom's problem took her to jail rather than a graveyard.

"Hey, smell bomb! Turn around when you're addressed by your superiors." The latest taunt came from Jacinda Zubrowski, who sat two rows behind me on the bus and two seats behind me in homeroom, and never failed to comment on my smelly, secondhand clothes.

The poor kid sitting next to me—I didn't even know his name, he was some scrawny freshman who looked about twelve—slid closer to the window. Smart move. No reason he should be brought down with me. Then he scrunched his nose and said, on the down low, "There are showers in the gym locker room, you know." Little jerk.

I knew. I was hardly going to further expose myself— naked—in a public high school locker room. I'd rather smell bad.

"Anybody hungry for some mixed nuts?" a male voice—one of Redmond's friends—asked, and the back of the bus group laughed. What a not clever way to speculate about my heritage. My mother was part Irish, German, African American, and Native American, but the shape of my eyes and my cheekbones indicated my biological father was Japanese. I'd never met him, didn't even know his name. "Mr. Tokyo," Mom called him. He was probably married like all of Mom's other boyfriends. Married men were her primary weakness, until she was introduced to painkillers. One of those men had been driving the car when they got hit from behind on the Beltway. He died. Mom suffered severe spine injuries. That's when the Beast took over. I blamed the dead married man.

An object much larger than a pencil hit the back of my head. I wouldn't have known exactly what it was, except the next one missed my head, grazed my shoulder, and landed on my lap. A bar of soap.

A new chant erupted in the back of the bus. "Smell bomb! Smell bomb!"

Happy birthday, Elle Zoellner.

• • •

On my fourteenth birthday, right before everything went to crap, I'd celebrated the day by kicking Reggie's ass in the 50M freestyle at our YMCA swim team practice, beating him by a solid 2.5 seconds. He'd had a cold—it wasn't his best practice—but still, I'd won! We had dinner at my house after, devouring special treat steaks and mashed potatoes. Reg and Mom sang "Happy Birthday" to me over a cake from Safeway, and my sweet cat, Hufflepuff, licked the icing off my finger. It was probably my last perfect day. One of the last decent days, period.

Ten months later, only a few hours after Huff had gone missing, our neighbor delivered his dead body back to me. Mom and the Beast had settled into BFF status by then, and we were living in the grungy apartment we had to move to after Mom sold our perfectly nice little house because she lost her job and needed time to "figure out the next thing." The next thing had turned out to be selling drugs on the Internet, which brought scary strangers to our apartment on a daily basis. While I was at school one day, Mom—in a drug-hazed stupor—left the apartment door open after a sale. Hufflepuff wandered out and was hit by a car. I could barely grieve. By that time, the Beast was so thoroughly in control of Mom's life—and mine, by extension—that crying and blaming wasn't worth the effort.

It was amazing how life could go from good to fine to bad to miserable to unbearable so quickly, each transition seeming so much like the obvious next step for the circumstances that it wasn't until you reached the end of the line that you could see how thoroughly brutal the downward spiral had been. Could it get worse? Of course it could. It probably would. But I had no way out until I turned eighteen, and that was a long two years away. For now, I could only keep my head down, and try to survive. Study hard. Work my way out, and up.

The bus came to a stop. It was the best part of my day—when we reached Redmond's stop. Usually I tried to scrunch into an even smaller, unnoticeable form at the front of the bus. But today was different. Suddenly, I'd had enough of this particular devil I knew. I put my foot out into the aisle as Redmond passed by me to exit. He tripped hard, banging his head, fumbling to stand back up as the other kids on the bus howled with laughter. He was so mad that I imagined his head surrounded by fireball emojis. The slight grin I couldn't tamp down probably incited him further. Before stepping down the stairs to get off, Redmond glared at me and announced, "Go ahead and laugh, EZ. You're trash. Nobody gives a shit about you."

My heart pounded with shame. His comment burned.

Still worth it. It felt incredibly satisfying to end this bus ride with a skunk's bang. Hated, but legendary.

Sometimes when nobody gives you a birthday present, you have to give one to yourself.

• • •

Five minutes later, the bus turned onto the street where Foster Home #3 loomed. The houses here were small, single-story brick houses like the one I'd grown up in back in nearby Greenbelt, Maryland, but the street in Greenbelt was a million times nicer, with kids playing on the sidewalk, well-kept lawns, flower gardens, white picket fences, and neighbors who looked out for one another. This block felt like the horror movie version of my old neighborhood, with houses in various states of disarray, front yards filled with dirt and weeds, nasty neighbors who kept big dogs barking behind chain-link fences, and broken-down cars in the driveways. Foster Home #3's neighborhood felt like Redmond's swagger—angry and mean.

Which was probably why the fancy car parked in front of "my" house seemed like a mirage. It was a black Mercedes sedan with a white-gloved chauffeur standing outside the passenger door, seemingly waiting for someone to get out. Even weirder was the sight of Mabel Anderson, my social worker, who usually arrived for visits in a beat-up old Toyota Corolla with screechy brakes and holes in the seat covers, standing next to the chauffeur. Friday was supposed to be her visit day, not Tuesday.

The kids on the bus moved to the side with the better view, pressing their faces against the windows: Had someone won the lottery?

The bus came to a stop and the driver opened the door. I stepped down to the street, suspicious. The bus drove off. As I approached Mabel, the chauffeur opened the Mercedes's back passenger door and Masashi Araki emerged from the car. My heart dropped. It was like seeing a ghost from happier times.

Uncle Masa, as I called him, had been a friend of Mom's, before the Beast, when Mom worked at the restaurant where Uncle Masa was a regular. He used to take me swimming or ice skating, depending on the season, and always threw in a trip for pizza or ice cream after, with no worrying about how much it cost. One time I straight out asked Mom if he was my father. "Oh God, no" was all she said. A couple years ago, Uncle Masa got posted from the Japanese Embassy in Washington, DC, to Geneva, Switzerland. He sent me postcards regularly, but then Mom sold our house, leaving no forwarding address because of debt collectors, and I stopped hearing from him.

"What's going on?" I asked Mabel.

"I've brought news for you," Mabel said. "This gentleman would like to be the one to explain."

Uncle Masa approached me and bowed. That's how I knew he was real. He never hugged me when he saw me, like an American uncle would; he always bowed. "You've gotten tall!" he said, and grinned, like nothing terrible had happened since I'd last seen him. "We're the same height now."

"What the hell are you doing here?" I asked.

"There's no need to curse," said Mabel, who didn't take anyone's shit, especially mine.

Fuck her.

From his suit jacket pocket, Uncle Masa took out a blue United States of America passport wrapped in a silky white ribbon and handed it to me. "I'm here to take you to live with your father. In Tokyo, Japan. Happy birthday!"

chapter two

"You know my father?" I asked quietly, trying to hold back the rush of emotions swirling in my heart, my stomach, my brain, every cell in my body.

"I do," said Uncle Masa. "And he would very much like to know you."

"Is this a joke?"

"I wouldn't joke about a matter this serious," said Uncle Masa.

"Well, maybe you should. Because the idea of even having a father is a joke *to me*. Where has that guy been all my life and why the *fuck* would I go live with him?"

Mabel never smiled or frowned; it was like her face's only mission was just to get through the day without emotional expression. Tersely, she said, "You know the rules,

Elle. You're free to vent your anger, but I will not tolerate impolite language."

"I'm not going," I said to Mabel. "You can't make me."

"I have no intention of making you go. It's your choice," said Mabel.

I started to walk down the street, just to get away from this nonsense. Hadn't I been through enough already? But Uncle Masa hurried after me. He made it past me, turned around, and bowed again, trying to block my way. "Listen to me, Elle."

I saw the living room window blind creep open at Foster Home #3's no-hot-water-except-on-Wednesdays house. Foster Parent was clearly spying.

"Your father would be honored for you to come stay with him in Tokyo," said Uncle Masa, sounding very formal, like he was the butler for this "father" of mine.

"You've got to be kidding me. I haven't seen you since I was in middle school—and by the way, my life went to hell in that time—and now you're here with an invitation for me to live with my father, when you never even told me you *knew* my father? No way. Just, no. And . . . and . . ." I was starting to sputter. There was too much to say, to ask, to know already. "And why is he suddenly ready to be in my life . . . but can't even be bothered to show up in person?"

Reggie's dad was a military hero killed in an ambush in the Middle East when Reggie was only five. Reggie had his dad's photos, his medals, his letters. Reggie's dad was real. He existed. He loved his son, even though he left Reggie way too early. But Reggie had all the proof—and the memories. All I'd ever gotten was evasive answers about "Mr. Tokyo" from my mother, who shut down each conversation by saying the subject hurt her too much to talk about. I'd never thought of myself as a person who had a father. Girls on TV had them, not people like me. Dads: just some fantasy created by Hollywood.

Mabel caught up to us. She said, "My understanding is your father wasn't able to be part of your life in the past. Now he is."

"What's his name?" I asked.

Mabel rifled through some papers in the notebook she always carried. "Kenji Takahara." After all these years of wondering who my real father was, I couldn't believe I was finding out from a social worker of all people. There was an actual name attached to this fantasy.

"Why should I believe this Kenji Takahara guy is my father?" I asked. "I mean, *come on*. Absent biological fathers don't just drop out of the sky."

Uncle Masa looked up to the sky. I forgot how he took statements literally. His English was excellent, but it was not his native language and he often didn't get turns of phrase. "Come with me," said Uncle Masa. "I'll show you."

I let him lead me back toward the fancy car. He opened the back door, retrieved some documents from his briefcase, and handed one to me. "Here is your birth certificate. Your father's name is right there. Kenji Takahara."

There it was, a birth certificate issued by the State of Maryland, with my name and date of birth on it. Mother: Brandy Zoellner. Father: Kenji Takahara.

Uncle Masa held up more documents for me to inspect. "You see? This is your mother's signed consent form authorizing you to go live with him. This is your plane ticket."

"Wait. What? You *saw* my mom? When?"

Uncle Masa said, "I haven't seen her. I've been in touch with her through a lawyer." He bowed to Mabel. "She saw your mother to get the form signed."

Even *I* hadn't seen my mom since she'd gone to Jessup Correctional Institute three months ago. Every week Mabel gave me the option of going. Every week I declined. Not ready. Too mad. I was grateful Mom was alive, of course—but her addiction had ruined both our lives. I knew prison was difficult—how could it not be? But to see her face-to-face would require too painful an acknowledgment of how difficult my own life in foster care, without her, had also become. All Mom's fault.

I looked accusingly at Mabel. "Why didn't you tell me any of this before?"

Mabel said, "I was instructed not to, in case it didn't work out. We didn't want to give you false hope."

"I don't believe you." I wasn't sure if I was addressing Mabel, or Uncle Masa, or the whole rotten universe.

"Then you can verify it with your mother yourself," said Mabel, looking at her watch. "She's expecting you, and I assured her I would deliver you to her this time. Visiting hours today end at four p.m. If we leave right now, we'll get to Jessup in enough time."

"What if I say no?" I asked Mabel.

Mabel looked toward #3's house. The blinds closed suddenly.

The chauffeur held open the passenger door for us to get in.

Mabel confidently stepped into the car.

Go directly to Jail, do not pass Go.

chapter three

"How do you manage to make even a prison uniform look glamorous?"

I thought I'd lose it at my first sight of Mom, but even though my eyes welled, I was pleasantly surprised. When she emerged into the visiting room, she looked like my real mom, before the Beast. Sober. With color in her face again, her hair washed, and some meat on her bony hips, I remembered how beautiful my mom once was.

She wasn't allowed to give me a hug, but her big grin reached into my chest and grabbed my heart, hard.

"Jail's cheaper than rehab," she said as she sat down at the table opposite me. "I tried for the Betty Ford Clinic, you know. I hear it's real fancy there, but the judge said no." I didn't laugh. It was a good joke, but I was the one paying the price for her need for rehab. Mom said, "How you doing, kid? God, I'm happy to see you. Finally."

There was so much—too much to say. So, I kept it simple. "I'm sorry I smell bad."

"You smell like foster care. *I'm* sorry." I promised myself I wouldn't, but I could feel a sob coming on. Mom sensed it—maybe she felt the same. She reminded us both, "Zoellner women are tough."

"Because we have to be. I know. I remember." The truth was harsh, but the reminder served its purpose. I felt calmer just hearing the normalcy of her old rules. "So, apparently now is when you're going to tell me about my biological father?"

"Bingo!" said Mom, looking happy to change the subject to the one she could have brought up years ago but never did.

"Kenji Takahara? Who was he to you?"

"I'm not going to lie. I was a hot-looking thing back in my day." She smiled and checked my face to see if it was warming up. It was. She always knew how to play me. I felt the crinkle of a smile hearing Mom's boasting in fine form again. "I was nineteen and had gotten a job as a hostess at a fancy restaurant in DC. I had no polish, but I was pretty. I met him there. He was studying International Affairs or something at Georgetown University. Honestly, the best-looking guy I'd ever met, and he wore the most exquisite tailored suits he had custom-made in London when he was just a student! We fell hard for each other."

"You *loved* him?" This might be the most shocking news of all. I'd always assumed I was the product of a married-man affair, or a one-night stand, or worse.

"I was crazy for him. Had the time of my life with him."

"Why'd you never tell me any of this before?"

"I *did*. I told you it hurt too much to talk about, and I wasn't lying. Eventually, I planned to tell you. When you were eighteen and ready to take off into the world."

"That's such a selfish answer."

"You know me best, baby."

The guard next to us checked his watch, and I felt our meager time ticking away. "So what happened with you and him?"

"I got pregnant. I was thrilled. He panicked."

I couldn't believe I was finally hearing this story—in jail of all places. I was riveted and eager to hear more. "Why?"

"He was from a prominent family in Japan. They threatened to cut him off if he stayed in DC with me, or worse, married me."

"So what'd you do?"

"I'm not a total idiot. I lawyered up, as best I could.

Got a settlement from him in exchange for his freedom. His family paid for our house in Greenbelt. I owned it outright. We had fourteen good years there, right?"

"Sure. At the house you eventually sold to pay for your drug addiction."

Mom bowed her head. "I know," she said quietly. "At least it allowed me to raise you on a waitress's income."

"While you were still employed, yes." I didn't owe her any response other than brutal honesty. Zoellner women are tough, right? "So what happened to this Kenji guy?"

"He did as he was told by his family. Returned to Tokyo and opted not to be part of our lives."

" 'Opted' is a nice way of saying 'abandoned.' "

"I don't disagree. But things have changed, and the door is open for you to go to him."

"How do you even know that?"

"When I knew I was going to jail, I tracked down Masa through the Japanese Embassy in Washington and let him know the situation. He was Kenji's best friend."

Another blow. How could I ever trust "Uncle" Masa, who'd been part of my life once, yet withheld this crucial information from me? Mom saw my mad face and said, "Don't blame this on Masa. He was only ever good to us, and you know that. He made all the arrangements to take you to Japan to live with Kenji."

"Why now?"

"Because, duh, you're in foster care?"

"No, I mean if he didn't want to be a father before, why would he want to be one now?"

"I was told by Masa that the timing wasn't right before for you to be part of your father's life, but now it is."

"Why?" I asked again.

"How should I know?" Mom said, agitated. "Just be glad the opportunity exists."

"*Opportunity?* To live with a *complete stranger* on the other side of the world? What the *fuck*, Mom? What if I don't want to go?"

"Go! Living with him now is your best option." I shook my head. I still wasn't buying it. Mom added, "You being in foster care is my worst nightmare come true."

"So it's all about you?"

"It's all about *you!*" Mom said angrily. "How'd your towel work out?"

It was a bizarre question out of nowhere, but I knew exactly where she was going. Before I was officially made a ward of the State of Maryland, when I was packing my few belongings, I begged Mom to let me bring my favorite towel, a plush, expensive blue towel she'd bought for our house after a restaurant patron left her an unexpectedly big tip. Mom told me not to bother packing it, because anything nice I had would get stolen.

I glared at her, then admitted, "Foster witch-mom said

it was hers and then accused me of stealing it from her."

"I was afraid that would happen. Fuck." The towel issue seemed, by the look on Mom's face, to be the one that might finally make *her* cry. "Is that how you want to live, with people that petty?"

"I don't know what I'm supposed to want," I snapped. "Literally *everything* I know about my life has changed in the past few hours."

"Take this chance. Don't be me, Elle," Mom pleaded. With her other hand, she gestured to her prison uniform.

An announcement came over the loudspeaker that visiting hours were over.

No! We'd only gotten started on our visit! We'd barely scratched the surface of the story of her and my father. I hadn't told her anything about my own life except about my stupid fucking towel being stolen. I wanted to scream in frustration. I wanted to take my mother out of this place with me.

Mom stood up. "I hate this. I can't even hug my baby. Please tell me you'll go, Elle. Let me know so I can finally get some peace."

Just kill me now.

"I'll go," I said, only making up my mind in that instant.

Her face had a look of bittersweet relief. "Tell Kenji I hate him for getting to be the hero—and so many other things—but that you're a good girl and I'm jealous he gets to have you all to himself."

I shook my head at her but offered a small smile. "I'm not going to tell him that."

Mom smiled back and blew a weepy kiss my way as she was led away. "Happy birthday, Elle my belle. I love you."

"I love you, too, crazy lady."

Her back was to me as she walked out of the visiting room, but I could hear her laugh, and I was happy she couldn't see the tears springing from my eyes.

• • •

I found Mabel outside in the parking lot, doing paperwork on a bench, while Uncle Masa and the Mercedes idled nearby.

"So?" Mabel asked me.

I couldn't believe I was about to say this, but what else was there to do? I had a chance to meet the father I always wanted to know, to never go back to Foster Home #3, and never find out if Foster House #4 would indeed be worse than its predecessors. I said, "Let's go."

"Your foster home is on the way to the airport. The driver said we have enough time for you to stop and get your stuff."

The first lesson I'd learned in foster care was to keep whatever was most important to me with me at all times. All I really cared about were my old photos—of Mom, Reggie, Hufflepuff—and they were safely zipped away in the school binder inside the backpack I'd left sitting on the seat of the Mercedes.

"Let's not," I said. "Burn my stuff, for all I care."

chapter four

If the luxury Mercedes ride was a precursor to my future life in Japan, it was already winning over the last three months of my life.

I decided to think of this fucked-up situation as an opportunity—like my mom had said—rather than a terrifying question mark. I wasn't going to disappoint Mom and get sent back to foster care. I'd figure this Kenji guy out and be a good (enough) daughter till I finished high school and could strike out on my own.

"So how do you know this Kenji Takahara?" I asked Uncle Masa. We'd dropped Mabel back at her office and were en route to Dulles Airport, moving slowly through rush-hour DC-area traffic.

"He's not 'this' Kenji Takahara," said Uncle Masa. "He's your father."

"Right. My father." Connecting those two words—*my* and *father*—together was a lot to wrap my brain around. "How long has he been your friend?"

"He's not just my friend. He's my cousin. His father and my mother were brother and sister. So, in a way, I am almost your real uncle."

I knew Uncle Masa was trying to be nice and welcoming, but I had big trust issues with my "uncle" who'd reappeared out of nowhere and was now whisking me to a new life with a father I didn't know, in a country where I didn't speak the language. But I understood that Uncle Masa was trying to do right by me, and I needed to remember I'd always trusted him. He would be the only person I knew in my new world, and my one connection to my old one. I wanted to hear his side of the story.

"So how did you know my mom really, then?"

"I was with Kenji at the restaurant where they first met. And I stayed in touch with your mother after Kenji returned to Tokyo."

"Did he know that?"

"Yes. He encouraged it. He wanted to know about you."

"Without actually being there for me. What a guy."

Like turns of phrase, sarcasm was often lost on Uncle Masa. "Yes, he is a guy," said Uncle Masa. The mistake was funny, but I wasn't laughing. Because:

"How come he didn't want to know me himself?"

"Kenji's father oversaw the family business, and he made the decisions. He decided that Kenji should return home, finish his studies in Tokyo, and cut off contact."

So Grandpa was a dick. Strike one, Takahara family.

I said, "Kenji Takahara could have chosen otherwise."

"He was very young and it was falling on his head."

"What?" I asked, confused.

"You know, the situation was too much for him."

"You mean he was in over his head?"

Uncle Masa smiled. "Yes. You always helped me with my English, remember?"

I said, "I remember that even while you were visiting with me, I still grew up without a dad. Even if he was young and in over his head, he could have stayed."

"That is not the Japanese way, to disobey parents."

Strike two.

"So why now? Why does he want me to live with him now?"

"His father died last year. Now Kenji is the boss of the family and the family business. He makes the decisions. He had been trying to find you, but there was no record of where you'd gone."

"Mom changed her cell number and didn't leave a forwarding address for us. Because she owed so much money."

"We were fortunate that she was trying to find me while he was trying to find you."

"All these years, he could have tried harder. He's a deadbeat."

Uncle Masa searched the word *deadbeat* on his phone. "He's not a deadbeat," said Uncle Masa, frowning.

"Is he married? Does he have other children?"

"No. No."

"What does he do?"

"He's in real estate. The Takaharas are a prominent business family in Japan."

Once again on this stranger than strange birthday, I felt overwhelmed. It was hard enough to accept the fact that my father was about to exist in my life, without also trying to figure out who he was as a person, where he came from, what he did, and . . . and . . . I needed a break, to an easier topic. I stared out the window of the Mercedes at the gray skies over Maryland. "What's the weather like there?"

"Hot and humid in summer, cold in winter, beautiful cherry blossoms in spring."

"Just like here."

It would probably suck just as much.

Strike three.

chapter five

Life moves fast once you turn sixteen, I guess.

Suddenly, I had a father I'd never known about. Suddenly, I was leaving Maryland, the only place I'd ever lived. Suddenly, I was at an airport for the first time, being whisked past a long-ass security line and over to a quick and efficient security line for first- and business-class passengers, and soon enough, I was going to be on a plane for the first time. Would my seventeenth birthday ever live up to this crazy one?

Uncle Masa took me to a special lounge waiting area for "International First" customers. Already I felt like an outsider, and I was still in my own country. Everyone in the private lounge looked rich, well-dressed, and comfortable, like they belonged in this immaculate, glass-windowed oasis overlooking the planes taking off and landing, and where a buffet of *free* food was available, along with rows of Japanese and English newspapers and magazines. The majority of people in the lounge also looked and spoke Japanese. A monitor hung on the wall showed the terminal's upcoming departure times to cities like Vancouver, Paris, London, Rio de Janeiro, Beijing, and Mexico City. I'd never much imagined the world beyond Maryland, yet here all these people were, casually waiting to fling themselves to every corner of the earth, and I was about to be one of them.

An older Japanese couple sat opposite me and Uncle Masa, drinking tea. The lady kept looking at me disapprovingly, but every time I met her stare, she gazed into her teacup. She and her husband spoke to each other in Japanese—about me, I was pretty sure. I kept hearing her say the word *hafu*.

I wanted to hide my unsophisticated, never-been-on-a-plane self under a blanket while Uncle Masa sat beside me, working on his computer.

"What's *hafu*?" I whispered to Uncle Masa.

He didn't look up from his work. "I can't hear you."

I spoke louder but decided on a different question. "Can we call Kenji Takahara?"

"No. He'll be working right now. Phone calls with him are by appointment, unless you want to speak with the receptionist at his business."

"Why would I want to do that?"

"That's what I thought."

"What does he look like?" Genuine curiosity began to crowd out everything else. "Do you have a picture of him on your phone?"

"I don't."

"Can I see his online profile?"

"His security team advises him to keep a low online profile. He's not on Facebook or Instagram or any of those other platforms."

That my father had a receptionist wasn't that interesting. That he had a *security team* was mind-blowing. Who *was* this guy?

"So let's google him."

"You can try but 'Kenji Takahara' is a very common Japanese name. You probably won't see your father there."

"I'm getting the feeling you and the security team don't actually want me to see this guy."

Uncle Masa laughed and finally looked up at me. He handed me his computer. "You're welcome to try."

I googled "Kenji Takahara." As Uncle Masa had promised, there were too many hits to decipher which one was my father. I turned to the Google Images page. The screen flooded with photos of men named Kenji Takahara.

"Is he here?" I asked, turning the screen toward Uncle Masa.

He pointed to a photo of a man wearing a suit and a construction hat, cutting the ribbon at an empty lot. "That's him. The day they broke ground on the new hotel."

"I can hardly see his face."

"Then the security team is doing their job properly."

I could tell this was a Google job that would require a lot more time and energy than I had at this moment, and I wanted to take advantage of having computer access. So I gave up on "Kenji Takahara" hits and logged on to my Gmail account to send Reggie a quick email.

Dude, you're not going to believe what is happening! I am at the airport now, waiting for a flight to Japan to go live with my dad, who I just found out about. I'm so sorry there was no time to see you and say good-bye! Email me back and let me know when you can log on to the computer at the home and we will arrange a video chat. I will be in Tokyo then! Love, Elle. PS—I AM NOT JOKING! Sayonara! (Look it up.)

"Here she is," said Uncle Masa, rising from his chair as a young Japanese woman approached. She handed a file folder to him and bowed.

Uncle Masa told me, "Elle, this is Emiko Katsura. She's your father's assistant in Tokyo, and she came to help me with all the arrangements. She'll be flying back with us."

Emiko Katsura bowed to me as well. Was I supposed to bow back? Set a date for royal tea? She appeared to be in her early thirties, and she wore a simple navy pencil skirt that showcased her trim figure, with a crisp white oxford blouse, cherry-red stiletto-heeled shoes, a gold charm bracelet on her wrist, and diamond stud earrings. I didn't know how anyone could walk in heels that high. She had long, smooth ombré hair—raven-colored at the top, honey-colored toward the bottom, with full strands of chestnut-colored highlights. She looked like that Beyoncé song—"I Woke Up Like This."

"Do you keep pictures in your locket charms?" I asked, fixated on her pretty gold bracelet. If I had one of those, I'd put pictures of Mom and Reggie and Hufflepuff in it, and anyone who wanted to steal the bracelet from me would literally have to fight me to get it off my wrist.

"I do." Emiko opened it to show me a small bridal photo of herself and a Japanese groom who looked about the same age as Emiko but boring and not nearly as stylish. "My wedding day."

"Nice," I said.

"We've been doing some shopping. This is for you."

I returned Uncle Masa's computer to him and took the bag Emiko handed me. It was a Louis Vuitton duffel that I was pretty sure was not a fake, based on its smooth feel and expensive-store smell. Emiko and Uncle Masa started speaking to each other in Japanese while I rifled through the bag. It was filled with new clothes—shirts, sweaters, jeans, socks, and underwear, all in my size. I lifted a James Perse T-shirt and held it against my face. I had no idea a T-shirt could feel so soft, like a kitten rubbing my cheek. I placed the T-shirt back in the duffel bag and saw that there was also a Louis Vuitton toiletry bag with a hairbrush, toothpaste, and even feminine products. This duffel bag was better than a birthday present. It was like a windfall for the past three Christmases combined. Guilty much, Kenji Takahara?

"I hope these items will be acceptable to you for the time being," Emiko said. "I didn't know your style, so I tried to make safe choices."

"They're okay," I said, trying to sound unaffected. "Thanks." My style was Old Navy clearance rack, but I didn't want her to think I could be impressed so easily with luxurious new clothes. "Is there a bathroom where I can change?"

Emiko said, "The front desk attendant can direct you. They have spa facilities if you want to relax while we wait. We've still got another hour to go before boarding."

"Does the spa have a shower with warm water?" I asked, joking.

"Of course," said Emiko.

SHUT! UP!

"I can take a shower in there, for real?"

"Yes. The attendant will give you a robe and slippers and any other items you require."

"I might need a massage," I said, joking again.

Emiko said, "The attendant can book that for you."

"Wait, seriously?" I'd never get a massage. Strangers touching me? No way. But the fact that a massage was even a real option here and not a joke was ridiculous. We were in *an airport*.

Uncle Masa said, "My credit card is on file at the front. Get whatever service you'd like. Emiko and I will be working in the bar area meanwhile. You can find us there when you are finished."

• • •

New plan. I was going to live at the International First Lounge.

The shower "stall" in the spa area was a spacious, white-tiled, private room with a showerhead centered over the ceiling, so it felt like bathing under a glorious rainfall—not too hard, not too soft, but just right. The lather of the sweetest-smelling lavender body soap felt like a purification, wiping Foster Home #3 clean off my skin. Argan oil shampoo and conditioner left my hair feeling light, smooth, and born-again clean.

After the shower, I chose from a whole rack of white towels. (Who could ever need that many towels for one shower?) The towel was unbelievably soft and plush; I wanted to sleep in it. Since I couldn't take the shower stall with me, I stuffed the wet towel into the Louis Vuitton duffel bag in case the towels were terrible in Tokyo. Then I thought better of it and placed a second dry towel in my bag, in case someone stole the first one.

I felt like a different person when I emerged from the spa back into the main area of the lounge. Clean, refreshed, whole. A not-sorry towel thief. I saw Emiko and Uncle Masa in the bar area at the far end of the lounge, but they were deep in work, so I checked out the rest of the lounge. There were free soda and tea machines, a virtual reality game pod, a snack buffet, massage chairs. While I didn't want strange human hands touching me, a chair would be more than excellent. I plopped down into the recliner chair, turned it on, and whoa, the vibrations seemed to be soothing my every muscle, and then . . .

"Time to board." It was Emiko standing over me. I must have fallen asleep on Heaven Chair. "Would you like something to read?" She showed me a stack of fashion and business magazines.

"I don't think I'm really interested in Harvard Business School alumni magazine, but thanks. Did you go there?"

I was being sarcastic when I asked but she answered me sincerely. "I got my MBA there." She went to Harvard

Business School and now she was just an assistant? That seemed crazy. Maybe she wasn't that smart.

"Do we have to go?" I asked. "I like it right here. This might actually be the best place I've ever been."

Uncle Masa said, "That's because you've never been to Tokyo." He held out his hand to help me out of the chair. I reluctantly stood up. At least I'd always have the towel(s) to remember this divine sanctuary called the International First Lounge.

• • •

Our group was called to board first. I tried to act casual as I followed Uncle Masa and Emiko to the plane, like I knew what I was doing and did it all the time, but I was actually shaking with fear. That ginormous *thing* on the tarmac I could see through the window was supposed to carry people across an entire ocean? Did. Not. Seem. Possible.

The Japanese air hostess waiting at the entrance looked like a Disney princess wearing an ANA Airways uniform suit, with a tiny figure, smooth black hair, impeccable makeup, and a glittering smile. She addressed Emiko and Uncle Masa in Japanese when they boarded, but somehow knew to speak English to me. "Your seat is across the aisle from theirs," she said, gesturing down the path ahead. As Emiko and Uncle Masa placed their briefcases in an overhead bin across the aisle, on my side, I walked past some bedlike private pods, walked by the bathroom, and saw the rows of seats, three on the right side, three in the middle, and another three on the left. I looked down at my ticket, trying to figure out which seat was mine, but then I felt a tap on my shoulder. I turned around. "Back this way," the air hostess said to me. I followed her back to the private pods at the front, where the seats seemed like mansions in comparison to the cramped dormitory rooms in the rear of the plane. "Two-A, for you."

"Seriously? For me?"

She pointed at my ticket. "First class. Yes."

Okay, lady, whatever you say. I'd no idea that first-class tickets meant seats that were entirely different from the other cabins on the plane. As the next boarding group filed past the first-class cabin, I settled into my solo seat. It pulled out into a bed, was partitioned for privacy, had its own TV screen that seemed to show every movie I'd ever wanted to see, and—WHAT?—my own pair of noise-canceling headphones to use during the flight. *For free!*

Uncle Masa sat in the middle pod across the aisle from me, and Emiko sat next to him in an identical pod. Row two was only four seats across, but in economy, as they called it, the rows had nine seats in the same amount of space.

"I don't mind switching back there if someone needs this seat," I said to Uncle Masa. It seemed unfair that most passengers would be crowded together on such a long flight while we had the sweet life up front. I was excited (if terrified) just to be on a plane. I'd be fine in ecomomy. Seemed more like where I belonged. (So long as I could take those headphones with me.)

"Don't be silly," said Uncle Masa. "That's your seat."

Phew. I hadn't really wanted to change seats.

I'd only just figured out how to plug the headphones into the sound system when a male voice came through them announcing that boarding was complete and it was time to take off. He said it in English first, then Japanese. As the plane pulled back from the gate, a safety video played on my TV monitor, showing how to use the oxygen mask and how to find the inflatable raft under my seat.

What?!?! Why did I need to know that information?

Why would we need inflatable rafts for a jetliner that was supposed to be flying OVER the ocean, not in it?

My heart pounded hard as the captain came over the intercom, asking the crew to take their seats for takeoff. I braced my hands against the sides of my seat and felt beads of sweat on my brow. This was it. No turning back now. The plane moved forward, going faster and faster, and then, like it was nothing, the huge behemoth lifted off from the ground and we were in the air.

Holy freaking amazing! I'd never been so simultaneously scared and awed in my whole life. I wanted to throw up and cheer at the same time.

I looked out the window at the DC area below, getting farther and farther away from view. *I'll miss you, stupid only home that I've ever known. Take good care of Mom and Reggie for me. Pray I don't fuck this up.*

chapter six

Here.

We were being driven to Kenji Takahara's home from Narita International Airport, in a chauffeured car service again. I'd slept almost the entire flight, to my wanted-to-watch-all-movies regret, so I was wide awake now and full of questions. The car drove on the left side of the road, which made me feel dizzy every time I looked up to see oncoming traffic on my right. I needed the distraction of conversation, and I had about five million questions. So far Uncle Masa and Emiko hadn't answered the most obvious one, so I finally asked it. "Why didn't Kenji Takahara come to greet us at the airport?"

"It's four in the morning," said Emiko. It was also, I'd learned, with the time difference, two days in the future from when we'd left.

Uncle Masa said, "Narita is too long a car ride there and back. He doesn't come to you. You go to him."

"Seems kind of rude," I muttered.

"Not rude. Practical," said Uncle Masa.

"I have lots of questions for him about living here."

Emiko said, "I've prepared an orientation notebook for you. Would you like to see it now?"

"Sure," I mumbled. I already knew Uncle Masa and Emiko could answer lots of my questions. But I wanted Kenji Takahara to do it.

Uncle Masa turned on the light in the backseat as Emiko took a white three-ring binder from her briefcase and handed it to me. Inside the clear sleeve on the front cover was a piece of paper that said ELLE ZOELLNER: JAPAN. I opened the notebook. It was divided into sections with tabs labeled "Etiquette," "Tak-Luxxe," "ICS," "Dining," and "Transportation." Each section was filled with brochures and printouts. Each printout page was laminated, and each brochure was tucked into a plastic sleeve attached to the ring binder. Indestructible. It would probably take me a week to read through the whole thing. "*Dining?* I need etiquette orientation for *that?*"

Uncle Masa said, "In Japan, there are different customs for eating. Like how you hold your chopsticks, how you drink your soup."

"I think I know how to eat," I said. (I didn't actually know how to use chopsticks.)

"There's a lot more about Japanese customs in the binder than just dining," said Emiko. "For instance, did you know it's considered unlucky to use the number four in Japan?"

"What does *four* have to do with anything? How random."

Emiko said, "Our rules may seem odd to you, but etiquette is one of the defining principles of Japanese life. Japanese pride themselves on a very ordered way of living. Observing etiquette rules makes that possible."

I started to read one of the printouts in the Etiquette section. "I can't wear my own shoes in the house? In my own home or anyone else's?"

Emiko said, "It's the custom to take your shoes off in the *genkan* of a home—which is like an American entryway or foyer. You leave your shoes in the genkan but not facing the door."

"What am I supposed to wear if I have to take my shoes off? What if my feet are cold?" I'd barely gotten off the plane, and I was already starting to panic that I could never acclimate to this new world.

Emiko said, "Wear socks, or there will be slippers available in the genkan."

"What if there's not?"

Emiko said, "There *always* are. That's the Japanese way."

"But if the home has a tatami floor, then only wear socks, not slippers," said Uncle Masa.

I didn't even know what a tatami floor was. I turned the page in the notebook. There was an illustrated brochure all about bowing. It went on for three pages! How could there be that much to know about bowing? "I don't understand bowing," I said, hoping the implication was clear: *and I don't feel like reading a boring brochure about it.*

"As a foreigner, you won't be expected to," said Uncle Masa. "Just remember it is customary to bow as a greeting or to say thank you."

"And don't hug Japanese people," Emiko said. "Such an unfortunate American habit."

Like I'd want to hug her and all her stupid rules that were on the verge of giving me an anxiety attack.

Maybe Uncle Masa saw the I'm-about-to-full-on-freak-out expression on my face, because he told Emiko, "We should tell her about her new school."

I couldn't believe I hadn't thought about that yet. "How can I go to school here? I don't speak Japanese."

Uncle Masa said, "Your classes will be in English. It's an international school, for students from all over the world. Expats, like you."

"What's an expat?"

"It's short for 'expatriate.' People from one country who live in another."

Emiko said, "Look at the divider labeled 'ICS.'" I turned to the ICS section in the notebook, where there was a brochure that said "International Collegiate School Tokyo" and had a picture of uniform-wearing private school kids standing on a green lawn quad in front of a flagpole with the Japanese flag at the top and various other country flags like USA and the UK below it. "It's an old ICS brochure I found at the Washington embassy. ICS has locations all over the world where expats send their children, for an American-style education."

"In case I'm not smart enough for a Japanese education?"

This lady had no sense of sarcasm. "Japanese education is very rigorous. You would find it very challenging."

Okay, now she was just insulting me. "I don't like school uniforms," I shot back, looking at a photo in the brochure of private school kids wearing matching clothes. "I don't want to wear one."

Emiko said, "In Japan, you are a reflection of your family. To refuse a uniform would make your respected father look bad. You must follow the rules. That's why he wanted you to have this notebook. So you don't offend anyone by mistake."

Didn't they realize this whole conversation was offensive—to *me*? What did this Kenji Takahara guy want—a daughter or an obedient geisha?

More of the city was coming into view, so I chose to focus on that rather than Emiko's Etiquette Edicts. There were tall, narrow apartment buildings and short, wide apartment buildings. Warehouses. Bright lights toward the city center. It was hard to believe so many buildings could exist in such a condensed space. The car drove on an elevated highway that seemed to go on forever, and as the buildings got taller and taller, the sky burst with city lights. The landscape felt very alive. Sleepy Washington, DC, had no super-tall buildings, so I'd never seen a skyscraper before except on television, but here, they towered across the skyline in abundance, a vertical city shining in the dark early morning. Many of the skyscrapers had electronic advertisements displayed on their facades, with sweet young Japanese women demonstrating cosmetic products. We passed a building ad with a Japanese businessman who had a huge white cat's face poking out from behind his head, and a slogan written in Japanese that looked very happy based on the pink-and-red coloring of the letters.

Hold up. Excuse me?

"What's that ad for?" I asked.

Uncle Masa said, "It's a political ad. That man is running for parliament."

"Why the cat?" I approved, obviously, but it made no sense.

Emiko said, "Cats are revered in Japan. You will see many shops with cat figurines on display. They're called *maneki-neko*, or 'beckoning cats.' They're considered good luck."

I didn't like all their rules, but a country that revered cats had potential.

The car exited off the elevated highway and down into the city streets, filled with vehicles and people on bikes, and lots of pedestrians on the sidewalks, despite it being before dawn. I saw no houses, only tall apartment buildings and skyscrapers. "Where does Kenji Takahara live?"

"See the tab labeled 'Tak-Luxxe,'" said Emiko. God forbid she just tell me.

I opened the notebook to a travel brochure printed in English, for a luxury hotel/residential suite establishment called Tak-Luxxe, which occupied the upper floors of a fifty-five-story skyscraper building named Harmony Tower, in a Tokyo neighborhood called Minato. The brochure boasted that Tak-Luxxe was an Asian boutique hotel luxury brand in high demand by the world's most discriminating travelers, and it had pictures of posh hotel suites, a sky deck pool and garden, and restaurants like a sushi bar, patisserie, champagne bar, and Japanese steakhouse. "This is nice," I said after glancing through the brochure. "But what's it got to do with where I'll live?"

Uncle Masa said, "It *is* where you'll live."

"In a *hotel*?" Had I been scammed? I *knew* this was too good to be true. I wasn't a total bumpkin. I'd heard about trafficking, where young girls were taken from their homes and forced to become prostitutes or slave factory workers. "Real homes don't come with travel brochures. Have I been *kidnapped*?"

Uncle Masa laughed, but I didn't see what was so funny.

Emiko said, "If 'kidnapped' means living in one of the most exclusive buildings in Tokyo, then perhaps. I wish *I* could be kidnapped there."

Uncle Masa said, "Tak-Luxxe is the Takahara family business. They have several luxury hotels throughout Asia. Tak-Luxxe Tokyo is their flagtrain."

It took a second, but I figured it out. "Do you mean 'flagship'?"

"Yes, flagship! Your father lives in a penthouse apartment on the forty-ninth floor."

I processed those words: *penthouse apartment on the forty-ninth floor.* I'd never been in a building so tall, much less lived in one. What if I had vertigo? On the other hand,

I'd just survived a fourteen-hour flight and time-traveled to two days in the future, so maybe I had superpowers I'd not been aware of previously.

The car pulled into a discreet driveway on a side-street entrance for the looming Harmony Tower, which I recognized from the brochure. Bellhops wearing Tak-Luxxe uniforms immediately opened the passenger doors. We stepped out of the car, and Emiko and Uncle Masa exchanged a series of bows with the bellhops, who then unloaded the luggage and placed the items on brass rolling carts.

"My turn to go home," said Emiko. "I'll see you again later today. Call me if you need anything in the meantime." She handed me her business card and then bowed to me.

I didn't bother to bow back. Or hug. Especially not hug. "I hope you'll have more brochures next time!" I chirped.

"I will!" She stepped back inside the chauffeured car and was whisked away.

I looked up. And up up up, trying to discern how high forty-nine floors was.

My father was somewhere up there in the clouds.

chapter seven

"Why different elevators? And how many lobbies does this one building have?" I was starting to feel like a three-year-old with infinite *Why* questions.

Uncle Masa and I stood in a small lobby where there was one set of elevators marked for floors forty-four through forty-nine that required a swipe card to call, and opposite, another set of elevators marked for floors thirty-six through forty-three, with a sign in Japanese and English that said the Tak-Luxxe Hotel lobby was on the thirty-sixth floor.

Uncle Masa said, "Tak-Luxxe isn't just a hotel; it also has apartments. Your father lives in the penthouse apartment." Uncle Masa swiped his card on the set of elevators for floors forty-four through forty-nine. "This is the private set of elevators for Tak-Luxxe residents. The other side has public elevators for guests, to take them to the Tak-Luxxe hotel lobby."

More rules. Of course.

"Then what happens on floors one through thirty-five, and where's their lobby?"

"Those Harmony Tower floors are office space owned by Takahara Industries. It's a separate lobby, very big. The entrance is on the main street, not the Tak-Luxxe side street."

That people even *lived* in a building so complicated blew my mind. There was nothing about this partitioned skyscraper that screamed HOME to me.

Some Japanese businessmen entered the elevator lobby and pressed the button for the Tak-Luxxe hotel floors. They bowed to Uncle Masa, and he bowed to them. They got into their elevator, and we got into ours.

"Seriously, I don't get the bowing," I said after the elevator door closed. "Why's it such a big deal?"

"Bowing shows respect. How far a person bows is also an indicator of the status of the person being bowed to."

"Status like how?"

"Age, economic status, job rank."

"How could someone possibly know enough about a person they just met to then know how to bow to them?"

"It's something you learn from the time you're a child. It becomes a basic instinct."

"Seems complicated."

"You're right, it's complicated," said Uncle Masa. "But you won't be expected to bow as Japanese do it. You are gaijin."

"What's gaijin?"

"Foreigner."

"But my father is Japanese."

"I know that. You know that. But Japanese people will see you and know you are not pure Japanese. Right or wrong, that's how it is here."

WTF!? What an unwelcome surprise pop of information to the newcomer: You can assume you will be judged here by what your face tells the natives about your race—that you're not really one of them.

Did I make a huge mistake coming here?

My sense of panic built as the elevator raced upward. I was about to meet Kenji Takahara. My FATHER. Did I look okay? What if he didn't like me? What if he turned out to be an asshole? What if I bowed wrong or said something stupid?

The elevator door opened.

I gulped.

No turning back now.

We stepped into a simple, elegant hallway with wood-paneled walls, a large orchid arrangement on a centerpiece marble table, and tasteful walnut-colored carpeting with no blemishes, not even the smallest stain or tear. This place was so clean. Like, lick-the-walls-and-floors immaculate. I'd grown up in a barely tidy house where the cheap Ikea rugs and furniture were covered in cat hair, and then I'd gone on to foster homes that were sparsely furnished and "clean" only when social workers' visits came due. I already felt like I didn't belong here, and I'd yet to see my new residence.

Gaijin.

I could barely breathe I was so nervous.

Uncle Masa walked toward a doorway where there was a peaceful Buddha sculpture surrounded by small, jade plants in ceramic vases at the corner wall. He started to place his swipe card against the door's console, but I put my hand up to stop him. "Wait."

He pulled his hand back. "Why? Your father is waiting in there for you."

"I know." I took a deep breath. I wanted to throw up. This wasn't a fever dream. "Do I look all right?"

"You look fine." That wasn't the answer I wanted. I meant, *Do I look like trash?* Maybe he read something in my face because Uncle Masa added, "You look strong, like always."

Uncle Masa swiped his passkey card against the console. The door clicked, unlocked. He pushed the door open, and we stepped inside the penthouse apartment into the marble-floored genkan that Emiko had told me about. On the other side of it I could see a posh living room with beautiful Oriental vases filled with tall flower arrangements and sleek, minimal furniture that looked like it should be on the cover of an interior design magazine. The apartment didn't look lived-in at all. I was afraid to step farther inside. I'd probably tarnish or break anything I touched.

"Take your shoes off," Uncle Masa reminded me as he took off his own and stepped into a pair of slippers neatly lined at the wall.

What did these people have against shoes? The soft slippers were the most comfortable things I'd ever had on my feet, and suddenly the No Shoes rule made total sense; their slippers were so much better than shoes. Uncle Masa beckoned me inside the living room. I cautiously stepped in and noticed a man was standing in the corner.

His posture was perfectly straight, his hands clasped behind his back, and he looked like he was surveying his domain, a lord on a forty-ninth-floor perch. Uncle Masa said something in Japanese, and Kenji Takahara turned around.

He was shorter than I expected, not much taller than me, but I had my mom's 5'7" height. I could see his chest moving up and down. He was *real*. Maybe he was as nervous as I was? Despite how cool and collected he looked in his elegant dark gray suit that was clearly custom fit to his exact size, with a black silk tie and silver cuff links, he looked as awkward as I felt.

"Hi," I said.

"Welcome," Kenji Takahara said. He bowed to me.

I didn't bow back for fear of doing it wrong, and because I didn't want to lose sight of his face. I couldn't believe how much he looked like me: the shape of his eyes and mouth, the high cheekbones. I wondered if he was thinking the same thing? No DNA test needed here. The evidence was staring us both in the face.

He didn't look like a dad. He looked like a wealthy businessman, but a ridiculously handsome one who could have been advertising men's hair gels on an electronic billboard splashed across a Tokyo skyscraper.

Then he killed me—by smiling. I could see how my mother fell for him in an instant. All he'd probably had to do was smile at her.

Someone should say something, but I had no words and he didn't seem to, either. I thought my anxious stomach would be my problem in this situation. It was so much worse. I burst into tears. I'd managed to suppress full-on sobbing when visiting Mom *in jail*. So why did the cryfest have to come forth now, at the worst time, in a sleek sky castle where it seemed like I was meeting a king? I wanted to be casual but aloof, not some transparent emo teenager.

Kenji Takahara looked at Uncle Masa like, *What am I supposed to do?*

Uncle Masa patted my back comfortingly. "It's a lot to take in," he reassured me. With Uncle Masa by my side, I managed to get my tears under control and regain my composure, even though I wanted to grab the perfectly cornered hanky from Kenji Takahara's chest pocket and blow my snot all over it. Uncle Masa spoke to my father in Japanese.

"I'm so glad to meet you, Elle," Kenji Takahara finally said as I wiped the embarrassing tears from my face. His English was more accented than Uncle Masa's but confident at the same time. "I've wanted to know you for so long. You're beautiful like your mother."

Great, a fresh new round of tears.

Seriously.

Was. He. Trying. To. Kill. Me.

I had frizzy black hair and too-thick eyebrows and I bit my fingernails when I was nervous. Nobody had ever called me beautiful. This handsome father person thingie must be looking at my expensive new clothes but not really seeing me.

"You must be tired," said Kenji Takahara.

Not really. I wanted to sit him down right now and hear how this king had gotten my mom under his spell and conjured me before the magic died and no one lived happily ever after.

"I'm fine," I said. Was our communication already like this? How are you? *Fine.* How was school? *Fine.* How's it feel having your life radically change on your birthday with no warning whatsoever? *Fine.*

"Excellent. Masa will show you the apartment. I'm sure it will be nicer than what I was told you're used to. I have to leave for work."

Wait, what? I didn't grow up in a fancy place like this, but it wasn't the ghetto, either. *Don't act like you know me, Lord Skyscraper.*

"You're going to work at five in the morning?" I asked.

"There are dignitaries just arrived from Dubai who have leased five office floors in Harmony Tower. They will expect me to greet them personally."

But you couldn't be bothered to greet your own long-lost daughter at the airport?

Kenji Takahara bowed at a depth that gave me no indication of what he considered my rank to be. And he left. Just like that.

What was with him flying me all this way to be with him, then bailing on me? "He's *rude*," I said to Uncle Masa as soon as the penthouse door had closed. "He basically said I grew up in a dump. How would he know? *He was never there.*"

"He's not rude," said Uncle Masa. "Intense personal situations are difficult for anyone. Especially him." That made sense. Kenji Takahara had quickly left my pregnant mother when his family ordered him to go home. What a big baby. "You'll get used to him."

Great. Another parental relationship where I was supposed to be the mature one. "I'm not supposed to get used to him. He's supposed to get used to *me.*"

I walked—more like, skulked—around the living room and its adjoining dining area, inspecting, disappointed that I had to discover the place for myself without my father showing me around. Sofa, glass coffee table, side armchairs, TV and TV console table, vases with plants, museum-quality Japanese art on one wall, smoothest-wood-ever dining table and six chairs around it: check. Photos, books, mess, anything that indicated an individual with interests occupied the space: nonexistent.

"He's like instant ramen," I pronounced.

"What do you mean?" Uncle Masa asked.

"One minute to cook, one minute to experience, and then it's gone."

"He's nothing like ramen."

"I'm hungry." Saying the word *ramen* had reminded

my stomach that I hadn't eaten in forever. I walked into the kitchen. Spotless, empty counters. Stainless steel appliances including a fancy stove and oven that looked like they had never been used. I opened the fridge. It had basic condiments, some soymilk, and a takeout salad in a container. That was it.

Uncle Masa followed me into the kitchen and saw the contents of the fridge. "I'll advise Emiko to go grocery shopping. Make a list of what you like, and she'll take care of it. Could I interest you in some genuine Japanese ramen now?"

"I'm so hungry, you could offer me instant ramen and I'd probably eat it straight from the packet without bothering to add hot water."

"You will have the real thing, if you can wait about ten minutes."

"Hah! No ramen place will be open this early in the morning." Restaurants in Maryland closed by ten at night and didn't open again until eleven in the morning, as any latchkey kid with a single-mom waitress knew.

"This is Tokyo. Awake and working all the time, like New York."

"Ten minutes? Come on."

"Have you heard of room service? Watch!" He walked over to a house phone on the kitchen wall, picked up the receiver, and spoke to some unknown person on the other end in Japanese. In the middle of the conversation, he stopped and asked me, "Are you one of those Americans who needs a dark sugar water with her meal?"

I remembered that's what Uncle Masa used to call Coke—"dark sugar water." "I sure am!" I also remembered that the only time I ever got Cokes as a kid had been when Uncle Masa took me out to eat.

Once his call finished, Uncle Masa gestured for me to join him in the hallway. "Come with me. I'll show you the rest of the apartment while we wait for the food." We walked down a hallway off the genkan that led to three different bedrooms—a large master bedroom, a small bedroom that was furnished as an office, and finally, a medium-size bedroom that had a twin bed, a dresser and chest, and a desk with a chair. The furnishings were top quality and the room was immaculately clean but otherwise unremarkable. I'd never actually stayed in a hotel, but I'd seen them on TV, and this apartment seemed like one, just with more space and nicer furnishings. We stood in the hallway as Uncle Masa gestured to the room with the twin bed. "This will be your room. We left it plain so you could decorate as you wish."

I ventured inside, and he turned on the light. The bedroom was small but had everything I could need. I opened the closet. It was filled with clothes—jeans and skirts on hangers, blouses with tags still on them, and hanging shelves filled with meticulously folded shirts and sweaters. A cubby had boxes of shoes—sneakers, sandals, slippers. "Did someone leave their clothes here?" I asked Uncle Masa.

"Those items are all for you. Emiko can return whatever you don't like or exchange anything that doesn't fit." My head was about to explode. Was this for real? Then he added, "And there's a new iPhone in the desk drawer for you."

"Are you *serious*?" I ran to the desk and opened the drawer. Indeed, there was a new iPhone in it, still in the box. I picked it up and kissed it. "Thank you, thank you, thank you."

"I think Emiko took care of all the items you'll need to start your new life here, but let her know if there's anything she forgot."

She forgot to tell me that my father was apparently going to make up for *all* the birthdays he'd missed in one fell swoop.

Uncle Masa wasn't kidding about ten minutes for food delivery. In what felt like exactly-to-the-second that period of time, the doorbell rang. A uniformed Tak-Luxxe waiter did the bowing game with Uncle Masa at the front door and then wheeled in a cart with bowls that had silver tops on them and two Cokes in glass bottles. Uncle Masa told him, "You can leave the food here. We will set up the food ourselves." He and the waiter then exchanged some words in Japanese. When they were finished, the waiter bowed at me and said, very proudly I thought, "Have a nice day!" before bowing to Uncle Masa and then leaving.

Uncle Masa put place mats on the dining table as I brought the food over. I lifted the silver top from my soup bowl. The scent of the steaming broth was exquisite. The bowl teemed with thick, fresh noodles, tender meat, a soft-boiled egg and green onion garnishes floating at the top.

We sat down and clinked Coke bottles. *"Kanpai,"* said Uncle Masa.

"What's that mean?"

"Cheers."

I took my first spoonfuls. Cheers was right. "OH MY GOD!" I exclaimed.

Uncle Masa misinterpreted my outburst. "Too spicy for you?"

"Hardly! I can't believe how flavorful the broth is. And these noodles are so fresh. I've never had noodles so good." I gulped down more broth followed by noodles, then added, "Honestly, it never occurred to me that there was a better level of ramen than instant, but this is probably the best meal I've ever had in my life, except for that time when Coach Vickers took the Y swim team for Ledo Pizza after we won our district championship."

He laughed. "Do you still swim? I remember how good you were."

"I stopped after Mom's accident, and then we moved. It got too hard to keep up with practices."

"You'll swim again here," he said confidently, which would have excited me, except I was cracking up watching Uncle Masa eat his own noodles. This elegant man wearing an immaculate, finely tailored business suit, who had lived all over the world and spoke several languages, was *inhaling* his noodles like a three-year-old, leaving spots of broth all over the bottom part of his face.

"You slurp your noodles up! I can't believe it!"

"This is considered the proper way to eat noodles in Japan. Also fine to do this. . . ." He lifted his large bowl and drank directly from it. I gasped. Then he placed his bowl back on the place mat and darted his chopsticks into his meat so that the chopsticks stood directly up. "But not fine to do that. Also, when there is a small bowl of soy sauce placed by your food, dip your food into it. Don't pour it over the food."

"You're joking. Right?"

"No."

I was starting to appreciate that Emiko had made me

an Etiquette Notebook. Apparently, I had a lot of reading to do. And eating. Lots more eating.

I said, "I wonder if the cafeteria food at my new school will be this good."

"You'll find out tomorrow."

This shocker was almost as disconcerting as my new father walking out on me less than five minutes after meeting me. "No way, I can't start school so soon. Don't I need time to, like, adjust to the new place?"

"That kind of laziness is not the Japanese way. You will have today to rest, and tomorrow you can get right back to schoolwork."

We'd left Washington on Tuesday night. The flight had been fourteen hours. But tomorrow was Friday! So confusing. And how stupid to start a new school at the end of the week. But maybe it was for the better. I didn't need extra days to worry about how I'd fit in (or not) at yet another new school. Better to just dive in. "Will Kenji Takahara take me there?"

"I doubt it. He'll be working and your new school is about an hour away."

He'd rejected me before I was even born, so I didn't know why Kenji Takahara not making time to take me to a foreign school on my first day felt like a fresh burn—harsher even than sending me to a school with such a

62

long commute. "Will you take me?" I asked Uncle Masa hopefully.

"Sorry, no. I'm returning to Geneva early tomorrow morning. I'll be back in a few weeks to check on you, and we can always FaceTime."

A few weeks? I'd only just reconnected with Uncle Masa, and now I was losing him again. My heart felt stomped all over. "So I'm on my own?"

"Yes."

Just like back home.

Aside from the fact that here no one was going to forbid me from taking a shower every day, had anything really changed for the better?

I looked out over the Tokyo skyline beckoning from my forty-ninth floor. Even from that height, I could see people through the windows of the other nearby tall residential and office buildings, going about the start of their days. In this city of millions and millions, including my newfound father, I was still all alone. Just like back in my old world. There was odd comfort in realizing that.

I survived there. I could figure out how to survive here.

chapter eight

I had always loved *reading* about orphans. Being one was awful. Every day in foster care, I'd prayed for some magical escape from that life, never thinking it would actually happen. But it did.

The next morning, I woke up in my new bedroom in a forty-ninth floor penthouse overlooking Tokyo. I took a long, hot shower in my own private bathroom, and that was already magic enough. I was about to go to my new school. I'd checked out the pictures in the International College School (ICS) Tokyo brochure that Emiko had put into my binder. It wasn't quite Hogwarts. It looked more like Disneyland. I was starting the day jet-lagged and disoriented, still wondering how the hell did I end up *here*, but I didn't care. I was too grateful to be awake inside this dream.

Oh, and sayonara, Maryland public school bus from hell. Now my mode of transportation was a chauffeured Bentley to my first day of school in Tokyo, Japan. I would be sharing a morning car ride with a girl named Akemi Kinoshita who lived with her parents on the forty-sixth floor of Tak-Luxxe. Their idea of a "car pool" was the slickest and most regal car I'd ever seen, with no less than a black-suit–wearing chauffeur at the helm. Reggie would pass out when I told about the Bentley. Probably I'd leave out the part about how my own new father couldn't be bothered to escort me to the driveway for my first day of my new school, but my car-pool mate's father was there to greet me.

"You are Elle?" an old man standing outside the Bentley asked me. I nodded. "I am Akemi's father. I hope you will help her with her English." His own English was halting and heavily accented. I looked inside the vehicle, where a girl who looked about my age was seated. The man who'd greeted me as her father looked old enough to be her great-grandfather. He wore an elegant business suit, but his face was wrinkled and his posture hunched.

"I'll try!" I said. "And thank you for the ride share."

"You're welcome. Have a good day." He bowed to me and left, as the chauffeur held the passenger-side door open for me. I stepped into the back seat of the Bentley.

"*Konichiwa,*" I said to the private school girl sitting

next to me. *Hello* was one of the few Japanese words I'd learned so far. The rear interior of the car was more like a luxury pod, lined with leather, including on the ceiling of the car. My car-pool mate's seatback had a folding table with a tablet rising up from it, and she was watching an anime movie on that tablet.

"Hey." Akemi (pronounced *Ah-kay-mee*—I thought it was one of the most beautiful names I'd ever heard) didn't seem too interested in me; her attention was focused on her movie. Emiko had told me that Akemi was a sophomore, but she barely looked old enough for middle school with her hair tied back in a bow, and pastel *kawaii* "cute style" ribbons and lace bedazzling her school uniform and backpack.

I hoped Akemi wasn't one of those supposedly innocent girls who the minute she was removed from her family's sight let her hair loose, removed layers of clothing to show off a banging bod, and became a wild party girl. Or maybe that wouldn't be so bad. Wild party–girl Akemi might be a lot more fun than drive-to-school girl Akemi, who hardly had two words to say.

If Akemi's English wasn't very good, her collection of one-word responses didn't give me much indication how to help her.

Me: "Akemi, how do you like ICS-Tokyo?"

Akemi: "Fine."

Me: "What's your favorite class?"

Akemi: "Art."

Me: "What do you like about art?"

Akemi: "Blue."

Me: "Have you always lived in Tokyo?"

Akemi: "No."

Me: "These school uniforms actually don't suck. I didn't expect that."

Akemi: "Sure."

I wasn't kidding about the school uniforms. I'd never thought I'd want to wear one, but these designs were fun. Pleated, forest-green-and-navy-blue plaid skirts that were knee length but slit on the sides, with black safety pin latches instead of buckles holding together the slits, and white oxford shirts that had *ICS-Tokyo* spelled out in green-and-gold along the arms. The skirts could be worn with matching navy-blue knee-high stockings or leggings, and the oxford shirts had navy-blue cashmere not-ugly-at-all vests to wear over them when the weather was cold. The best part were the shoes: either saddle shoes or combat-style lace-up boots. I'd chosen the boots for my first day.

Akemi pulled out a Japanese fashion magazine from her backpack, opened it to a particular page, and then handed the magazine to me. The photo spread featured a teenage girl named Imogen Kato. Her name was proclaimed in a bright font in English, but the rest of the article was in Japanese, so it wasn't like I learned much about her, other than she had a half-Japanese face like mine, crazy hair colors, and an incredible array of clothes options in her bedroom closet. Akemi said, "Her mother designed the ICS uniforms."

Akemi said it like Imogen Kato's mother was some big deal, so I asked, "Who's her mom?"

"Shar Kato."

"No way! Shar Kato designed these uniforms?" Why would a world-famous fashion designer with a global empire bother to design school uniforms?

Akemi said, "Shar Kato went to ICS. She always tries to support the school. Now her daughter, Imogen, goes there, too."

Whoa. Was I going to school in Tokyo or Hollywood?

"Is Imogen Kato nice?" I asked her.

Akemi shrugged. "Imogen is a junior. I don't have classes with her. She's one of the popular girls. They don't talk to me."

"Oh." Got it. Understood. Been there. "How long have you gone to ICS-Tokyo?"

"Since we moved to Tak-Luxxe last year. Before, we lived in Osaka and I went to Japanese school. My father wanted me to learn better English when we came to Tokyo, so he chose ICS-Tokyo."

"Your English sounds pretty good to me." She spoke

cautiously and with an accent, but she didn't sound like she struggled with the language.

"Thank you. I am comfortable with speaking, but English grammar and reading are hard for me."

"I'll try to figure out a way to help you with that. Do you like ICS?"

"I prefer Japanese school. They are not all about popularity and sports, like an American school."

Suddenly, I had a flash of inspiration. Konichiwa! I was starting a new school in a new country on a totally new continent. Thousands of miles and a whole ocean away from where I came from. No one here knew my social rank back home. I could be someone new here. Clean slate. Fresh start.

Akemi said, "Maybe Imogen will like you. She's hafu like you."

"What's hafu?" I felt like I kept hearing that word since my journey to Japan, but always whispered, like it was a bad word or something.

"Half Japanese, half something else. Imogen is only hafu in junior class. But now you, too." There were plenty of multi-racial kids at the schools I'd gone to in Maryland, so I thought it weird that Akemi felt the need to point out that I was one of only two in my new class. I wondered if this was a particularly Japanese distinction to make.

"Is the workload hard at this school?" I asked.

"*Neko no te mo karitai,*" Akemi said.

"What's that mean?"

"It means 'borrowing the cat's paws.' Like, you are so busy all the time, you would even borrow your cat's paws to get some help. That's what the homework at ICS is like."

"Neko no te mo karitai," I repeated. Cool phrase. "You're the cat's meow," I told Akemi.

She scrunched her face, confused. "I don't understand."

"It means, 'you're awesome.'" Her face brightened into a big smile. "Maybe we could exchange Japanese and English sayings?" I suggested. "Help each other learn the funny things in each other's languages, not just the basic words."

"*Â, yokatta,*" she said. Now I scrunched my face in confusion. "It means, 'Oh, good!'"

"Â, yokatta," I repeated. "It's on."

"It's on," she repeated in an American accent. She yawned. "I usually nap on the way to school. Excuse me if I close my eyes for the rest of the trip?"

"Go for it," I said.

"Go for it," she repeated, again in an upbeat American accent. Then Akemi hit STOP on her movie and closed her eyes for the rest of the journey.

The distance to school was significant, about twenty miles from the Minato district of central Tokyo out into the suburbs, if suburbs could be considered more tall apartment buildings, more industrial buildings, and less skyscrapers. As the car traveled west (according to the GPS on my new iPhone), I started to appreciate the vastness of Tokyo. It seemed more like a collection of small cities than one giant city.

Living in a penthouse in the sky was cool, but I enjoyed my first opportunity to see beyond the Tokyo skyline. Here at ground level, I cracked my passenger window for fresh air, which I couldn't do on the forty-ninth floor, and observed the streets where people hurried by foot to their destinations. I loved that there were cat symbols everywhere: feline figurines in window storefronts, cat posters, and cat ads. Even the construction signs were cats—pink-and-white Hello Kitty figures hanging off barriers, to keep pedestrians from stumbling into holes in the road. I hurt from missing my old cat, Hufflepuff. HuffleFurface would have felt right at home here.

It turned out Uncle Masa was right. With traffic, the commute to ICS took nearly an hour. My pulse skipped in excitement as the Bentley entered the school grounds through a wrought-iron gate. OMFG! I'd seen photos of the school online, but they didn't do justice to how big and beautiful the campus was. The grounds were expansive and luxurious, lush and green. The stone building at the forefront of the campus looked like it belonged on an old, storied British university campus. At the high schools I'd gone to in Maryland, there was always a modern, behemoth central building that had been expanded with unattractive additions to accommodate student over-enrollment. They all had crowded and decaying classrooms, smelly and gross bathrooms, and a football field. That was it. Already ICS-Tokyo felt magical to me.

I gently nudged Akemi. She woke up, saw where we were, and then rolled her eyes. "*Chikusho,*" she mumbled.

"What's that mean?"

"Fuck," she whispered.

Already I liked my new neighbor and car-pool mate.

A long car-pool line of cars waited to let out students in an orderly fashion, consisting of the soccer mom minivans I'd been expecting, but also more than a few luxury SUVs—Mercedes, BMW, Lexus. I felt like Rory Gilmore when she first went to posh Chilton, coming from a background that in no way mirrored this level of privilege. I'd always been a good student, at least before my life went to hell, so maybe ICS-Tokyo could be my launching pad to Yale, like Chilton was for Rory. An orphan can dream, right? *Work hard, Elle Zoellner,* I told myself. *Take advantage of this opportunity. You landing here was no less than a miracle. Don't screw it up.*

The Bentley pulled into the passenger exit lane, and I didn't wait for the chauffeur to get out and open the door for me. I wanted to run, leap, and fly across ICS's sweet green lawn. I started to open my door, but Akemi said, "Wait for the driver. It's a rule."

New Elle didn't care about this old rule. I opened my door anyway and instantly, something slammed into it so hard I let out a little yelp, thinking I'd broken the door. I got out and saw a guy my age on the ground. He must have been running along the curb because I hadn't seen him before I opened the door. He looked like a Japanese character from the anime movie Akemi had been watching earlier, with a messy mop of black hair that had thick strands of icy-blue streaks and dark brown eyes that scowled at me.

"Watch where you're going," he fumed. Once he stood up, he paused long enough to check me out, and his face turned weirdly red. "Great, now I'm late. Maybe don't try to kill me next time you're in the car-pool lane." He scraped the gravel off his knees, slammed my passenger door closed, and ran off toward the pool area in the distance. (This school had a pool! Did I have time to check it out before the first bell? Wait, did they even have bells here?)

"Nice to meet you too, asshole," I murmured.

The chauffeur opened the other passenger door for Akemi to get out. "Don't worry about him," she told me. "That's Ryuu Kimura. No one likes him anymore."

chapter nine

I sat in the office of Chloe Lehrer, the dean of the Upper
School, waiting to meet with her. The grounds of the
school might have been lush and manicured, but her office
drowned under a refreshing chaos of books, paperwork,
and folders, which looked familiar to me from many visits in school administrators' offices when starting new
schools. On the dean's walls, there were framed under-
graduate and master's degrees in education, and framed
photos and commendations from the dean's previous gigs
at ICS-Hong Kong, Miss Porter's School in Connecticut,
and the Swiss International Scientific School Dubai. Her
desk was decorated with framed photos from her college
days at Harvard.

"Hello and welcome, Elle." I turned around and

saw an older, late-thirtysomething version of the young woman whose college pictures I'd just been inspecting— red-haired, ivory-skinned, stern teacher face. "Nice to meet you."

"Nice to meet you, too, Ms. Lehrer."

"Call me Chloe. We go by first names here."

"Okay . . . *Chloe*," I said reluctantly. Back in Maryland I was pretty sure I'd get detention for calling a school administrator by her first name.

Chloe sat down and glanced through my file. "I've looked through your record. Your standardized test scores are top five percentile across the board. Honors everything. You had good grades back in Maryland, until last year. What happened?"

"Life got a little crazy," I said, defensive. I'd been through enough of these interrogations every time I started a new school, and I didn't feel like telling the stupid story all over again.

"I see you moved schools a few times."

"Like I said, crazy." I saw a letter from my social worker back in Maryland in the file, so I knew this Chloe person must have known why I'd come to Tokyo. What was I supposed to say? *And now Mom is in jail and my absent father magically appeared out of nowhere, so hopefully my good grades can resume?*

"I'm guessing you just need some time and consistency in your education to get back on track. You'll have to work hard to catch up. Are you up for that?"

"Totally," I said, like a confident Rory.

"That's what I like to hear." Chloe turned around from her desk to unlock a file cabinet below her wall of fancy university degrees. She extracted a brand-new MacBook still sealed in its original box and handed it to me. "Here's your computer for school."

"For serious?" Who just *gave* a new student a brand-new MacBook?

"It's included in the cost of tuition." Merry Christmas, Happy Hanukkah, and Best Kwanzaa ever to you, Elle Zoellner. "Any questions for me so far?"

"Can anybody use the pool here?" I asked, balancing the precious Macbook box carefully across my knees.

"The pool is for the whole student body. Of course you can use it." She smiled but I felt like an idiot for having asked. "Your social worker in Maryland wrote to let me know you're an excellent swimmer, so I've assigned you to swimming for your morning fitness class."

"Thanks. That sounds great." I tried to sound casual, like getting to use a pool every morning was something that happened to me all the time. In the world of NEVER.

"Are you interested in joining the swim team? Most students here participate in school sports."

I shrugged. "I guess." The idea was exciting but intimidating. I hadn't swum competitively since the Beast entered my life and I dropped out of the YMCA swim team.

A teenage girl barged into Chloe's office without knocking. She held out her MacBook. "It's broken. I need a new one."

"What happened?" asked Chloe.

"The boys were being assholes, standing up and rocking the boat in the Chidorigafuchi moat on the class trip to the Imperial Palace yesterday."

"You shouldn't have brought your laptop on the boat."

"But I *did* because I have so much *damn* homework."

"Please don't curse, Imogen," Chloe said.

Chikusho, I thought. This was the famous Imogen Kato, right here! She saw me and glanced down at the magazine I'd been looking at while waiting for my meeting with Chloe, open to the photo spread—of her. God, how embarrassing. I closed the magazine abruptly. It was definitely the same girl, although now her hair was platinum blond with dark roots instead of a mixture of auburn with honey and green apple–colored streaks. Beneath her plaid uniform skirt, she wore deep purple-and-blue-and-silver leggings that had prints of galloping gray unicorns, and over her blouse was a worn-out, oversize, cream-colored cardigan sweater with the belt tied to the side instead of center. Apparently, the uniform dress code was not that strict at this school.

She looked down at the magazine I'd just shut. "How *meta*," she moaned. I had no idea what she meant. But she smiled at me and said, "Hi, I'm . . . guess who? Imogen Kato." Then she returned her gaze to Chloe and said, "Sorry. The boys' *darn* fooling around caused me to drop my computer in the water and now all my data is lost."

Chloe said, "I'll have the IT department work on retrieving your data. Meanwhile . . ."

The dean pulled another brand-new MacBook from her file cabinet and handed it to Imogen as if she was giving her a sandwich to replace the one her dog had eaten, and not a thousand-dollar-plus machine the likes of which I never dreamed I'd own for myself.

"*Go zai mas,*" Imogen said. Besides *konichiwa* and *sayonara*—"hello" and "good-bye"—I'd also learned that *arigatogozaimashita* was "thank you" in Japanese but often got slang-ified to what sounded like go zai mas in casual conversation when people spoke quickly. That was pretty much the extent of my Japanese language knowledge so far, and I wouldn't learn much more here—classes at this international school were taught in English.

Chloe said, "Elle, Imogen has been assigned as your orientation buddy. You'll shadow Imogen today before starting your regular schedule next week."

Imogen returned to Chloe's office door and held it open for me. "Let's go, rookie." She didn't sound like having me as her charge for the day was the worst chore ever. I thanked Chloe, then stood up and walked out of the office with Imogen, following her outside the administration building. "We'll start with a quick tour of the grounds. Not all the school tour guides are as popular as me, so consider yourself lucky."

I said, "I'm pretty awesome, so consider *your*self lucky."

Excuse me, private school girl Elle, who are you now? I had no idea where that confidence came from. Was there something in the water in Japan giving me new superpowers?

Imogen laughed. "You're spunky. I like you."

"I like your sweater," I said. The sweater was so not posh. It looked lived in and loved.

"It's so Lebowski, right?" Imogen said. I nodded, even though I had no idea what she meant. "I stole it from my father." We walked along a path lined with green bushes and fresh flowers. "So, what's your deal here? Mom's Japanese and Dad's American, and she finally wore him down to get a job here so she could return to the civilized world of Tokyo?"

"Hardly. I've always lived with my mom. She's American. But she . . ." I paused, deciding whether I was ready to tell this magazine girl that my mother was in jail.

I wasn't. "She was having some problems, so I came to live with my Japanese father here."

"What's he like?"

"I don't know really. I only met him yesterday. Before I came to Tokyo, I'd never been farther from Maryland than a sixth-grade class trip to Williamsburg, Virginia."

It was hard to imagine how far I was from Maryland now. Not just in distance, but already in experience.

Imogen laughed. She paused, expecting me to say more. When I didn't, she said, "Are you fucking serious?"

"I'm fucking serious. Last week, I didn't even know who my father was."

"Whoa," said Imogen, sounding as impressed as she was shocked. "Well, if you ever feel like elaborating on that story, I'd love to hear it. Meanwhile, you saved the first part of my day."

"How'd I do that?"

"Being your guide got me out of stupid yoga class."

"You have yoga class here?"

"I signed up for morning phys ed yoga because I thought it would be extra sleep time, but they actually expect us to do balancing and standing and really fucking hard inversion poses. There's barely a second for *savasana* before it's time to hit the showers and go to the next class. *Namaste*, bitches!"

Imogen might as well have been speaking in Japanese for all that I understood her. As she walked us across an outdoor path between buildings, it seemed like all the students who passed us treated her reverently, calling out, "Hey, Imogen!" and gushing over her new hair color and funky accessories, or getting out of her way entirely. She had a cheerful greeting for each and every one of them; no wonder she was so popular.

I said, "You have an American accent. Did you live there?"

"Nah. The fam stayed in San Fran for a few months when my dad was doing an art installation project down in Silicon Valley, but otherwise I've always lived in London, where my mum's originally from, or here in the past few years, cuz my dad prefers Japan to Eurocentric absolutism."

Right. Whatever that meant. "Where'd your American accent come from, then?"

"It's a common international school affliction. A lot of non-American kids have American accents here. Your accent becomes fluid when you're surrounded by people from all over. Like, I have more of a British accent when I'm talking to Mum, and I speak to my dad in Japanese, but he teases me that my accent sounds Australian. When I'm at school, I sound American."

"Have you always spoken Japanese?" I wondered if she'd learned it after she'd moved to Tokyo from London, and how hard it was.

"*Mochiron!*"

"Huh?"

"Of course."

Classes had started, so we were the only people roaming the grounds besides a few latecomers I noticed dashing into buildings. I was still wrapping my mind around the concept of a school that felt like a lush, remote countryside resort but was located in the middle of a huge city—and the fact that I was an actual student here. I feared the instant we walked into a classroom with students, I would immediately be ratted out as "smell bomb," even though I'd taken a long shower earlier in the morning and used perfumed lotion all over my body right after. I smelled like a freaking gardenia-scented angel.

We reached a silver, three-story building that was shaped in curves and reflected the sun. The sunlight made the UPPER SCHOOL gray lettering on the awning appear yellow and sparkly. "This building looks more like a modern art museum than a school building," I said.

"I know! When ICS-Tokyo got too big, they had to build a separate structure for the Upper School. The board tried to get Frank Gehry to design it, but they were only able to get some knockoff instead."

"Uh-huh," I said knowingly. Was Frank Gehry a famous spaceship designer? Because the building looked like it could lift off from the ground and fly up into space.

Imogen said, "Most Upper School students take phys ed in the morning, so we'll be able to check out the classrooms." We walked into the building, which looked like a regular school hall with classrooms and lockers on either side, except everything was shiny, new, and immaculate. Imogen opened the door to the first empty classroom. "This is the technology and robotics lab."

The classroom had a ceiling-mounted projector facing toward a full screen on one end of the room. On the other end was a whiteboard taking up the entire wall, with mathematical equations written all over it. Lining the remaining walls were cabinets labeled with supplies like routers, motherboards, memory cards, and graphic cards. There was a large table in the middle of the room, with chairs surrounding it, creating a communal feel. The empty wall spaces were covered with posters of robots and communication devices and photos of students with their lab projects.

"This is amazing!" I exclaimed. "Have you built a robot here?"

"I'm not a tech person. Big yawn. Are you into art and music?"

"Theoretically, but I suck at both."

"Great, then we can skip those rooms. They're so sincere it makes me sick."

She led me out of the classroom and down the hall. At the end, we reached a library, visible through long, clear windows. "I can't take you in because I'm on two-week probation for too much loud talking in there, but the first floor has private study rooms, the second floor is all the books no one reads, and the third floor has the Japan Center, which has pretty much everything you'd want to know about Japan. And a nauseatingly eager staff of librarians to help you with any research projects."

We returned outside, where we walked past a football field. Imogen said, "This field's for American football, soccer, and Aussie-rules 'footy.' The South Australian kind of footy, not that Indian rugby knockoff the Sydney and Queensland people play."

"Obviously," I said. My know-nothing brain was starting to hurt. It had no idea it knew so little until this walk with Imogen Kato.

A running track rimmed the football field, where students ran and hurdled, advised by a teacher on the sidelines.

"Faster!"

"Higher!"

"Two seconds off from yesterday! I *know* you can do better."

"That teacher seems intense," I said.

"He's a trainer, not a schoolteacher."

"There's an on-site trainer here?"

"Trainers plural. Those track and field bozos asked for a triathlon trainer. Big babies."

Two girls our age ran off the track and came up to us, breathless. One was Indian, with long black hair streaked with red and pulled up in a messy bun, and the other was a black girl whose hair was braided into beaded cornrows. They had perfect complexions. I swear, a zit spontaneously broke out on my face from just admiring their pretty, smooth ones. Imogen told me, "Elle, meet the Ex-Brats, Jhanvi Kapoor and Ntombi Amathila. Besties, this is my new charge, Elle Zoellner."

"Hey," both girls said.

I paused before answering, half expecting them to lob an insult my way just as a rite of passage to the new girl. When none came, I said, "Hey," back. To show what an amazing conversationalist I was . . . not.

Jhanvi, the Indian girl, asked Imogen, "Did you do the Latin homework?"

"*Sane quidem,*" said Imogen, pronounced sah-nei kwee-dem.

"What's that mean?" Ntombi asked.

"No doubt," said Imogen. To my confused face, she added, "In Latin."

"Can I copy your answers before fifth period?" asked Jhanvi.

"Of course," said Imogen. "I'll leave my homework in your locker."

Jhanvi said, "Thanks. I was up all night studying for my calculus exam, so I never got around to it."

A whistle sounded behind them and then the coach yelled at them. "Hey, Jhanvi and Ntombi! This is a class, not social hour. Back to work."

Both girls rolled their eyes, said good-bye to us, and returned to the track.

Imogen told me, "You'll meet lots of teachers and staff and students today. But really, the Ex-Brats are the only people who matter."

Her haughty confidence was equally frightening and inspiring.

"The Ex-Brats? That's what you call . . . your group?" What word did the cool kids use here for *clique* or *gang* or *popular crowd*? Was there a Latin word for it?

"Yeah. My mom went to this school when she was my age. Her father was a diplomat at the UK Embassy in Tokyo. 'Ex-Brats' was what he used to teasingly call

Mom's friends at ICS-Tokyo. So I adopted the expression for mine here."

"Clever."

"Aren't I?"

We reached the other side of the campus and went into the Athletic Building. Classes were going on inside the rooms, so we peeked through the windows in the doors. All the schools I'd gone to in Maryland had one central gymnasium, and that was it for indoor fitness areas. ICS-Tokyo had dedicated yoga, Pilates, dance, and martial arts studios; a fully equipped gym with weights, treadmills, stationary bikes, a basketball court, and a wrestling room. We came out on the other side of the building, where there were eight tennis courts, with middle school boys playing on one court and girls on the other. Several of the girls sitting inside the fence close to our walking path waved at us. "Hi, Imogen!" they called out.

"Hello, my young flock," she said, and bowed to them. They bowed in return.

Our walk finally led to my personal Holy Grail. The pool. I already knew I a little bit liked ICS-Tokyo. Now I *loved* it. The pool was a twenty-five-meter competitive swimming pool with ten lanes and glistening water. The familiar old smell of chlorine was intoxicating. Most of the swimmers were congregated in front of a teacher at the pool's ledge, instructing them in doing leg lifts with foam noodles. A lone dude swimmer on the outermost lane practiced his butterfly stroke, looking powerful and confident.

I wanted to jump in that pool so badly and hide from these worldly strangers who had been everywhere and knew everything while I knew nothing. "I thought there would be more Japanese students here," I admitted. The student faces I'd seen so far at ICS-Tokyo did not reflect the school's host country.

Imogen laughed. "Hah! 'Pure' Japanese parents usually only send their children to 'pure' Japanese schools."

"But you're Japanese." I was so confused.

"My dad's Japanese but my mom's British. I'm hafu, not pure. Trust me, if there's Japanese students here, either they're hafu, or if they're 'pure' Japanese, then they go to ICS because their parents were brought up abroad and they're more open-minded about an international education. Or their parents are crazy rich and want their kids to learn English." That explained Akemi. Imogen paused, and then her naughty eyes lit up, and she conspiratorially leaned in closer to me. "Or they go here cuz their dads are yakked and think ICS is more prestigious."

Honestly, I'd gotten more of an education about Japan in one hour with Imogen than I'd gotten in a whole binder put together by Emiko, the Harvard Business School graduate. I couldn't wait to find out the answer to my next question. "What's 'yakked'?"

"*Yakuza.*"

"What's a yakuza?"

"Not *what*. *Who*. Gangsters with rich lives and nice offices." I chuckled. Imogen really was *high-lar-ious*. Then she said, "Not kidding. Yakked like that guy's dad." Imogen pointed to the lone dude swimming butterfly at the far end of the pool. When he came up for air, I saw it was Ryuu Kimura, the guy I'd accidentally tripped in the car drop-off line earlier.

"He's a really good swimmer," I observed.

"Don't bother with that guy. He's *uzai*."

"What's uzai?" I wondered if it meant *gangster's-strong-son-with-amazing-biceps*.

"Gloomy. Annoying. Ryuu used to date my best friend, Arabella Acosta. Arabella was so destroyed after he broke up with her that she went home to Bolivia to recover. I don't know what she ever saw in that moody loser. He's been iced out by the Ex-Brats ever since Arabella left."

"He does seem intense," I said, remembering his scowl at the car-pool line and observing his purposeful stroke in the pool now.

"Ryuu's probably a sociopath. Time and future disturbing news headlines will tell."

chapter ten

Sane quidem it was a surprise that Imogen's nemesis was also her science lab partner.

"Not my choice, of course," said Imogen as we went into her second-period class, AP Environmental Science. "We're not allowed to pick our lab partners because it gets too, like, political."

"Can you ask to switch?" I said. I eyeballed Ryuu Kimura sitting alone at their lab table, which had a bench that seated two people. I couldn't imagine sharing a small lab partner bench every day for a whole semester with someone I despised.

Imogen said, "He's actually a brain and a really good lab partner, so we have a truce in the classroom. It's business. And my business is getting an A in this class, and that's more likely to happen with him as a lab partner."

"Got it." I appreciated her logic. I used to get teased in Maryland for taking school too seriously. Here, it seemed like a student could be proud of working hard.

We reached their lab table, and Imogen placed a folding chair at the side of it and sat herself down on it. To Ryuu she said, "Lab partner, meet Elle. She's my charge. Elle will be taking my regular seat next to you today, so try not to fart or anything while she's there."

Ryuu said, "I had a bean burrito for breakfast. We'll see what happens." He looked down at the small space between us on the bench and then his eyes met mine. "Good luck."

His eyes were so brown and his lashes so black and thick, his mop of black-and-blue-streaked hair was still wet, and he smelled so much like chlorine, I almost wanted to swoon. I could see why Arabella's heart was broken when this moody but gorgeous boy dumped her.

The teacher approached our table, a tall, blond-haired, skinny dude who looked fresh off an Iowa cornfield. "I hear you're Elle?" he asked me, extending his hand to mine to shake. "I'm Jim and I teach Upper School science. I've been told you're not in this class on your regular schedule, but I will see you starting next week for fifth-period Marine Science. You're going to love it! We're studying the mating habits of the humpback whale. Things get pretty frisky in those GoPro videos we watch!"

I could feel a horrendous blush cover my face. I didn't want to hear about humping and whales and mating when Ryuu Kimura sat right next to me.

"Great," I murmured, with no enthusiasm.

Jim handed me a piece of paper. "Here's our AP Environmental Science syllabus if you want to see what we're doing in this class and try to get into it next semester. Welcome to ICS-Tokyo!" Jim then returned to the front of the room to begin the lesson.

Ryuu told me, "We're working on our climatogram biomes today. It's cool, you'll like it." Why was he suddenly being nice to me after practically chewing me out this morning in the car-pool drop-off line?

"Don't flirt with her," Imogen warned Ryuu. (He was *flirting* with me?) "Elle is my personal charge, so *back off.*"

"I never backed *on*," he answered, but not angrily, just matter-of-factly. Imogen didn't seem to get under his skin at all. He moved his rear end closer to where Imogen sat at the side of the table, and he let one rip in her direction.

The fart was disgusting, but I couldn't help laughing.

"You're the worst," Imogen told him.

"Go zai mas," Ryuu said.

Jim silenced the classroom to begin class. As he started

to lecture, I looked at my own class schedule for the first time, which Chloe Lehrer had given me earlier that morning. I had Swimming for Personal Fitness class, then Algebra 2 with Trigonometry, Spanish (which I'd taken back in Maryland), Marine Science, English 11, a study hall period, and Visual Arts. My schedule had no advanced placement classes on it. Imogen's classes were almost all AP classes. I knew I'd been given an easier class load to help me acclimate to my new country, but I didn't want to be in the slower classes forever. I was going to work my ass off here.

Then I glanced down at the AP Environmental Science syllabus and almost immediately scaled back my competitive ambitions. The amount of work required in this class was huge! It also might have been written in Latin or Japanese for all that I understood half the words used in it. My eyes circled the room, inspecting all the students. Nobody seemed bored or distracted on their phones. They seemed to be dutifully paying attention, like they were actually interested in what Jim was saying. The energy was completely different from any classroom I'd experienced in Maryland.

Class was only five minutes in, and already I felt tired. How could I ever catch up here? Was I overwhelmed or was it jet lag or both?

My mind felt fogged, and my body heavy and exhausted. I let my eyes close for a moment's relief but almost immediately felt myself listing to the side. I shook myself awake, but I couldn't fight the fatigue onslaught.

Within minutes, I fell asleep on Ryuu Kimura's shoulder.

chapter eleven

"I am *not* joking!" Imogen exclaimed to the Ex-Brats during lunch. "Sweet Elle fell asleep *directly* on Ryuu Kimura!"

Jhanvi and Ntombi could not stop laughing. I didn't know if their laughter was because they pitied me or just thought the situation was genuinely funny. I did not think it was funny. I could not be more embarrassed.

"What did he do?" Jhanvi asked.

"He just let her sleep!" said Imogen. "She was probably out for ten minutes before Jim came over and gently tapped her awake."

"Why didn't *you* wake her?" Ntombi asked Imogen. (Exactly! I thought.)

Imogen said, "She looked so cute and content, I

couldn't. Also, I loved watching Ryuu squirm, trying to figure out what to do."

"I'm so mortified," I said.

"Don't be," said Imogen. "Everyone here is jet-lagged at school at some point. People fall asleep at their desks all the time."

"Just not usually on Ryuu Kimura's shoulder," said Jhanvi, still laughing as Ntombi made a *yuck* face.

What I found funny was that I was sitting at the popular girls' regular table on the outdoor patio like it was no big deal and happened all the time. By virtue of being Imogen's charge, New Elle was insta-popular, and when I really thought about it, that kind of made up for falling asleep on Ryuu Kimura's shoulder.

Ntombi, who'd only been half-paying attention to Imogen's story while she texted on her phone, suddenly squealed. "Luke's parents are coming to Tokyo this weekend, and he convinced them to bring him along!" Her wrists were covered in bangle bracelets, and between those and the beads at the ends of her cornrowed hair, every time she moved, there was a subtle chorus of mesmerizing clicking.

Imogen told me, "Ntombi's mom is Namibian ambassador to Japan, but she used to be ambassador to Korea. Ntombi's boyfriend, Luke, goes to ICS-Seoul. Ntombi used to go there till last year." She turned to Ntombi. "Are you gonna be one of those girls who forgets her friends when her boyfriend's in town?"

"I sure am," said Ntombi, smiling and returning to her texting.

"We have a field hockey game this weekend against the British International School," Jhanvi reminded her. "You're not going to miss that, right?"

Ntombi shrugged. "Might!"

"Not cool," said Jhanvi.

"You're the one who cares about field hockey, not me," Ntombi told her.

Jhanvi said, "Ugh, it's São Paolo all over again. We were on track to win the championship until our team captain started dating some minor league soccer star."

"Was São Paulo totally boy crazy?" I asked Jhanvi.

Jhanvi's face looked confused. "São Paulo's a place, not a person."

"Right," I said, like, *I knew that.* "When'd you live there?"

"Before Lisbon but after Beirut."

"Wow, you've lived in a lot of places! Are your parents in the military?"

Jhanvi scoffed but I couldn't imagine why anybody would be offended by the suggestion that their parents served in the armed forces; seemed like an honorable job to me. "Hardly. My dad's an engineer. He doesn't enlist.

Major companies enlist *him*. He builds skyscrapers. Once a new one is finished, we move on to the next city. But I don't care when the new Tokyo building is finished, I'm *staying* here. Tokyo is the best."

"You can live at my house," Imogen told her.

"Thanks, *Joushi*," Jhanvi said. "I love you so much, even if you refuse to play on the field hockey team."

Imogen said, "My weekends are saved for my karate trainer. Field hockey sticks are too primal for me."

Ntombi said, "Joushi should have taken Arabella's place on the team when she returned to Bolivia. We need her aggression."

"Who's Joushi?" I asked, looking around to see if someone new had joined our table.

Ntombi didn't look up from her texting, but she pointed at Imogen and said, "It means *boss* in Japanese."

"Where are *you* from?" Jhanvi asked me.

"Washington, DC," I said, which sounded worldlier than Maryland.

"Most boring city in the world," said Jhanvi. "But the best American high school field hockey teams are from Maryland." I should have just said I was from Maryland.

"Did you go to ICS-Washington?" Ntombi asked.

I shook my head.

Jhanvi asked, "Sidwell? Georgetown Day? Holton

Arms? I have a field hockey friend from São Paolo who transferred there."

If they had verifiable friends at those schools, I wasn't going to lie about the school I'd gone to. I said, "I went to Temple Park . . . Prep School." So maybe I fudged Temple Park High School a little to sound fancier than it was.

"Never heard of it. What brought you here?" Jhanvi asked.

"I came to live with my father. He owns this place here called Tak-Luxxe."

Finally . . . finally . . . it was like I'd said something right. There was a look on their faces, like I was one of them. "Not too shabby," said Jhanvi. "My father says it's one of the best-constructed new buildings in Tokyo."

"I've eaten at one of the restaurants at Tak-Luxxe," said Ntombi. "The views up there are sick."

Imogen said, "We could probably throw amazing parties at Tak-Luxxe. I'm taking a vote to bring Elle into the Ex-Brats. All in favor say aye." Neither Ntombi nor Jhanvi answered. "The motion passes! Let's eat."

Not surprisingly, given every other facility I'd seen at ICS-Tokyo so far, the cafeteria was more like a nice restaurant buffet. No sloppy joes and lukewarm Tater Tots here. Instead, there were buffet trays filled with delicious and healthy offerings like chicken, fish, tofu, vegetables, with a full salad bar, and an espresso machine. My lunch today was my new favorite: a bowl of hot ramen. Not as good as from Tak-Luxxe room service, but still damn fine. I dug into my ramen so my mouth would be too full to showcase my lack of worldliness, even if I was Tak-Luxxe's newest resident, which apparently was an impressive status.

The Ex-Brat girls all had identical takeout containers—rectangular-shaped and about the size of a box of chocolates, with a plastic red liner inside the box to separate beautifully arranged food items like sushi, tempura, rice, and dumplings. The boxes looked more like ornate gifts than ordinary lunches. Curiosity won out over my sense of intimidation. I had to know. "What are you guys eating?" I asked them.

"*Konbini* lunches," said Imogen. "Konbini are convenience stores."

"So much cuter than ICS caf food," said Jhanvi, using chopsticks to pick through a carefully arranged box filled with sushi and edamame.

"*Itadakimasu!*" said Imogen, bringing a gyoza dumpling close to her mouth. Then she clarified for my benefit. "That means, like, 'bon appétit.'"

"So where's your mom?" Ntombi asked me.

"D-I-V-O-R-C-E?" asked Jhanvi.

"She's in a correctional institute," I admitted, using the more polite term. I didn't want to go there, but it was no use lying about where Mom was. These kids seemed to know everything and they'd probably find out anyway. Better for me to say it first, and own the truth.

The girls laughed hard.

"You are *such* a brat, Elle," said Imogen.

"I'm serious," I said. Their faces turned to shock. I added, "Not for murder or anything. Drugs."

"Whoa," all the Ex-Brats exclaimed. It was weird, but I could feel the energy from Ntombi and Jhanvi toward me turn from dismissive to . . . awed?

"That's harsh but so cool," said Imogen.

"Is it like *Orange Is the New Black*?" asked Jhanvi.

"I love that show," said Ntombi.

I didn't get a chance to tell them I'd only visited my mother once in jail, and my impression was that it was anything but cool. It was a million times more dreary and less glamorous than on TV. Two Lower School students—seventh grade, by the particular plaid of their school uniforms, with each grade distinguished by a unique pattern—approached the Ex-Brat table, holding out lunch boxes filled with different kinds of Kit Kats.

"What's the trade today, kids?" Imogen asked them.

One of the girls said, "We have ginger ale and soy sauce."

Imogen inspected their offerings. "Interesting. Ginger ale is a rare find."

"Do it, Joushi," said Jhanvi.

Imogen told the girls, "I'll trade you two red bean for two ginger ale and soy sauce. *Each.*"

It was an unfair 1-flavor-for-2-flavors trade, but the younger girls eagerly handed over the four Kit Kats to Imogen, who in turn retrieved two mangled red bean Kit Kats from the bottom of her backpack, and gave them to the girls. The seventh graders squealed in excitement and ran away.

"Suckers," said Imogen.

"Why would they make that trade?" I asked.

Ntombi looked at me like I was an idiot while Jhanvi informed me, "A trade with an Ex-Brat is a very valuable social commodity to a seventh grader."

Imogen passed around a Kit Kat for each of us. "I haven't tried soy sauce yet. I'm stoked."

Jhanvi said, "I tried sweet tofu last week. *Loved.*"

Ntombi said, "Good trade, Joushi. Red bean is disgusting."

Imogen said, "I kind of like 'em. Which one do you want, Elle-san?" I knew that adding "san" to a last name was a way of saying "Mr." or "Ms."—the staff at Tak-Luxxe called Uncle Masa Araki "Araki-san." I hadn't been in Japan long, but I was sure what Imogen had just called me was this group's form of hipster slang, and not a proper Japanese nickname at all.

I didn't know which to choose. I'd never imagined Kit Kats could come in so many interesting flavors. I feared each and every one. "Ginger ale?"

Imogen handed me a ginger ale Kit Kat. I unwrapped it and took a bite. It was a simultaneous burst of sweetness and bitter in my mouth. "How is it?" asked Ntombi.

"Surprisingly good," I said between bites. "More ginger-y than soda-y."

"Move over." Two athletic-looking guys—lean, strong, preppy hair—sat down on either end of our bench and placed their own konbini bento box lunches on the table.

"Who's the newbie?" asked a dark-haired, olive-skinned guy. He was clean cut and classically handsome, straight out of a Ralph Lauren ad.

Imogen said, "This is Elle. She just started at ICS today. We've decided to take her in because we are so wise and generous. Her dad owns Tak-Luxxe."

"Cool," said the guy, like he met girls whose fathers owned boutique luxury hotel companies all the time. "I'm Oscar Acosta."

"Did you see our girl while you were away for the weekend?" Jhanvi asked him.

Oscar said, "No. Arabella didn't come to the match. She's still brooding over that loser." He veered his head in the direction of Ryuu Kimura sitting alone in the courtyard, propped under a tree, eating cafeteria rice balls and reading a Haruki Murakami novel—in French. The Ex-Brats smirked in Ryuu's direction. He looked up briefly, noticed their glares, and returned to his book. He seemed like he couldn't care less. I kind of admired him for that.

Imogen told me, "Oscar and Arabella are twins."

"You went to Bolivia just for the weekend?" I asked him. Who *were* these people?

"Of course not," said Oscar.

The other guy told me, "We went to Buenos Aires. Polo match. Hi, I'm Nik."

"Hi, Nik," I said. Nik was cute, with intense blue eyes, razor-cut black hair, and the muscled body of a weight lifter.

"Hey, Elle-san," Nik said. He smiled at me flirtatiously. "You're cute."

"Not yet, Nik," said Imogen. "She only just got here." The others laughed.

"Where were you guys this morning?" Jhanvi asked the boys. "Didn't see you in Global Relations class."

Oscar said, "Our flight was late. Delayed departure from Buenos Aires because of a storm." His accent leaned toward American, but with shades of British and Spanish.

"Did you fly commercial?" Ntombi asked them.

"Hardly!" said Nik. "Zhzhonov Air."

The other Ex-Brats laughed. Once again, I was confused. For all I understood of their conversation so far, they might as well be speaking exclusively in Japanese.

Imogen to the rescue. She told me, "He means he flew private. The family has their own jet. His dad is Alexei Zhzhonov."

Suddenly going to school with Shar Kato's daughter was almost ordinary. While I'd never heard of so many varieties of Kit Kats, even my unsophisticated bumpkin self had heard of Alexei Zhzhonov. He'd invented the latest chip technology used in practically every mobile device in the whole world. He was on the cover of that Harvard Business School magazine that Emiko Katsura had tried to pass off on me to read on my flight over.

"Do your bodyguards look as jet-lagged as you?" Ntombi teased Nik. "Did you drag them here with you or are they finally allowed a day off?

"Very funny except not at all funny," replied Nik. "I only have bodyguards when I travel to third world countries. They stayed on the plane after we got off to take Mom and Dad to Ukraine." Nik then focused his gaze on me. "But I'll be *your* bodyguard any day, new girl."

"Shut up, you lecherous creep," said Imogen.

"I love you, too, Joushi-san," Nik said, stealing a dumpling from her bento box with his bare hand, which Imogen playfully slapped.

I looked around to the other tables and saw Akemi studying nearby, all the other kids at her table oblivious to her. She looked lonely and I remembered her saying during our car ride that the cool kids never talked to her. "Maybe we could invite my friend Akemi over here to join us?" I suggested, then added, "She lives in my building." Thinking that might give her more Brat-cred.

The Ex-Brats exchanged disturbed looks. Imogen said, "There's no need to be a humanitarian aid worker here, Elle-san."

chapter twelve

Was I a prisoner like my mother but with better amenities? I had to wonder.

I couldn't wait to use my new MacBook after school to see if I could find Reggie on G-chat, but as soon as I returned to the penthouse after my first day at ICS-Tokyo, I found Emiko Katsura waiting there, with plans.

Back home, before the Beast, Mom would take the day off from work on my first day of school. She'd pick me up at the end of the day, and we'd go home and have hot chocolate and freshly baked cookies, and we'd talk about my teachers and the other kids in my classes and what I'd be studying. I wished I could call Mom this very second and tell her about Imogen Kato and the free laptop and falling asleep on some rude-but-hot dude's shoulder during AP Environmental Science. I wished hard that whatever she was doing at this moment, she was on her best behavior so she could get paroled as early as possible.

Kenji Takahara apparently had no immediate parental curiosity about my day. His assistant, Emiko, said, all business, "I've allotted time now for your Tak-Luxxe orientation. Let's go."

"I was planning on doing my own thing this afternoon," I said.

Emiko shook her head. "You'll have leisure time later. Now, schedule. Takahara-san wants you to receive instruction on how the building works."

"He should show me himself," I said. WTF? What a terrible host *and* new parent.

"When there's time, I'm sure he will."

"Is there ever time?"

There was a look of appreciation for me on Emiko's perfect face. "Now you understand."

I wanted to try to reach Reg and start to put my bedroom together, but I knew arguing would be pointless. Besides, I was curious to explore Tak-Luxxe. Like a good prisoner, I followed the warden for a tour of the fanciest jail ever.

Tak-Luxxe was like its own little city up in the sky. We started on the fiftieth floor, which bustled with employees wearing uniforms, businesspeople, and sophisticated travelers and residents. Emiko explained to me that the lower floors, thirty-six through forty-five, were hotel rooms, and the upper floors, forty-six through forty-nine, had private residences like the one I now lived in. Above the private homes, the very top floors, fifty through fifty-five, of Tak-Luxxe had restaurants and clubs and spa services.

Emiko led me first through the Ikebana Café on the fiftieth floor, the twenty-four-hour restaurant offering panoramic views over Tokyo and a giant ikebana flower display in the center of the room. The buffet had the most sumptuous food displays I'd ever seen. Hot trays filled with delicate beef and fish dishes, sautéed vegetables, dumplings, potatoes, and pastas. A noodle station with a dedicated chef who made ramen and udon soups customized to a diner's request, heaped with meats, tofu, and vegetables. There was a full salad bar offering raw greens and vegetables, and a fruit station that had a wide range of cheese and crackers alongside that. There was even a dessert station that had a chocolate fountain spilling luscious sugar glory down three levels, with a huge assortment of house-made cookies and pastries to dip in it.

The restaurant was filled with people of all ages and nationalities—it seemed like a dozen different languages were being spoken in the expansive room. The people were mostly dressed like Emiko, in sophisticated business clothes. I felt out of place in my school uniform and my inability to distinguish who was speaking French or Japanese or Korean or Arabic or Elvish for all I knew.

"What's that Eiffel Tower–looking thing?" We'd reached the far end of the Ikebana Café at the windows. I pointed at the glass toward a triangle-shaped red-and-white tower in the near distance. The city was spread out before us, and I figured I might as well use this Harvard Business School assistant to give me a primer on the view. Does anyone ever leave this place? I started to wonder, glancing at the forever-sealed windows.

Emiko said, "That's Tokyo Tower. It's an observatory and a TV tower and a tourist attraction."

"That mountain in the distance looks familiar."

"That's Mount Fuji, one of the most iconic places in Japan. You see it in Japanese art all the time. It's one of Japan's proudest symbols. Good view today. If the weather is cloudy or overcast, you can't see it at all."

"What are all those bright lights over there?" I saw a green park in the distance, then behind it, neon signs everywhere, and tall buildings with holographic advertisements displayed on the sides, like constantly running, very colorful movies with no sound.

"That's Shibuya and behind it, Shinjuku. Have you ever seen Times Square in New York City?"

"On TV, yeah."

"Those areas are like that. Lots of bright lights; very,

very busy; and many people packing the streets."

She turned around from the window view and walked toward the center of the room with the giant ikebana.

"How long's Tak-Luxxe been around?" I asked, following her. "Everything looks so shiny and new."

"It is. This location has only been open for about a year. They also have locations in Kuala Lumpur, Singapore, and Shanghai, but this one is the family's prize."

"Why's that?"

She looked at her Apple Watch, like she was bored with my lack of knowledge. She said, "Takahara-san's father started this business in Tokyo. The city is special to the family. But the previous Tak-Luxxe in Tokyo was in an old building with not nearly as much space or grand views. Now Tak-Luxxe Tokyo's hotel rooms are almost always booked, especially as this location offers guests access to Destiny Club."

"You say that name like it's some kind of sacred mecca."

"It is, by Tokyo's vertical city standards. Here, we only have room to build up and not out. There isn't the space here for big country clubs like you have in the US. So Tak-Luxxe offers Destiny Club in Tokyo. You're in it now!"

I followed her to the elevator bank. Employees zipped by us wearing chef, waiter, desk attendant, and other Tak-Luxxe uniforms.

"I don't get it." I saw no sign announcing, "Destiny Club."

She pressed the UP button. Emiko said, "Floors fifty through fifty-five are Destiny Club. It's available to Tak-Luxxe hotel guests and residents, and to members who pay an annual fee to come here."

"Hold up. People pay a fee just to eat in a restaurant?"

"This restaurant is just one part. Destiny Club is a complete experience." I gave her what Mom calls my *oh, come on* look. Emiko said, "Yes, I know I sound like the Tak-Luxxe brochure, but it's true. It is a recreational and social club that has world-renowned restaurants, private clubs, business lounges, meeting rooms, gaming rooms, a spa, and a state-of-the-art gym."

"How much is a membership?"

"They pay a fee. Destiny Club membership costs about ten million yen per year."

The elevator door opened and I almost choked. "WHAT?"

"It's not as much as it sounds like. Ten million yen only equals about a hundred thousand dollars."

Equally choke-worthy. "That's still a *crazy* amount of money."

We stepped inside the elevator. Emiko said, "It's not a crazy amount of money to this type of clientele."

Mom used to think she'd hit pay dirt if she had an

extra fifty dollars before her paycheck ran out. It seemed criminal that people could spend a hundred thousand dollars on luxuries when there was so much poverty in the world. What made them so lucky to have that much while others suffered really hard? What made *me* so lucky to now be part of that world?

As impressed as I was by Destiny Club, it was intimidating. The place didn't seem like real life. It looked and felt like a haven where unfairly wealthy people went to be separate from everyone else. Everything was so ordered and impeccable. Beautiful, but soulless.

Emiko looked at a text message on her phone. "Takahara-san will be available to dine with you at seven this evening," she said.

We got out of the elevator on floor fifty-five, where there was a sign on the wall that said SKY GARDEN.

"Is that how it will always be?" I asked her. "I find out from you when my father is available to see me?"

She didn't hear my frustration. She answered, "Probably."

"What if I want to see him *right now*?"

She looked at a calendar on her phone. "Not possible. He'll be at the private men's club."

I followed her into a garden in the sky . . . literally. It was like a miniature city park in a glass atrium, filled with lush plants and private seating areas. But I couldn't focus on the beauty of the room. I said, "Private men's club? Where's that?"

"It's entered through a hidden door just past the racquetball courts."

"Can I go see it?"

"No. *I've* never even been inside there, and I've worked here for two years."

"Who goes there?"

"Businessmen."

"What do they do there that needs to be private?"

"Smoke cigars and do business."

"Is there a club like that here for women, too?"

"The women's locker room at the spa is private."

"No, I mean, like a private women's club for smoking cigars and doing business stuff."

"Japanese women don't need that." And this woman went to Harvard?

"*I* wouldn't mind it." We walked through the garden, which led to another door, where there was a pool built under an atrium roof. The pool was lovely but small, and had an adjacent hot tub. No guests were using it at this particular time. Such a shame. The views out the glass walls were more impressive than the pool itself, but I was thrilled that I'd have the option for a quick dip here when I wasn't enjoying the ginormous competition-size pool at ICS-Tokyo.

Emiko wasn't interested in debating whether the private men's club was anti-feminist if a similar club was not also available for females. Despite her painfully polite facade, I felt confident she would be relieved to ditch me and my questions. She handed me a long brown envelope from her briefcase. "The remaining items you'll need are in here. Your swipe card for access to your home and the Tak-Luxxe facilities, a PASMO card for taking taxis and the subway, and an American Express card to pay for any expenses like clothes and food."

"My own credit card? I can't pay for that!" I rarely had more than a couple bucks in my pocket. I had no idea what to do with a credit card.

"It's Takahara-san's account. Your . . . father pays." She hesitated to use the word *father*, like it couldn't possibly be true.

I actually understood her hesitation. I came to Japan to meet my father and all I got was his assistant and a lousy credit card. It didn't seem real to me either that Kenji Takahara was my father. Since I wouldn't seem to be getting much attention from the man himself, I asked Emiko, "What's he like?"

"Who?"

Even I had a hard time saying *father*. "Takahara-san."

"Very hardworking. A good boss."

"I mean, like, as a person."

Emiko looked stumped. Finally, she said, "He likes jokes. He can be funny. He likes it when his guests are having a good time here." I never would have guessed that about him. He seemed nice enough, but all business.

"Does he have a girlfriend?"

"Not that I know of."

"Does he have any family here?"

"Yes. I'm sure you'll meet them soon. His mother and sister live one floor below you, on forty-eight."

Wait. I had a grandmother and an aunt here, too? Nobody thought to tell me that? And why hadn't they bothered to come meet me?

Despite the royal treatment and my new gold Amex card, I couldn't shake the feeling that I was less than a family member here at Disney in the Sky.

chapter thirteen

I found my way to a sushi bar called Ryoga on the fifty-second floor of Destiny Club at exactly 7 p.m. It was a small restaurant—just a long countertop, with eight high stools, all occupied, and a chef working behind the counter. The men wore suits and the ladies wore dresses. I looked like a vagrant in my jeans and T-shirt.

I spied Kenji Takahara at a private booth in a corner of the restaurant, where a cream-colored curtain that wasn't closed all the way separated the area from the main countertop table at the center of the restaurant. I hesitantly ventured inside. "Hi?" I said. "You were expecting me?"

He put his phone down on the table and stood up and bowed. "I've been looking forward to our visit."

Our *visit*? I lived with him now. Or did he not remember that?

I didn't want to stare, but I also wanted to never stop looking at his face. It was so familiar and completely foreign to me at the same time. I still couldn't believe he existed and had invited me into his world. Maybe not his life, but his world.

We two sat down across from each other at the table big enough for eight people. I asked, "How come we're eating back here and not in the main area?"

"I realize the restaurant might look plain, but it's very exclusive. Seats reserved months in advance. The chef is Michelin-starred."

"Who's Michelin Starred? A famous *Top Chef*?"

He laughed warmly. "No. The chef's a third-generation sushi master, rated by Michelin, a very important travel and food guide."

"Then good for you for snagging him!"

He laughed again. "Thank you!" he said, and I almost wanted to die with happiness at the bemused smile on his face. I made that happen. He gestured to our table. "This table is for special clients. Or me and my special guests." He paused. "And you are not dressed properly for dinner in the main section."

I hadn't been told to wear anything in particular, so I'd worn what was comfortable. At least I'd known enough not to show up to dinner wearing my ICS-Tokyo uniform. "Excuse me," I said sarcastically.

"Did you sneeze?"

"No."

A waiter came in, bowed, and spoke to my father in Japanese. Goblets of water were brought to our table. "Where's the menu?" I asked.

"No menus here. What kind of sushi do you like?" I'd seen sushi in the prepared foods aisle at Safeway, but it always seemed way too expensive to buy, relative to how small the portions were.

"I don't know. I've never had it."

"That's good. Ryoga Restaurant is *omakase*."

"That's the best kind of sushi?"

"It means, 'I leave it to you.' The chef makes the choice for you. It's the best quality and intervention that way."

"Do you mean 'invention'?"

"Yes. So how was your day?"

Finally, a legitimate dad question.

"Good. They had this girl, Imogen Kato, show me around. Her mom is a famous designer."

"Shar Kato!" He beamed. "Her daughter will be an excellent girl for you to have as a friend. We're trying to get Shar Kato to design new employee uniforms for Tak-Luxxe. See what you can do to help our case." I wasn't sure if he was kidding.

"How was *your* day?" I asked him.

"Since my father died last year and I took over running

the company, my life is work, all the time work. I hope I don't . . ." He hesitated, like he was trying to find a word. "In Japan it's called *karōshi*."

"What's it mean?"

"Death from overwork. Usually a heart attack."

"Yes, please don't karōshi." Mom worked a lot, too, before the Beast, but she always found time for me. "So . . . when am I going to see you?"

"You're seeing me now! We will have dinner together every night. Get to know each other that way." Well, that was something. He seemed married to his work, but at least he had a plan for us to spend time together. We were never going to be a "normal" family—whatever that was—so I figured I could try to appreciate the situation for what it was. He'd taken me in and was sending me to a really nice school and I could help him out by not being so desperate for him to immediately be like a real father. Whatever *that* meant. I'd never had one—how should I know? Kenji said, "Tell me about yourself. What do you like?"

"Eating, for one," I said as our first plate of sushi was set in between us.

He handed me a set of chopsticks. "Do you know how to use?"

"I'm learning." I cautiously took one of the sushi pieces as he took the other with his chopsticks.

"Eat each piece in one bite," he advised.

"Don't worry, I read that part of the binder. I also now know to eat sushi in the order it was put out, always finish it, use soy sauce sparingly, dip the sushi upside down into the sauce, and don't linger after the meal."

"Excellent!" he proclaimed, not getting that I was trying to mock the rules.

I placed the first piece of sushi in my mouth. HIGH HOLY HEAVEN! It was like a dance of flavors and textures—salty, rich, sweet, chewy yet silken—all at once. "This is maybe the best thing I've ever eaten," I said after swallowing. To be fair, food that good *did* deserve rules for eating. Each flavor ping caused epic delirium to my taste buds. Ramen was *okay*. Sushi was *the bomb*.

"Eating is my favorite activity, too," he said. "What else do you like?"

"Cats. Swimming. Beyoncé. What about you?"

"Dogs. Baseball. Beyoncé."

A dog person who loved Beyoncé wasn't hopeless, but I had a more pressing concern. "What am I supposed to call you?" I blurted out. Was there a Japanese word for Father-I-Only-Just-Met-and-Don't-Yet-Feel-Comfortable-Calling-Dad?

"What do you want to call me?"

"Kenji, I guess?"

He smiled. Seriously, with that charismatic smile and

handsome face, he missed his calling as a J-Pop music star. "Then call me 'KenjiIGuess.'"

I giggled. Good sense of humor: check. A new plate of food was brought to our table, looking even more delicious than the previous plate. I said, "I also like Coca-Cola, KenjiIGuess."

To the waiter, he said, "Coca-Cola," and held up two fingers. Then he said something else to the waiter in Japanese. When the waiter was gone, he said, "I told him not to tell Chef Shiro we were having Coca-Cola with his masterpieces."

"Is that a sushi rule? No Cokes with the meal?"

"No, that's a basic rule of fine food dining. But I'm the boss. I get to break the rules."

Interesting. I liked this rebellious side of Kenji.

I asked him, "What kind of student were you when you were my age? Where did you go to school?"

"I went to boarding school in America, actually. Andover. My sister went there also. Our parents wanted us to perfect our English. My sister was a star student, but I was just all right. Not the worst. Not the best. I preferred sports and partying with my friends. What about you?"

"I used to be a good student. Until things got bad with Mom, I got almost straight A's." I paused. I appreciated how open he was being with me, and I wanted to reciprocate that. "Thank you for the opportunity to go to school here. I really like ICS-Tokyo."

"You're welcome," he said, looking pleased. He took a deep breath and then announced, "But even more important than getting good grades is getting along with my mother."

"Is she hard to get along with?" Was that why I hadn't heard anything about her yet? He was hiding her from me . . . or vice versa?

"She's . . . not always easy," Kenji said tactfully. "She's the true boss of the family. When I found out what was happening with your mother, I said let's bring Elle here and see how she does. My mother wanted to pay to send you to boarding school instead."

I need a drink, my mom would have said at this point in the conversation. She would have meant something a lot stronger than Coca-Cola.

"So how come I'm here, then?" I asked, not sure whether I still felt the same level of gratitude. Instead, I felt nervous and anxious, like I was about to be sent to a new foster home again.

"Because I finally got Mother to agree that we could have you here temporarily, to see how it goes."

My heart dropped into my stomach. Temporarily? I didn't know my coming to Tokyo was possibly a temporary measure. Wasn't that something I should have been told *before* I chose to get on the plane?

"Don't look so concerned! I'm sure you and she will get along fine."

He didn't sound too convinced, but I would fix that. I was here now. And I was determined to make it permanent. At least until I finished high school and could get a scholarship to college. Then I would go home and wait for Mom to get out, and we'd resume our lives together.

"I know we will," I said confidently. I'd do whatever it took to make this new family like me.

chapter fourteen

True to the Japanese dining etiquette, we did not linger after the meal. Once we'd consumed the last plate of awesome sushi, Kenji glanced at his watch, resigned. "Time to meet the rest of the family."

"Don't you want to have an after-drink first?" I asked, hoping to stall whatever had him looking so oddly nervous. "Isn't sake the thing here?"

For the first time, Kenji gently touched my hand across the table. He pulled it back just as quickly but looked me squarely in the eyes. "I don't drink. I'm in recovery."

WHOA.

I was *not* expecting that. Kenji looked like such a healthy and confident man. Not vulnerable like Mom was once. He was the Lord of a Skyscraper, for God's sake.

What pain could he possibly need numbed by alcohol? He had everything.

So I had two parents who were addicts. The odds that I could become one, too, were 100 percent not good.

He added, "It's why I couldn't be a father to you before. I was in bad shape until I got sober about three years ago."

I knew it wasn't a decent excuse, but it helped. There was an actual reason, other than sheer abandonment, that he hadn't been part of my life before now.

"Do you go to meetings? I could go with you . . . for support." I'd have done anything during the time of the Beast to get Mom to try sobriety. I'd have baked cookies and babysat for anyone in recovery who would take Mom to one of their Alcoholics Anonymous or Narcotics Anonymous support groups.

"That's not done here," Kenji said. He stood up and very abruptly said, "And that's all I have to say on the subject. I just wanted you to know."

I wondered if he'd confided in me because he wanted to be honest and open or because he wanted me to be aware that he could fall off the wagon at any point, or both, but I knew not to press the drinking issue further, even though there was so much more I wanted to know. He'd said what he felt he needed to say. He was obviously sober now. I followed him to the lobby, toward the elevator.

"What are their names?" I asked him. "Your mom and your sister?"

"My mother is Noriko, and my sister is Kimiko, but she's called Kim when speaking in English. She's the second in command at Tak-Luxxe after me." *Nori and Kim?!* I resisted the urge to crack a Kardashian joke. We stepped into the elevator and got out at the Tak-Luxxe hotel lobby on thirty-six. "We need to make a stop at the concierge desk. I forgot something."

I followed Kenji to the front desk. He had an air of authority walking across the room, receiving deep bows from employees as he passed by them. I recognized the concierge from earlier in the afternoon. "Are you also a waiter in Ikebana Café?" I asked him. He looked just past college age, with light brown skin, dark hair, and deep green eyes.

"Indeed," he said. "I'm Dev Flaherty. I do a little bit of everything here. Wherever the boss needs me, there I am." He saluted Kenji, who laughed.

"Are you American?" I asked Dev.

"Yep. Representing Boston's Irish-Indian Americans' finest."

Kenji told him, "This is my daughter, Elle. She'll be living here now."

Dev's face brightened. I felt mine blush. Not because Dev Flirty, I mean Flaherty, was so cute, but because Kenji had introduced me as his daughter.

Dev said, "Awesome. Welcome. Anything you need at all, I'm your guy. Just ring the house phone and ask for me. I speak English, Japanese, Hindi, Spanish, and French, so you can even call me if you just need help with your language homework." Then he addressed Kenji in Japanese, and after whatever they discussed, Dev opened a cabinet behind the concierge desk. From it, he retrieved a gift box wrapped in flowered wrapping paper and a gift bag and handed them to Kenji. "*Gracias,*" Kenji said to Dev.

"*De nada,*" Dev answered.

"Just testing your Spanish," Kenji said with a laugh.

Kenji placed the box in the gift bag and handed it to me. "Let's go, we're late. Mother hates late."

I noticed Dev's face squint in surprise, and I was surprised, too. Kenji was clearly flustered. It was disconcerting to see in a man who otherwise seemed so measured and controlled.

"What's the gift for?" I asked Kenji as we walked to the private elevator for the residential suites.

Kenji said, "I forgot to ask Masa to buy *omiyage* from the airport for you to give to Mother. In Japan, it's tradition to bring a gift as a sign of respect when you visit someone's home or work."

"Why did we have to put the gift in a bag if we're only taking it upstairs and it was already wrapped?"

"It should be given in a bag for discretion." He said this seriously and as if it was obvious, like the gift bag contained valuable jewelry or something very expensive and important, and not an already-gift-wrapped box.

"I could make them a gift instead," I suggested. "I make great chocolate-chip cookies! The secret is a pinch of cardamom. I learned that on Pinterest."

"Nice idea, but too late. My mistake. We need a gift now. The concierge desk always keeps a stock for me. You will give the gift bag to Mother."

"What gift am I giving?"

"Chocolates from the airport in Dallas. My mother and sister won't eat them. They don't like American chocolates."

"So why are we giving it to them?"

"Because it's Japanese tradition. The gift-giving is more important than the gift."

"That makes no sense."

It did to Kenji, apparently. He added, "Give the gift with two hands but don't give it right away. Wait until you are seated and everyone is comfortable."

"These are a lot of rules for a chocolate gift that no one will like."

Kenji smiled. "You learn quickly."

"American chocolates are the best," I boasted. I wouldn't mind a Hershey bar right now, in fact.

Kenji chuckled. We stepped into the elevator. "That's because you've probably never had chocolates anywhere besides America. The best chocolate comes from Belgium or Switzerland. England, also good. Japan's chocolates are excellent, but they import from the best countries like Belgium and Switzerland."

"You've insulted my country's chocolate."

"Your country's chocolate tastes like wax. We'll go to the patisserie after this meeting and I'll prove it to you."

"Really, KenjiIGuess?" He wanted to do something with me not on his Sacred Schedule?

"*Rilly,*" he said, mimicking my American accent. He was funny. I was funny. Another thing we had in common!

The elevator door let us out at forty-eight. The floor had two units on either side of the hall. Kenji walked to the one on the right. He softly sighed, as if resigned, and then rang the doorbell. A matronly Japanese woman opened the door. She wore an elegant suit, with her black hair in a bun, but with that poofy-at-the-front style that old people seem to favor. She had a stern face, with painted-on black eyebrows and plum-colored lipstick, and she looked like she'd just bit into a Sour Patch Kid and only then remembered how much she hated them. "You're ten minutes late," she scolded Kenji in English, then glanced in my direction like it was my fault.

"Sorry," I mumbled. Both my mom's parents died when she was still a kid, so I'd never had grandparents on her side, or imagined what having a grandparent would be like. If I had, my imaginary granny probably would have been sitting in a rocker sewing me an awesome cape that had "Granny's Super Girl" stenciled on it, and not scowling at me the first time I met her.

Kenji and Granny spoke a few words in Japanese. Then, in English, he said, "Mother, this is Elle. Elle, this is my mother. She says she would like you to call her Mrs. Takahara."

Okay, Grandma. Glad to get that out of the way. Thanks for the warm welcome. Glad I didn't waste too much energy being excited about having more family in Tokyo.

I bowed slightly because I felt like I was supposed to, while Mrs. Takahara inspected my face closely. I wondered if she had the same reaction I had to seeing Kenji for the first time: The resemblance between us could not be denied. Her sour expression certainly didn't indicate pleasure at this sight.

Kenji and I stepped inside the foyer, changed our shoes to slippers lined at the floor's edge, and stepped inside the living room. It was exactly the same apartment layout as Kenji's home, but the furniture was more formal and Japanese. As we walked into the living room, we were greeted by Kenji's stunning sister, who looked a few years younger than Kenji. She extended her hand to me and said, "Welcome to Japan, Elle. I'm Kim." Her words were more welcoming, and unlike Mrs. Takahara, her English was confident and without accent, but her formal demeanor in no way suggested elation to meet her niece.

"Hi," I said. "Nice to meet you." *Please like me!*

Kimiko Nakamura made Emiko Katsura look almost frumpy. She wore a soft pink suit and had a slender figure accentuated by her perfectly tailored clothes, and shoes that had a gold plate on them that said Ferragamo. Her long black hair was so smooth and lustrous that a genuine hair model would probably want to snatch it from her head.

Kim gestured for me to take a seat on the sofa. Tea service had been set up for our visit. "How do you take your tea?" Kim asked me as Mrs. Takahara perched on a chair at the opposite side of the coffee table.

"Do you have Coke?" I asked.

"I don't think so," Kim said. "Mother doesn't approve of sodas."

To me, Mrs. Takahara said, "You're pretty and skinny now. Drink tea, not soda, so you stay that way."

"How about water?" I was frightened of the tea.

Everything in Japan seemed so ritualized, and I didn't want to do the ritual wrong and offend. I tried to stop my foot from tapping and my fingers from twitching nervously.

"I'll get a water for you," said Kenji, walking toward the kitchen. He returned with a glass of water and then sat down next to me. Kim took the chair next to her mother's so the two of them sat opposite us.

It seemed as good a time as any, so I took the gift box from the bag and handed it to Mrs. Takahara using both hands. "A gift for you," I said. Crap! I was supposed to leave the box in the bag.

Mrs. Takahara received the box with both hands and a disapproving face. "American chocolates?"

I nodded. Mrs. Takahara said something in Japanese that probably translated as *Hmmmph*, then placed the gift box on the floor behind her chair. Already forgotten. "You wore that to dinner?" Mrs. Takahara asked me. I looked down at my new jeans and blouse—an outfit that cost more than my mother's weekly waitress earnings.

"Yes?" I said.

Mrs. Takahara said to Kenji, "You allow those clothes in Destiny Club? Why have a dress code if you bring your own . . ." His mother apparently couldn't bring herself to say the word *daughter*. "Guest to dinner like this?"

Kenji looked annoyed as he and Mrs. Takahara

exchanged some words in Japanese. I couldn't understand their conversation, but I did distinguish the words *hafu* and *gaijin* being used.

Maybe I'd have better luck winning over Kenji's sister. I said to her, "You have the smoothest hair I've ever seen. Do you use a special shampoo?"

Kim said, "No special shampoo, but I've been getting Japanese hair treatments since I first went off to university, when I was just a few years older than you. I can arrange one for you, if you'd like."

I had no idea what a Japanese hair treatment was, but I said, "Sure! Thanks!" mostly to be polite.

"Your hair is wild," Mrs. Takahara said to me. "It needs work."

Geez, lady! Where'd you learn manners?

Kenji looked around the room and then said to Kim, "Would Mother like some whiskey with her tea?" Then he shot me a knowing look. A lyric from Beyoncé's "Daddy Lessons" song. I felt my heart rate calm as a small smile curled on my mouth.

"No whiskey!" said Mrs. Takahara to Kenji. And then it sounded like they were bickering in Japanese again.

Politely, Kim asked me, "How was your first day at ICS?"

"Good. The campus is amazing."

Kim said, "I've known Chloe Lehrer since my freshman year at Harvard. I put Kenji in touch with her, and she helped with getting you admitted quickly so he could send for you."

I was starting to see that what had been a sudden, shocking decision for me to come here had involved a lot of planning and negotiation on the other end before Uncle Masa was sent over to retrieve me. All those months since Mom went to jail and I went to foster care, people had been trying to find a better solution for me. I'd probably never see my two parents in the same room together, but somehow, without me knowing it, they'd made this new life possible for me.

"Thank you," I told Kim, truly meaning it.

"How was your ride to school this morning?" I didn't think Kim cared about my ride; she was trying to distract me from Kenji and their mother's Japanese conversation.

"I totally didn't expect a ride to school in a Bentley!"

"Right?" Kim laughed.

Mrs. Takahara had finished whatever scolding she was doing to her son, and she turned back to me. "Why is your skin dark?"

My skin was not dark, but it wasn't exactly lily white, either. On a skin-shade scale of one to ten where one was the lightest white and ten was the darkest brown, I was probably a three. "My mother's father was part Native American and African American," I explained.

Mrs. Takahara did not try to hide her shock and displeasure. "Like black?"

"Mother!" Kim and Kenji both cried at Mrs. Takahara, who ignored them.

Mrs. Takahara said, "You know about the Nigerians in Roppongi? They're bad, not honest."

To me, Kenji explained, "Roppongi is the nightlife district near here." He turned to his mother and in English said, "The Nigerians who run the shady nightclubs in Roppongi have nothing to do with Elle. And just because someone is Nigerian doesn't mean they run a club in Roppongi."

I appreciated him schooling his mother, but I'd gotten her message: guilt by association. I was beginning to understand why Kenji's parents paid off Mom when she got pregnant—so Kenji could leave and not bring a granddaughter who wasn't fully Japanese home to Japan. Joke was on Granny. Because here I was!

I wanted to storm out. But I glanced at Kenji, who was giving me a pleading look. I took a deep breath. I certainly didn't owe this iron lady the courtesy, but I could make the effort to attempt courtesy anyway, since Kenji was clearly trying to defend me.

I said, "I'm hoping to learn Japanese now that I'm here."

Mrs. Takahara glowered. "No. It's too hard to learn and we don't know how long you here."

My heart pounded so hard I was scared it might explode out of my chest. I wanted to know my father. I wanted to live here and go to ICS. It seemed like a good life. But was it worth the cost of trying to get this mean lady to like me? Already I didn't like *her*.

Maybe he did have some basic dad instinct, because Kenji read my face. He pointedly told his mother in English, "We should be honored that Elle wants to learn our language."

Warmly, Kim told me, "I wouldn't worry about learning Japanese for now. Mother's right that it's a hard language to learn, and between Tak-Luxxe and ICS, you'll mostly be dealing here with expats who speak English. I'm sure your school load will be heavy enough without taking on Japanese."

Now Mrs. Takahara started scolding both Kenji and Kim in Japanese.

And suddenly I wanted to learn their language more than ever. So they couldn't talk about me like I wasn't there. So maybe one day I could tell off my racist grandmother in her own language.

chapter fifteen

The first thing Kenji said when we finally left his mother's apartment were the exact words I didn't know I needed to hear. "We need chocolate after that."

The Destiny Club patisserie—Delights—had closed at seven, but arigatogozaimashita to Kenji's privileged key card, we had access to the sweet shop even after closing. Delights was a small store decorated with pink-and-white-striped wallpaper, pink-and-white paper lanterns hanging from the ceiling, and pink-and-white shelves and cases. (Should I tell Kenji how corny so many of the Destiny Club food place names were? Nah.) The glass cases displayed fancy tea cakes and individual chocolates, surrounded by shelves filled with colorful gift-wrapped boxes of sweets decorated with bows. The shop looked like a young girl's bedroom by way of Willie Wonka and an overdose of kawaii.

I would probably never be able to consider my grandmother "family," but a man who gave me private access to sweets heaven? He had righteous dad potential, despite his too-busy schedule. Kenji was obviously a regular at Delights. He knew exactly how to unlock and open the glass case, and how to take out the individual pieces using tongs, placing them in a neat row on a porcelain plate located in a drawer next to the glass cases.

I said, "I see you've got a sweet tooth?" He looked perplexed and touched his front tooth. I added, "It's an English saying. It means you like sweet foods."

He smiled like I had said something charming. "Yes! I have a sweet tooth!"

"I have one, too. My mom doesn't like sweets. I must have gotten the sweet tooth from you."

He looked pleased that I'd inherited this trait from him. "I've gained weight since Delights opened. I come here at the end of the night and I indulge too much." Interesting. Getting to know Kenji maybe had less to do with the time allotted on his schedule and more to do with dessert. Already I liked him more.

"You don't look fat to me."

"One year ago, before Delights opened, I wore a pants

size smaller." He pointed at a piece of milk chocolate in the center of the plate he'd set out. "Try that one first. My favorite. It's praline mousse."

Nothing about the words *praline* or *mousse* sounded like a Delight, but I took a piece on Kenji's advice, and he was absolutely right. It was nutty and creamy and delicate all at the same time. "Wow! Amazing!"

"Not like wax," said Kenji.

"American chocolate does *not* taste like wax," I insisted. I placed another chocolate into my mouth. It had a pistachio bit on top, and the inside was a meatier texture, with a wonderfully sinful taste. I was starting to see Kenji's point. These chocolates were next-level delicious. Penthouse-level delicious. (But I'd still never turn away a Hershey bar. Especially if it had almonds. USA!)

"Cappuccino?" Kenji asked.

I assumed he meant the chocolates. "Which one?"

He shook his head. "No. Would you like a cappuccino? I'm the secret late-night barista here." He smiled at me. "But don't tell the employees I know how to use the machine. They will insist on making drinks for me when they're not scheduled to be working in here."

"That's nice of them."

"It is. But they would do it because their real worry is I would break the machine."

"Would you?"

"Only once. Now, I am expert."

I decided to test him. "I'll have a decaf soy-milk capp, then. Dry."

"All foam, no steamed milk. We also have almond milk if you prefer other non-dairy options."

Not bad, Lord Skyscraper. "Soy is good, thanks. What do you have?"

He walked to the espresso machine and got to work priming it and grinding the coffee beans. "I like whole-milk cappuccino with lots of foam on top."

I watched him prepare our drinks. He was a true pro. He steamed the milk with ease and no spillage, and used a thin metal wand to dip into my mug and draw a heart in coffee at the top of the foam. I took a sip. My capp was the perfect temperature, hot but not too hot, and the foam on top full but not too stiff. I told him, "I hear Starbucks is hiring."

"You're funny."

"*You're* funny," I said, taking another sip of my coffee. So Kenji didn't know how to be a dad yet, but his coffee and sweets game was excellent. No complaints. Other than: "You realize your mom is a racist, right?"

He sighed. "I'm sorry. I should have warned you, but I hoped she would be more polite. She grew up in a small town in northern Japan. I don't think she ever saw a non-Japanese person until she arrived in Tokyo over forty years ago to go to university. But I don't believe she's really a racist. Just uncomfortable with people who are different."

"You mean, not Japanese?"

"Yes."

"She seems kind of Slytherin."

I didn't expect him to get the reference, but he totally did. He said, "Slytherin are not always bad. They are driven, determined. My father could not have built this business without my mother supporting him. Will you do me a favor?" At this point, I honestly felt like I'd do anything for this person I'd only just met yesterday who drew heart shapes in my custom dry capp and who totally got it when I said his mother was Slytherin. I nodded. "Give her time and try not to judge her."

"The way she judged me, you mean?"

"She is old and set in her ways. You are young and open-minded, I hope. She will get better as she gets more comfortable with you. I truly believe that."

"I think you're wrong."

"Was I wrong about the chocolate?"

He had a valid point.

• • •

After our post-Granny dessert hangout, Kenji and I returned to his—my—apartment, only for him to announce that he had to go back to work. At 10 p.m.! Did this man never sleep? "Are you all right by yourself?" he asked, like this basic parent question had just occurred to him.

I would have rather he stayed with me so we could watch TV before bed. I bet he was a *Game of Thrones* binger, but maybe I could get him hooked on *Gilmore Girls*.

But I had been raising myself since I was fourteen. Why stop now? Being alone in a penthouse with room service if I needed it was way better than alone in a foster home bedroom, hiding. Or alone in my old bedroom, shutting out the pain, with Mom knocked out by the Beast on the living room sofa. "I'm fine, thanks," I said. "What do you do at work this late?"

"I walk the tables at the Destiny Club private games' parlor. It's important for me to socialize with the big players at the high-stakes mah-jongg tables. They need to feel like they're friends with the boss. Especially when they're losing a lot of money!"

"Destiny Club is also a *casino*?" That piece of information had certainly not been included on my tour. My mother's favorite movie was *Goodfellas*. I knew this scene. "Like with mobsters and—"

"Emiko said you want a cat," Kenji interrupted. "Why?"

I forgot I'd asked Emiko if I could have a cat here someday and she'd immediately shut me down, saying they didn't allow pets in the Tak Luxxe. I was surprised she bothered to tell Kenji about such a random question. Was she reporting back every single thing I said? I knew he was deliberately changing the subject, but I didn't try to swing it back to casino talk, because what if he was about to soften the No Pets stance? I certainly could go along with that line of conversation. I said, "When I was a kid, I had a cat I really loved. He was pretty much my best friend."

"What was his name?"

"Hufflepuff."

"You really like Harry Potter." I nodded. Kenji clenched his hand over his heart, totally sincerely. "Me too. Have you taken Sorting Hat House Quiz?"

What?! No way! "Yes. Have *you*?"

"Every time I see it online." Me too! "Always the same answer. Ravenclaw."

"I always get the same answer, too! Hufflepuff."

"That means you are very loyal."

"And you must be wise."

"Wise enough to know that Ravenclaw and Hufflepuff are great allies."

I took out my new phone and showed Kenji a photo saved to my email folder, of Huff sleeping in my lap when I was eight. "That's Hufflepuff when he was about a year old. He was the best."

"Who shot the cat?" Kenji asked. His English was very good, but like Uncle Masa, there were blips.

I tried hard not to laugh. "Mom took the picture."

"Good photo. You were a very pretty little girl." He was focusing on the wrong part of the picture, and his face had taken on a sad look. "Masa used to send me photos of you. They made me very happy."

"Oh." I didn't know what else to say to this acknowledgment that he'd wanted to be part of my life but had chosen not to. It felt weird to know that Uncle Masa had been sending photos of me to this stranger. I wondered if Kenji had ever thought about reaching out to try to meet me earlier. Given that he never did, there seemed to be an opening to turn his guilt to my benefit for a good cause. "So, can I get a cat?"

"No."

Not a big enough opening.

Yet.

chapter sixteen

My first night in Tokyo, I'd been so exhausted from the travel that I fell right to sleep. Now, on my second night, all alone in the apartment, my body felt tired, but my mind was hyped with so much new information. ICS! Ex-Brats! Takaharas! No way could I fall asleep. I went to the living room to look out over Tokyo, its tall buildings and billboards sparking across the nighttime sky. I could feel the city's energy wafting up to my lonesome perch on the forty-ninth floor. I wanted some company. And some fun.

It was 11 p.m. in Tokyo, which made it 10 a.m. Friday morning in Maryland. Yes! I knew Reg had study hall before lunch period. I sent him a G-chat message in case he was at the computer lab: You free to video chat?

You're not going to believe what I have to show you!

While I waited for him to respond, I did the obvious thing: tested this room service option. I picked up the house phone and dialed 0. A male voice answered and spoke in Japanese and then in English. "Hello, how may I help you?"

"Is this Dev at the concierge desk?"

"Sure is. Whatcha need?"

"Do they have ice-cream sundaes in Japan?"

"Absolutely. Shall I have Ikebana Café send one up to you?"

"Yes, please!"

"What flavors?"

"Omakase!" I said. "You choose."

I heard him laugh, then he said, "Should be up there in ten minutes." This Dev guy was like an expat magician.

"Thank you!"

I went into my bedroom. I didn't see any curtains for privacy, so I pressed a button next to the windows. I jumped in surprise when an automatic blind descended from the ceiling. Sweet Jesus! Now I was even more awake.

My phone alerted me to a video call from Reg. I answered. "OH MY GOD! REGGIE COLEMAN!"

Reggie came into view on my phone. I'd G-chatted

with him online but hadn't seen his face since I went into foster care. He had a little mustache action growing over his upper lip, and his face looked filled in from young guy to near-man. His hair was cut razor short, which nicely allowed for more focus to his deep brown eyes. His normally light brown skin looked darker, like he'd gotten sun recently. I hoped that meant he was getting lots of swim time. Nothing made him happier.

"ELLE ZOELLNER!" I could see from the background that he was in the computer lab at his school. "How the actual fuck did you end up in Japan?"

"I know, it's crazy. My social worker came to visit and Uncle Masa was with her—"

"That guy that used to come to our swim meets when we were kids?"

"Yeah! Turns out he's the cousin of my real dad, who had offered for me to come live with him since, you know, Mom's not so good at providing a home lately."

"I hear you."

Reg had it harder than I did back in Maryland, because he was just a few months shy of his eighteenth birthday. For most teenagers, turning eighteen meant being legally free to make your own decisions. A true adult. For foster kids, it meant the state was sending you out into the world on your own, whether you were ready and able to handle it or not.

"You should come live here," I offered.

"Hah, I'm sure your new dad would love that. Turn the camera around and show me your place."

"Watch this," I said. I pressed the shade button on the wall again and showed Reg the blind moving up and down over the skyline view of Tokyo.

"Dude, that's pretty cool. But I only have a few minutes until the teacher comes back and knocks me off this call. What else ya got?"

I knew exactly where to go next. "Look, my own bathroom!" I announced, turning the phone toward the door and flicking on the light. *"Inside my room!"*

"No way."

"It's true!" I walked into the bathroom. Never in my life did I imagine such a personal luxury could exist in a bedroom. The bathroom felt like Alice falling down the rabbit hole, but a rabbit hole provided by Santa Claus. I opened the glass door to the shower stall that took up a whole little room of its own. "The water pressure is perfect and I can take a hot shower as long as I want, whenever I want here."

"I'm dying."

I moved back to the main part of the bathroom and showed Reg the marble sink with a spotless mirror that covered the wall behind it. I opened and closed the storage closets filled with towels even softer and more luxurious than those second-rate ones I'd swiped from the International First Lounge at Dulles International Airport. I opened the other storage closet, and it was . . .

"IS THAT A WASHER-DRYER?" Reg asked.

"YAAAAS!"

I know, boys don't usually get excited about laundry. But we'd both survived foster homes, where you didn't know when or if you'd ever get to wash your own clothes. "Reg, here's the best part."

"You're not about to show me the toilet."

"Oh yes, I am! Trust me, you gotta see this."

I'd only been in Tokyo two days, but I was already obsessed with Japanese toilets. I walked into the private toilet vestibule inside the bathroom. The wall had its own console that said "Toto" and was covered in buttons that had Japanese lettering beneath picture symbols. I pretended I was a game show hostess demonstrating the buttons on the console. "This button sprays water on your butt! This one makes bird noises, I guess so you can feel like you're having a soothing, private experience in here. This one warms your butt when you're sitting on the pot! Guess what this one does?"

"Provides a robot to pee so you can pass a drug test?"

"Hah, good one! No, it sprays air freshener! This room smells like a scented bubble bath right now."

I turned the view around on my phone so I could see

Reg's face and he could see mine. He was shaking his head. "TMI," he said.

"Seriously, you have to experience it to appreciate it."

"I'll add it to my Bucket List. One: marry Rihanna. Two: experience a Japanese toilet."

The doorbell rang and I squealed. "Now watch this!"

I turned the view around again so Reg could see me answer the front door. A uniformed waiter bowed to me and rolled in a cart with a silver-domed bowl on top. "Where would you like this?" he asked me.

"In my belly!" Reg called out.

"On the dining table, please," I told the waiter.

He placed the silver-domed bowl on the dining table, bowed to me, and left.

I lifted the silver dome for Reg. The bowl had three perfectly scooped balls of vanilla ice cream, with warm chocolate sauce running over the sides, and whipped cream, chopped nuts, and a maraschino cherry on top.

Reg said, "Where exactly are you living now? Buckingham Palace?"

"It turns out my father owns a hotel business. He lives in their Tokyo property. Forty-ninth floor!"

"Show me!"

I ran to the living room and offered up the Tokyo skyline view for Reg's inspection. "If I get posted to Okinawa, Japan, I'll for sure come visit you," Reg said.

I turned the phone around to my own face again. "What do you mean?"

"Following my old man's path. I talked to a recruiter and I'm going to join the army as soon as I get my diploma. I could start basic training right after my birthday."

I plopped down onto the sofa. This was big. I'd been showing him the stupid Japanese toilets when he had major life news.

"You're not going to finish your senior year?"

"I got approved for early graduation in December. Foster privileges, you know."

I wasn't sure if I'd still consider it a privilege if Reg got out of high school early to join the army, only to then get shipped to war in Afghanistan or Iraq or somewhere terrifying. I said a silent prayer. *Please let Reggie get posted to Japan. Or somewhere safe. He's been through enough already.*

I realized all over again how lucky I was.

"That's great," I said. Reg had somewhere to go when he got kicked out of foster care. He had a future. But that future could get scary if it sent Reg to fight a war.

"What's your dad like?" Reg asked.

"Ask me in a month. I hardly know him yet. He kind of told me he used to be an alcoholic and that's why he didn't think he could be a father before. He's a bit stiff, but nice, and funny. He works all the time."

"If he's rich, you'll be taken care of. That's all that matters. Teacher's coming back in, I gotta go."

"There's a pool here, Reg."

He grinned. "I'm *definitely* coming to visit you. Bye, Cinderella."

chapter seventeen

It was early Saturday morning, and I was in a hard, deep sleep, but a rattling noise coming from I didn't know where tried to wake me. Asking my body to respond to this noise seemed not only cruel, but impossible. I couldn't get my eyes to open, trapped in that in-between of sleeping and waking. I was having such a nice dream. I was on my bed back in Greenbelt, before the Beast, cozy and comfortable, with Huff purring at my side. A freight train went by nearby, gently rocking my bed. The train got louder and louder and nearer and nearer until my eyes popped open and I bolted upright. Holy crap. The room was *actually* shaking. That was no dream!

I jumped out of bed and saw the water glass I'd left on my nightstand shaking and the water in it swirling around. I didn't know whether to hide in the closet or under the bed or what. Then the shaking and rattling noise eased, and stopped entirely.

OH MY GOD, THAT WAS AN . . .

Like I wasn't already terrified enough, a female voice spoke out of nowhere, saying something in Japanese, like a very loud ghost. I was already about to have a heart attack from the earthquake, and I couldn't figure out where mystery lady's voice came from. Then I looked up and saw an intercom speaker in the corner near the ceiling. After whatever she said in Japanese, her pleasant voice announced, in heavily accented English, "We have had small earthquake. Do not be alarmed. Please stay in place while we do maintenance check. We will make new announcement when elevators are operating again."

There was just an earthquake and some voice from out of nowhere was commanding me not to be alarmed? Sure, invisible lady in the ceiling. Sure.

I raced to the living room to look out the bigger windows there, and I inspected the street level. There seemed to be no rushes of panic or concern from the foot or car traffic below. Life seemed to be going by as normal, like, *Oh yeah, just a little earthquake, whatevs.*

Kenji appeared in the living room, wearing blue pajamas, his hair slightly disheveled. It was weird to see him wearing something other than a suit. I wore PJ shorts and a tank top, but I wanted to cover up. People who were family hung out together in their jammies. We were still practically strangers.

He said, "How'd you like that earthquake? Good shake, right?"

"I guess, if 'good shake' also means 'terrifying surprise'?"

"Was that your first earthquake?"

"How'd you know?"

"You look very pale."

"It was my first. Hopefully my last."

"It will be your first of many," said Kenji. He opened a storage closet door that I hadn't even realized was in the living room wall. "Emergency supplies, in there. If it's a big one, most important thing is to take cover under something like a table and cover your head with your arms for protection in case things fall."

"What do I use to protect my panicked heart?"

He laughed. "There's no need to panic in an earthquake. They happen frequently, usually not that bad. Just be prepared. Did you sleep well?"

"Yes, until a few minutes ago."

"Good."

Neither of us said anything. The silence of two strangers wearing their jammies was awkward.

Finally, I asked, "So what's up for today?" It was the weekend. I couldn't wait to take a shower in Heaven

Bathroom, put on my expensive new clothes, and try to make Kenji Takahara forget I had just arrived from foster care and my mother was in jail. I was excited to explore this new city beckoning outside the sunny windows with him. I wanted to go somewhere already.

He said, "I have to do an inspection with the building engineer. Then, meetings."

"On a *weekend*?"

"There's no such thing as a weekend off in my job. Kim made a hair appointment for you for early evening. We'll have dinner together after. Emiko will text you the schedule."

I tried not to let my disappointment show on my face. "So what should I do the rest of the day?" I didn't have homework yet.

"Why don't you text Imogen Kato and see if she wants to show you the city?"

• • •

After Kenji left for work, I gathered all my courage and texted Imogen. I mean, she'd given me her number and told me to text her anytime. She hadn't sounded fake when she said it.

Hey Imogen-san, what's fun to do on a Saturday and do you want to do it with me? Xoxo Elle-san

157

I waited five minutes. No answer. I felt sweaty and nervous and hungry. I decided to go out for some breakfast and leave my phone behind for the adventure, so I wouldn't be staring at it, hoping for a return text from Imogen. Hoping if she did send one, it didn't say something like *Why are you texting me, loser?*

I never thought it possible, but I wanted a break from delicious Japanese food. I wanted food not made by Tak-Luxxe chefs. I wanted good ol' American cereal, with lots of sugar and no pretending there was nutrition involved. The Ex-Brats loved konbini food from convenience stores. I remembered I'd seen a 7-Eleven on the main street, at the ground-level entrance to the offices on the lower floors of Harmony Tower. I went down to the side-street entrance for Tak-Luxxe, then walked around the corner to the office building entrance. I realized this was the first time I'd left Tak-Luxxe alone. Could I successfully get my own food without the benefit of English-language-speaking people accompanying me?

I walked into the 7-Eleven. The store looked familiar, with compact aisles densely filled with convenient foods, but all the packages were in Japanese. There was a fresh food section with meticulous arrangements of boxed lunches and noodles in beautiful packaging. The store felt way too classy to be a 7-Eleven, or maybe this was how a 7-Eleven was supposed to look, and the American versions were just sloppy? I chose a bottle of soy milk, a banana, and a single-serving bowl of what looked like the sugariest cereal based on the colorful Japanese lettering on the package, and I headed to the front counter. The young counter clerk bowed and said, "Hello!" brightly to me.

"Konichiwa!" I answered.

The clerk must have then assumed I spoke Japanese because he started speaking in Japanese to me. For all I knew, he could be saying, *You're very almost-Japanese looking, American!* Or *You have excellent taste in cereal!*

I shook my head and made an apologetic face. "No Japanese," I said.

The clerk also shook his head, but he smiled warmly. "No English. Only 'hello' and 'thank you' and 'bathroom,'" he said, pointing toward the restroom in the far corner of the store.

He rang up my purchases. I tried to hand him my new American Express card, still not entirely believing this plastic card could pay for my purchases, but the clerk didn't take it and for a moment I worried. Then he handed me a small tray the size of a wallet, and I remembered a rule from Emiko's binder: When paying for purchases in Japan, it was considered impolite to hand the money directly to the clerk; money should be placed on a tray first. I placed my Amex card on the tray, the clerk took it, swiped it, and then placed my items in a bag, along with napkins and plastic utensils, and returned the credit card to me on the tray. He bowed to me, I bowed to him. It was funny how proud I felt about the minor transaction, the kind I had completely taken for granted in America, but it felt like a huge accomplishment in this place where I didn't speak the language, barely knew my way around, and had never in my life used a credit card.

I returned to Tak-Luxxe, to enjoy my breakfast at the very top of the building, in the Sky Garden on the fifty-fifth floor. I wished Mom could see this sight. Her baby daddy owned this palace! She'd be so impressed. I tried not to think about where Mom was at this moment while I was living this life. The Sky Garden was a lush, glassed-in area that felt like a forest, with its own walking path around flora and fauna from all over the world, and little placards in Japanese and English describing what each plant was. The ceiling was also glass, and from all the way up on floor fifty-five, it felt like the sky hovered that much closer, as if I could reach through the glass and touch the clouds.

I approached a small table at the far corner of the Sky Garden and saw Akemi sitting nearby, studying a math textbook. She wore a demure, long-sleeved, knee-length white lace dress, black patent leather Mary Jane shoes, and on the floor was her school backpack that said

"ICS-Tokyo" and was adorned with pastel ribbons, bows, and lace. The woman with her looked like she was in her early thirties, and she was long and slender with a fierce beauty, and intense black eyes that looked like they could burn holes through me.

Akemi said, "Good morning, Elle." She didn't sound particularly enthused to see me, but maybe it was that I was used to American cheerfulness.

"Hi!" I said.

Akemi said, "This is my mother." The woman bowed her head at me, and I did the same.

"Nice to meet you, Mrs. Kinoshita," I said.

Mrs. Kinoshita said nothing. "She doesn't speak English," said Akemi.

Akemi's mom didn't smile, but she extended her hand to the available chair. I sat down, and then Akemi and her mother exchanged some words in Japanese, and Mrs. Kinoshita stood up and walked away.

Akemi said, "She's going to swim." The pool was in the adjoining area to the Sky Garden. It was too small for quality laps, but if Imogen Kato didn't answer my text, it's where I would probably spend my afternoon till my hair appointment. Who was I kidding? Imogen Kato wasn't going to hang out with me today. She was just being nice when she showed me around my first day at ICS because I was her day's assignment. Akemi added, "And my mother is not Mrs. Kinoshita. But she doesn't understand English, so it doesn't matter if you call her by the wrong name."

"Then who is she?" I asked, confused.

"Watanabe-san. The real Mrs. Kinoshita lives in Osaka with my father's real wife." Akemi relayed this information casually. "She is very old."

"Oh! Does she know about you?"

"Yes. That's why we live in Tokyo now."

And I thought my family was complicated.

chapter eighteen

I mogen texted me back!

My Saturday martial arts trainer has the flu. Sucks for him, good luck for you. Let's go to Ginza!

Imogen met me at the thirty-sixth floor lobby of Tak-Luxxe, wearing distressed denim jeans, a ratty old T-shirt that said "My Daughter Goes to Wellesley," a leather motorcycle jacket with the words *Shar* and *Kato* painted in graffiti style on the wrists, sparkling purple eye shadow rimming her eyes, and black lipstick on her mouth so her face looked rather like a very stylish bruise. She wanted to see the view from Ikebana Café. I couldn't believe Imogen Kato was actually here, by her own choice, with nothing to gain, except a new, very unworldly friend who didn't even know what an expat was until she arrived in Tokyo.

"You could throw some sick parties at Destiny Club," said Imogen.

"Totally." I'd never thrown a party in my life. Did not have a single clue how to. Would I even be allowed to? "So where are we gonna go?"

"Lunch. Priorities. Got your PASMO card?"

"Check."

"Been on the Tokyo subway yet?"

"No."

"The subway is def the fastest and easiest way to get around here. Don't be like the other Ex-Brats and take cabs or Uber cuz you're lazy and spoiled." I almost died from the compliment. She'd grouped me in with her lazy, spoiled Ex-Brat friends!

Imogen navigated us a few blocks from Tak-Luxxe and into the subway station. We walked through what felt like an endless underground corridor (connected to other endless corridors), with convenience stores, newsstands, and small restaurants lining the way. There were a lot of people walking through the corridors, but the flow of foot traffic was so orderly. People walked on the left and passed on the right, just like the cars. I noticed a lot of Japanese kids wearing school uniforms. I asked Imogen, "Why wear uniforms on Saturday?"

She said, "Japanese students go to school a lot more days of the year than us. I think they have school on, like, the second and fourth Saturdays of the month. Might not be actual classroom time, but test preparation and school trips. And lots wear their uniforms even when they don't have to. It's a Japanese thing—showing your place in society—and uniforms announce 'student.' I'd never wear mine on the weekend."

"But your mom designed the ICS-Tokyo uniform! They're so cool, for uniforms."

Imogen rolled her eyes. "Too too."

"Too too, what?"

"I don't know. Too obvious. Too cute. Too branded." Said the girl with her mother's brand announced across her leather jacket's wrists.

We'd reached the fare gate for the subway. Imogen demonstrated how to swipe the PASMO card to enter. I followed her through a surge of people, up a set of stairs, and to the train platform. I thought I'd be overwhelmed by the strange surroundings and the crush of *so many* people, but all the direction signs were in Japanese and English, and Imogen shuttled me through like a pro. I'd ridden the Washington, DC, Metro system—and heard about subway systems in other cities like New York and London—so I knew what mass transit was supposed to be: late, grimy, unpleasant disease factories with pushy, irritated passengers. But here, the trains and platforms were so clean they were almost sterile, and riders formed orderly lines where the doors opened to let passengers on and off. There were no homeless people lying around the stations or subway cars, no terrible odors, no overflowing trash cans. There was no pushing or jostling. It was like everyone had their own invisible lane and knew exactly how to use it, despite so little space relative to the crowd size.

When the train pulled up, a crush of people got off, but nearly as many were waiting to get on. Imogen stood behind me and gently pushed me onto the train. We sandwiched in, too close to strangers for my comfort, but Imogen didn't appear fazed, so I tried to follow her lead and be chill about a situation that made me want to panic. When it seemed like not another person could possibly fit into the car, a uniformed officer wearing white gloves stood outside the train and pushed at the people at the door, to squeeze them in. Finally, the door closed.

I told Imogen, "If an officer had pushed people on the DC Metro like that, there would have been a riot."

I didn't think I'd been talking loudly at all, but Imogen placed her index finger at her mouth to indicate quiet. Softly, she said, "Talk low on the subway. It's the etiquette here. And *never* talk on your cell phone while you're on a train. Big Japanese no-no." I was so squished I couldn't have dug out my cell phone even if I'd tried.

An older lady carrying giant shopping bags that

scratched against my legs pressed too closely to me, her face practically touching mine, her mouth covered with a face mask held up with ties behind her ears. "How come so many people wear surgical masks here?" I whispered to Imogen. It wasn't just this lady. It seemed to me that at least half the people on the subway car had surgical masks covering their faces—young *and* old, none of them looking particularly sickly.

Imogen said, "They wear them to protect themselves from germs, but also to protect you if they have a cold and don't want to spread their germs."

"That's so polite."

"That's so OCD!"

Smushed between so many people, I looked above their heads to distract myself from all the unwanted human flesh contact. The subway car was lined at the top, above eye level, with colorful electronic advertisements and anime showcasing parks, restaurants, beauty products. Above the train car door, an electronic map followed the train's progress on the subway line. Imogen groaned when one of the electronic ads displayed a series of photos for what looked like an art exhibition. The photos were of erotic sculptures painted in splashes of bright colors— hips and breasts and groins, rendered in swirls of loud pinks, neon yellows, electric purples. Imogen said, "Dad is such an art perv."

I didn't get it. "He likes those crazy sculptures?"

"Those *are* his sculptures." The ad flashed the exhibition name in English. *Akira Kato Presents: A Rainbow of Sensuality.*

And I thought it was awkward to see Kenji Takahara in pajamas.

A female intercom voice announced the next stop in Japanese, then repeated it in English. "Nihonbashi!" The voice was so cheerful it was like she'd just announced the train's arrival at Disney World. Imogen said, "That's us. Push, Elle. Go!"

I pushed my way through the people not getting off the train, stepping on a a few feet and tripping over someone's suitcase, then had to take a deep breath at the train station wall. "That was intense," I said.

"Wait'll you see how crowded it gets at rush hour."

"Ima take Uber, then."

"Sometimes I do, too," Imogen confessed. "Then I get pissed when I'm stuck in traffic."

We walked toward the exit. At the end of the platform, there was a sign on the floor that had Japanese lettering, and beneath it said WOMEN ONLY.

"Women Only?" I asked.

Imogen said, "That means late at night, the cars that arrive at this spot on the platform are just for women. So the polite salarymen who hit the *izakaya* bars after work don't suddenly think they can become subway grope monsters on their drunken rides home."

I thought of how often Mom complained about drunk guys hitting on her when she took the Metro home after late-night shifts and how she might have appreciated such a gender-exclusive transit luxury. I thought of her now in a jail cell while I was traipsing around Tokyo with a girl from a fashion magazine, and my heart clenched.

"You okay?" Imogen asked me as she led the way through the train station. She took hold of my arm. "I'm sure Tokyo is intimidating at first, but you'll get used to it. Why the sad face? Boyfriend you left behind in America?"

"Hardly," I said. I'd barely even kissed a boy. Not that I'd ever say that to this worldly force of nature. "My best friend back home is a guy, but he's more like a big brother."

"Photo evidence, please." I took my phone from my pocket and showed Imogen a picture of Reg and me, sitting on a diving board together after swim practice, two years earlier. "Boyfriend potential," Imogen announced.

"I'd be too scared we'd ruin our friendship like that. Do you have a boyfriend?"

"Not this week."

We walked through the crowded train station toward a set of doors leading into a big department store. Just inside, a set of uniformed women wearing fashionable skirts, jackets, and hats—looking rather like flight attendants, I thought—bowed to customers as they walked in from the subway station. "What's that about?" I asked Imogen.

"They're thanking customers for coming to this store. You'll see that a lot here."

"All the bowing feels weird," I admitted.

"Dude, don't hate. Japanese people have cultivated thousands of years of rules and protocol to protect the *wa*."

"Wa . . . what?"

"The wa is, like, the system of social harmony in Japanese culture. Did you notice how smooth and easy that subway ride was, even with packed cars and crowded platforms?"

"Yeah."

"That's the wa."

"That's *wa*-nderful," I joked.

"Don't be punny," Imogen said. We entered the Takashimaya department store through the basement level, and my eyes were joyfully assaulted by the sight of an epic number of beautiful food stalls lining the store aisles. "This is called a *depachika*—a Japanese food hall."

The depachika was like the Ikebana Café with all its different food types, but times a zillion, with confectionaries selling chocolates and cakes and sweets that looked like dumplings, and food counters offering dazzling displays of seafood, meats, salads, candies, and juices. There was even a grocery store, with exquisite-looking fruit individually wrapped and cushioned, flawless in appearance. The workers in each stall wore different uniforms, some with matching hats, and they called out "Konichiwa!" to passersby. I loved watching each counter's workers delicately wrap the purchases and hand them over to customers as if presenting a gift rather than just, say, a sandwich or a chocolate treat. As I marveled at the display cases of sweets—with so many varieties of chocolates, cakes, and candies—Imogen said, "The traditional Japanese sweets are called *wagashi*, which is stuff like *mochi*—rice flour cakes filled with sweet pastes—and jellied candies that look more like works of art than something you'd actually eat, and cookies that look gorgeous but usually taste bland."

"The cookie tins are so beautiful!" I marveled, admiring a case of tins with prints so intricate they looked like they could double as designer handbags.

"People give those cookie tins as omiyage. Do you know about the gift-giving thing here?"

I nodded. "I met my Japanese grandmother for the first time yesterday, and I had to give her a box of chocolates, which she basically said sucked."

"How rude," said Imogen.

"She wasn't very nice," I admitted.

"Hafu angst?"

"That. And being a racist bitch."

Imogen laughed. "Ouch. You need major carbs to compensate." We passed an array of stalls selling Belgian chocolates, German sweets, and then French pastries. "The *yogashi* are the Western-style confections like cakes and pastries. Some of the biggest names from all over the world have stalls here, like Ladurée from France and Wittamer from Belgium. I love going to the depachika for treats. It can be like a cheat weekend trip to Paris or Brussels."

"What do the Ex-Brats have when they eat here?"

"Hard to say because the Ex-Brats rotation changes all the time. I'm the only girl in our class who has been at ICS-Tokyo for more than five years. People are always moving away. Of the current crew, I never take Ntombi or Jhanvi here. They're always on a diet. So lame. When Arabella was here, we'd come to eat in the Din Tai Fung restaurant one level down. They make these dumplings with purple yams or sweet red bean paste that are just sick they're so delicious."

Yams sounded great. I found a food stall I liked and picked out a grilled yam and some fried tempura for lunch. I didn't need Imogen to help me translate. I just pointed at the items I wanted, the counter worker smiled and packaged everything, then showed me a calculator with the amount I owed. I placed my Amex card on the tray the worker handed me, relieved to have had my morning 7-Eleven experience so I was able to observe the proper paying etiquette in front of Imogen. She bought an egg salad sandwich, which was packaged so beautifully you'd think it was jewelry from Tiffany's. It was in a cardboard box that had a flower print on its sides and was wrapped in tight, clear plastic at the top so you could see the sandwich inside. The sandwich had the crusts removed and was cut into two square pieces standing upright in the box, with pieces of perfectly cut fruit arrayed on the side.

"Where do we eat?" I asked Imogen. I saw no tables for sitting and actually enjoying our lunch.

Imogen navigated us to an elevator. She said, "When in need of open space in Tokyo, go up." We got out at the top floor and stepped onto an open-air rooftop that looked like a park, with a green lawn, paths, and trees, and diners eating their takeout meals on benches or picnicking on the lawn.

"I officially love Tokyo," I said. *Itadakimasu!* Let's eat.

• • •

"Do you like cats?" Imogen asked me after we'd finished eating.

Seriously? Was my day that started off with an earthquake really this great?

"I only love cats like I love ramen and snow days and watching *Gilmore Girls* on endless repeat. While eating cake."

"I knew I liked you. Want to go to a cat café? None of the Ex-Brats ever want to go to the cat cafés with me."

"I'm so your girl. Let's do it!"

Imogen led us back to the subway in the basement level. I was giddy with excitement. I was having what felt like my first awesome day since before the Beast.

"How do you like your dad so far?" Imogen asked me.

"He works *all the time*."

"Typical. Did you find out if he's yakuza?"

What a strange question. "Why would you say that?"

She shrugged. "If he's in the hotel business, he's probably yakked. Or the businesspeople he associates with are."

I was offended. I hardly knew Kenji Takahara, and maybe he was a deadbeat dad who'd only shown up in my life a few days ago . . . but he wasn't a mobster. He wore beautiful suits, and he went to Andover and then to Georgetown. "He's not yakked," I declared.

"If you say so," she said.

When we got out of the subway, we walked in circles through throngs of shoppers and hipsters, trying to find the cat café, with no luck. "This new place just opened up, so I'm not sure exactly where it is," Imogen explained. Finally, she flagged down a policeman on the street and showed him her phone with an address on it. His face lit up. "*Nya, nya!*" To my confused face, Imogen translated. "Meow, meow!" He then escorted us to a building where the elevator was located in an alley. We never would have found the entrance on our own. He pointed up and then displayed seven fingers.

Imogen said, "Seventh floor, I guess." She bowed to the Japanese policeman as we got into the elevator. He bowed at us and returned to the street. When the door closed, she added, "God, I love Japanese law and order. I can't imagine a cop in London helping us find a cat café like that."

The elevator doors opened directly onto the cat café. There was a machine that dispensed slippers, and shoe cubbies where street shoes should be placed, along with a long list of rules in mangled English: *Please not loud voice. No feed cats, pay extra to feed treat to cats. Have super funs time!*

"Purr-fection," Imogen cooed as soon as we entered the cat room. A swarm of kittens played and napped on the benches and cat trees located throughout the room.

I hesitated at the door. I loved the sight of the furballs and their sweet whisker faces, but the vibe was weird and off. The cats all had short legs disproportionate to their size, like they'd been manufactured that way to look cuter, and they had little interest in playing. The room had upholstered benches lining the walls for seating, and was centered by a giant cat tree—bigger than the others—where the cats climbed and found perches. Cat toys were littered across the floor and in baskets so customers could play with the cats. I picked up a mouse on a string—Huff's favorite play toy—and tried to get some tabby kitties lounging on the high perches to engage with me. A few swatted but quickly lost interest, like they were too bored and tired from so many tourists coming to play with them. I paid extra to feed them some treats, but the cats just ate and then moved on, disinterested, fickle.

"Can we go now?" I asked Imogen after we'd been there for about ten minutes.

"We just got here." She was sitting on a window bench looking out over the street, surrounded by piles of furballs licking, playing, and scampering around her.

"I thought this would be cool, but honestly, it's creeping me out. I'm ready to leave now."

Imogen said, "So go. I'm staying."

"Then how do I get home?"

"Be a big girl. If you don't feel comfortable taking the subway by yourself yet, just take a cab."

"I don't speak Japanese."

"Just tell the driver 'Tak-Luxxe' and show him the address on your phone. He'll know."

She looked as irritated with me as I felt with her. But she also had a kitten crawling across her shoulder and she couldn't resist giggling. She sneezed. "I'm so allergic to these little jerks, but I don't even care!"

She also didn't seem worried that she was leaving me to maneuver this new, strange city on my own.

chapter nineteen

In the cab ride back to Tak-Luxxe, I googled *yakuza* on my phone. Imogen Kato didn't know what she was talking about. Yakuza weren't men like Kenji. Yakuza were gangsters, gamblers, and murderers. Yakuza had full-body tattoos, and they cut off the tops of pinky fingers of members as punishment for failure. They weren't businessmen who owned posh hotel properties.

When I returned to Tak-Luxxe, it was time for my hair appointment at the Destiny Club beauty salon, Utsukushii. I sat in the salon chair facing a mirror while the hairdresser, a Japanese lady named Tamao, inspected me. "You have very pretty face," Tamao said, fiddling with the length of my hair. Then she leaned in to my ear and whispered, "You look like Daddy! Very attractive. Don't tell him I said that."

I tried not to laugh. I said, "Maybe cut an inch off but otherwise keep it long, please. I don't like it too short."

"Two inches. Once your hair is smoother, it will look longer, so it's better to take more off now." I looked skeptically at Tamao in the mirror. Wasn't I supposed to be the boss of this decision? "You'll see," Tamao assured me.

An assistant came to Tamao with a rolling cart filled with hair-cutting supplies and some bottles with words in Japanese. I assumed this was the deep conditioner treatment I was getting. "Come with me for a hair wash first," the assistant said.

After the assistant had washed my hair, she raised my head up from the sink. I asked, "Shouldn't I get the conditioner first?" My wet hair was impossible to brush without conditioner. The assistant shook her head and said, "She will do it," gesturing to Tamao.

"Conditioner after cut," said Tamao, and led me back to the salon chair. She began brushing my hair, not nearly gently enough for my taste.

"Ow!" I cried out.

"Sorry," said Tamao. "Hafu hair is very difficult."

Ignorance, also very difficult, I thought. I asked, "Do you have a magazine?" I didn't feel like talking to this lady anymore.

Tamao brought me a stack of American, British, and

Japanese fashion magazines. "You will look like the girls in these pictures when we are finished!"

I hadn't asked to look like any of the girls in those pictures, but it felt too late to turn back now. I pretended to read a magazine, just so Tamao would stop talking to me. After she trimmed my hair, she applied the deep conditioner to it, which was a really weird, smelly goop that required me to sit with a cap over my head for an hour. I was about to put my earbuds in to listen to music while I waited, but an aesthetician approached my seat, pushing a rolling cart of beauty gadgets. "Face now," she told me.

The aesthetician gently tipped my head back, gave my forehead and cheeks a really nice massage that in no way indicated what was going to happen next, and then started plucking my eyebrows. "Hey, I didn't ask for this!" I protested.

"Mrs. Noriko Takahara request this service for you," she said. What the hell? But it was too late to demand the aesthetician stop, because then my eyebrows would look uneven.

"Just don't do thin eyebrows, please," I said, resigned but not wanting a pencil eyebrow look.

The aesthetician said, "Of course not. Just a little tweeze to shape. There, done! Would you like anything waxed?"

"No!" I said, horrified.

The aesthetician shrugged and walked away. I looked in the mirror. My formerly bushy eyebrows had been plucked and shaped into a more defined arch. They actually looked damn good. I hoped my hair would look as shiny as Kim Takahara's after they took the cap off.

When the timer went off to end the deep conditioning treatment, I assumed my hair would be rinsed, but instead Tamao brought me back to the chair at her station. She brushed and then started blow-drying my hair. When she'd finished, my hair was completely straight, and lustrous, just like Kim Takahara's. I *did* look like a girl in a magazine. "How do you like?" Tamao asked me proudly.

"It's nice." It would take some getting used to. I observed myself in the mirror and nearly didn't recognize the sophisticated girl with straight hair and admittedly amazing eyebrows looking back at me. "I mean, my hair's just going to be wiry again after I wash it, but I like it for now."

It was good to know if I ever wanted this smooth look again, all I had to do was go to the Tak-Luxxe salon to get it, but I wouldn't want this style all the time. I didn't look like me. Reg was going to fall out of his chair laughing next time he saw me on FaceTime.

Tamao said, "No, this straightening lasts a long time,

at least three months. Then you come back to us for touch-up."

"WHAT?" My blood boiled. "How come no one told me this was semi-permanent?"

"I thought you knew. That's what Japanese hair treatment means. Why do you look upset? Your hair is beautiful."

Tamao was not being insincere. The workers in the salon who'd been sneakily watching the boss's not-so-secret-anymore daughter the whole time I was in there were looking at me now with approval. "Lovely!" said Tamao's assistant as she ushered another client to the sink.

The client said, "I want her hair!"

I looked in the mirror. I knew I had moved to a different country to start a new life, but this new girl in the mirror was a stranger staring back at me.

• • •

"I protest!" I said to Kenji that night at dinner. We were seated inside the Destiny Club restaurant called Fantasy League, a sports bar on fifty that was decorated like the ultimate man cave, with wood-paneled walls, a beer bar in the center of the room, and TV screens hovering in every available space showing different sports games being played throughout the world: baseball, American football, soccer, golf, and cricket. "When your sister booked the hair appointment for me, she didn't also mention it was for a *semi-permanent* hair treatment. I thought I was just going to get, like, some fancy cut and blowout."

Kenji was more focused on his American-style hamburger with cheese melted down the sides than on my outrage over my new hair. "When I was at Georgetown, there was a sports bar on M Street that made delicious burgers. I modeled this restaurant and the menu here on it. We didn't add Fantasy League to the plans for the new building until after my father passed, though. He didn't like American burgers, so they were never on the menu at Tak-Luxxe. He was a snob for Japanese beef."

I wanted to learn more about his family, but not at this particular moment. Let's stay on topic, KenjiIGuess. "Like the hair appointment deceit wasn't bad enough, your mother also told them to pluck my eyebrows. I didn't realize that's what was happening until it was too late to stop it."

Kenji focused on his burger and also on the baseball game playing behind my head. Typical male avoidance. Then he said, "You like the Nationals or Orioles? I loved to go to baseball games when I lived in the Washington area."

Sigh. Men just didn't get it. I tugged on a length of my hair. "I didn't ask for *this*."

"It will grow out, eventually. But it looks beautiful."

"Or do you mean now I look like all the other rich ladies here?"

He put down his burger. Finally! "I never said that, but why would that be a bad thing? Is this hair drama a teenager mood? I was warned about those."

"Who warned you?"

"Mother." That witch. Of course she was going to bad-mouth me as much as possible to Kenji. Like she knew anything about me. I was going to do so well in Tokyo that Mrs. Takahara would choke on her own surprised pride.

I'd show Kenji some teenager moods. "It seems like you work all the time," I whined. "I bet you work Sundays, too."

"Usually."

"Is that why you don't have a girlfriend?"

Kenji laughed, even though I hadn't intended to be funny. "How do you know I don't have a girlfriend?"

"Do you?"

"There was a singer at the Destiny Bar piano bar. Her name was Eden Bechtel. We went out for a few years. She moved back to Texas four months ago."

"What did she look like? Do you have a picture on your phone?"

"Maybe?" He looked surprised by my curiosity, but

he took his phone out and scrolled through his photos. "There's one."

He showed me a photo of himself wearing a tuxedo, next to a stunning, statuesque, very tanned blond lady wearing a champagne-colored sequined gown. She was probably in her midthirties. If you put a waitress uniform on her, she actually looked a lot like my mother before the Beast. Kenji had a type.

"She's pretty. Why'd she leave?"

"She wanted to return home." He paused. "She wanted different things." Like a commitment? I wondered. "Mother didn't approve of her."

I had a sinking feeling in my stomach. His mother didn't approve of Eden Bechtel, and now she was *gone*. How long did *I* have to win him over so he'd let me stay? "Maybe you could take tomorrow off and we could do something together?" I asked him.

"You want to go somewhere with me?" He looked genuinely surprised. This guy went to Georgetown? He didn't seem so bright in this moment.

"Yes!"

"Will you stop complaining about your hair if we go somewhere?"

A slight smile pulled at the corners of my mouth. He really had been listening to my hair whine. "Probably."

"Do you like baseball?"

"I like to play it, but watching it on TV is boring."

A Japanese businessman wearing a nice suit entered Fantasy League and approached our table. Kenji stood up, and they bowed to each other, then spoke in Japanese. When they finished, Kenji bowed to the man again. Deeply. The guy must have been important. The businessman turned around and left, never once acknowledging me.

"What was that about?" I asked Kenji.

"Business" was all Kenji said.

"How come you didn't introduce me?" Now that I had proper hair and all.

"That man only cares about money, not about meeting my daughter." He looked at a baseball interview playing on one of the TV screens. "Hideki Matsui! Great hitter. Japanese outfielder who played for the Yankees." Classic male subject-changing. Reggie did the same thing when I complained about girls hitting on him at the pool and distracting from our swim practices.

"You like the Yankees?" I asked.

"I like Japanese players who are so outstanding they can play for the Yankees. I was very good at baseball when I was your age. My fantasy was to play in America." His face looked wistful.

"Really? What position did you play?"

"Shortstop. I had a very strong arm. I wanted to

become a professional player, but my parents refused. They thought athletics was not a real job."

"So you didn't like being told what to do! See? Get it?" I tugged on a piece of my hair again. (Wow, my hair was so smooth and soft.)

"My parents were right. I wasn't good enough for pro ball. Maybe Kim was also right."

Infuriating! "That I should look more Japanese?"

"Yes, to be honest."

Quietly, I asked, "Are you embarrassed by me?"

"No. Never. But Japan is different from America. Different expectations. The more you assimilate, the better it will be for you here."

At last I was ready to drop the topic. Pushing it further only reinforced what I was too aware of: He was spineless. I wondered if Kenji had mustered every ounce of courage he had to bring me here.

"I'd rather assimilate on *my* terms, not your mother's or your sister's," I said.

"Fair enough," Kenji said. "I can make some time tomorrow. I like to go to the batting cage to practice when I have time off from work. Would you like to join me?"

Part of me was disappointed that he didn't ask what I would like to do. Part of me respected that he didn't pander to the moody teenager. I took a bite of my hamburger. Good lord it was delicious—perfectly juicy and charred.

Like on a level where McDonald's didn't even exist, except in hell. Was a bad meal even possible in this country?

"Batting practice sounds awesome," I said. Perhaps we could work on strengthening Kenji's spine.

chapter twenty

On Sunday afternoon, Kenji and I took a cab to the batting cage. Like the subway, the cab was ridiculously clean, with white lace covers on the backs of the seats and a large GPS on the driver's dashboard. Nothing like the clunker taxis I occasionally took with Mom back in DC. As the cab drove along, I was mesmerized looking out the window. We passed temples with colorful flags adorning the grounds, gardens sandwiched in between tall buildings, restaurants with red paper lanterns hanging outside, and every variety of store. And so many people walking along the streets. The orderly density of people and buildings amazed me.

"How much farther?" I asked Kenji after we'd slowly moved through traffic for fifteen minutes.

"Not too far."

"Can we get out and walk the rest of the way?" It was a picture-perfect day outside.

"Sure. Good day for a walk. Crisp autumn air, not too hot, not too cold."

Kenji directed the driver and we got out and started walking. He walked at a quick pace, jostling seamlessly through the throngs of people while I struggled to keep up. "It seems like all the buildings here are either really new or really old," I said.

"So much of Tokyo was destroyed during World War Two. What you see now was either built recently, by Japanese history standards, or it's very old indeed."

He stopped our walk to peer inside a splendid white, wrought-iron gate with gold spokes, through which we could glimpse a building that looked like Buckingham Palace in London. The grounds were lush and parklike, surrounded by trees. Kenji said, "Tōgū Palace is through those gates. It's a state guesthouse now. You can't see it from here, but the crown prince and his family live on the grounds farther back behind the palace."

"Can we take a tour here sometime?"

"It's only open for visitors on New Year's Day and the emperor's birthday. The Imperial Palace, closer to where we live, has more access for tourists. It's even got a moat surrounding it. Beautiful gardens year-round but especially in spring when the cherry blossoms bloom."

We resumed walking. I didn't know when I'd have Kenji's undivided time and attention again outside of Tak-Luxxe, and I wanted to pepper him with as many questions as I could. "Have you always lived in Tokyo?"

"Except for a year in London, and my time in Washington, yes."

"What did you do in London?"

"I took a business course at London School of Economics."

"Did you like it?"

"I loved London but not school. I would have stayed longer, but my father wanted me here to work for Takahara Industries."

"What was your dad like?"

"Very strict. Rigid. Never satisfied. Always angry that I liked to have fun more than study."

"How did you do in school?"

"Decent, but it was hard for me. How about you?"

"I was a straight-A student until Mom started having problems."

"I bet you will be top of your class like Kim always was."

We'd reached a city park with sports fields and tons of people outside enjoying the autumn day. After so much concrete, it was refreshing to be surrounded by trees and green grass. We entered the batting cage building, where

Kenji paid at the front desk. I'd never been to a batting cage, so I had no idea what to expect. Would it be a literal cage?

The batting area was divided by small, fenced partitions large enough to hold a few people, with a mound in the middle of each cage, and all the partitions looking out onto a baseball field with a virtual stadium on giant screens behind it. "Batter up!" Kenji said. "You want to go first?"

"No, you go."

He stepped up to the plate, and a virtual pitcher appeared on a screen, sending a real ball Kenji's way. *Smack!* Kenji hit it hard—a home run! Virtual crowds cheered from the screen as a virtual uniformed player rounded the bases.

"That's a hard act to follow." I stepped up to the plate, and Kenji handed me the bat. I leaned into hitting position, remembering the form from when Reggie had once given me batting lessons.

"Relax your shoulders and focus on the ball," Kenji advised. Suddenly, a ball came whizzing by me. I swung but way too late. "You'll get the next one." Another ball came hurtling to me. Another strike. Kenji adjusted my arms and stance. The next ball came down. I hit it! Foul ball, but I got it. "Excellent!" Kenji said. "You have a strong swing like your father."

He set up for his next hit. He looked like I did when I swam: determined and happy.

"I think I'll stick to swimming," I said. "My coach at the YMCA used to say if I got good enough, I might get a swimming scholarship to pay for college."

"A scholarship is good, but I set up a trust fund for your college education when you were born. You get in, the money is there for you to go." He hit another home run.

WHAT?

I was determined to go to college but always expected I'd have to work part-time and take out huge loans. It would be a major struggle.

"Are you kidding me?" I asked.

"Why would I joke about something that important? You're very smart. You will get straight A's and go to an Ivy League school like Kim." He sounded completely confident of that prospect.

"Yale, not Harvard," I said, trying to share his confidence. Until one minute ago, I never imagined I could seriously consider anything more expensive than the University of Maryland. My head was reeling.

"Why?"

"Rory Gilmore went there."

"I don't know her," he said. "What would you want to study?"

"I'm not sure." I struggled to find words. "I'm sorry.

I can't believe you actually want to send me to college. I mean, thank you!" He bowed slightly to me, pleased. I added, "Science was always my best subject. I like helping people. Maybe I'd want to be a doctor?"

He put his bat down. "My daughter, the doctor." He beamed.

I was going to kick ass at my new school, if it earned me more of Kenji's look of pride.

OCTOBER

---

chapter twenty-one

Dear Mom,

*I'm sorry it's taken me so long to write you a proper
letter. I've gotten your two letters and I loved them. I'm
SO PROUD of you for joining the AA meetings. I know
that was hard for you. I'm so happy you've taken up yoga
and that you finally got off the waiting list to read the first*
Game of Thrones *book from the library. But sorry you're
having nightmares about dragons and white walkers.*

*Don't worry, I don't love Kenji more than you already. I
barely see him. Uncle Masa calls me almost every night
on FaceTime to check up on me. I think I see him more
than Kenji, who seems more like a roommate than a dad.
But Kenji's penthouse apartment has sick views over*

the city and I can order room service anytime I want.
(I don't, usually. But it's super sweet to know it's an
option.) And there's a maid who comes through every day
when I'm at school, so no one nags me about leaving my
clothes on the floor or not doing the dishes. ;)

Life in Tokyo is good. Crazy! But crazy good. My
ambition was to kick ass at my new school. Instead, I've
started out kind of having my ass kicked. The workload is
so much more than I'm used to. Even the subjects I was
already taking, like Spanish, I have so much studying
to catch up. Every night I have, like, four solid hours of
homework. On the afternoons I have swim team practice
after school, I usually don't even get home till after 5 p.m.
Then I have dinner with Kenji at 7 p.m. Doesn't leave a
lot of time for homework and getting to bed early enough
to wake up at 6:30 a.m. because the car to school leaves
at 7. Plus all the time I spend texting my friends from
school gets in the way of homework. Yes, I made some
friends! You are not going to believe this (I still don't),
but I have been hanging out with the "popular" crowd
because their queen, Imogen Kato, decided she likes
me. (Shar Kato is her mother! Remember how we used
to love shopping for the Shar Kato collection at Target
because we'd never be able to afford her fancy clothes at

*Saks Fifth Avenue, but we used to be so sure Shar Kato
didn't actually design the Target clothes herself? Well,
Imogen said her mom really did design them even though
she prefers not to use cheaper materials. Apparently,
her mom would never put her name on a line of clothes
no matter where they were sold unless she designed the
clothes herself. How's that for insider fashion gossip?)*

*I've been talking to Reg on FaceTime; he says hi. He said
he's going into the army in January after his birthday.
I'm excited for him but scared, too. Do you remember
Carmen Rodriguez, who was on our swim team at the Y?
(Really lazy backstroke and always complained about the
water being too cold?) She goes to the same school as Reg,
and they've been hanging out together a lot. He's always
talking about her now. I think he has a crush on her. I
really thought he'd have better taste in girls.*

*I get driven to school in the mornings with this girl
named Akemi, whose father sends us in a chauffeured car.
I know, insane. She's a year younger than me and shy.
Usually she sleeps in the car on the way to school—it's
a long drive in traffic. That's why I am using this time
right now to type this letter to you on my new MacBook.
No, I'm not joking. I have my own computer now.*

I printed out a photo for you of me in my school uniform . . . with my new hair. I got a Japanese hair treatment. I think the Japanese part means getting the treatment without having it first properly explained to you what it actually is. The treatment part is making your hair very straight and smooth. Reg laughed so hard when I showed him on FaceTime. He said I look like I think I'm in a magazine, not like me. I think I look like me . . . just different. But my friends loved it. Kenji said it makes me look more Japanese, and Uncle Masa said it makes me look very sophisticated. What do you think?

I haven't started off great in classes because I'm so behind, but I swear I'm going to get my grades up because Kenji said he would pay for me to go to college. Yeah, I'll give you a second to recover from that shock. I can go to college! But I gotta study. So, I gotta go.

Love you, more soon.

XOXO,

Elle

chapter twenty-two

"Zoellner! Show me what you've got."

The swim coach, Tanya Hopkins, was a former swim champion from Illinois who'd narrowly missed qualifying for the Olympics three years earlier, and then moved to Tokyo to join her English-teacher boyfriend in Japan. She called everyone by their last name. While the rest of the morning swim class of fifteen other students did warm-ups in the other lanes of the five-lane pool, I shivered, standing at the ledge of the farthest lane, waiting for the signal. Tanya held up her stopwatch and then said, "Go!"

I dove in and swam a front-crawl stroke to one end of the pool and back again. "Great form and outstanding flip turn," Tanya said to me when I'd finished the lap. "*And you knocked off one point two seconds from last week.*"

"Cool," I said, out of breath and exhilarated. I loved getting to swim *every day* for PE credit. Everything was right about this situation, except for Reggie not being here to share it with me. We always swam best when the other was in the water. I reminded myself that I still hadn't texted him pictures of the pool. I'd do that as soon as I finished with Coach Tanya. He wouldn't believe it.

"Let's see how your butterfly is coming along."

"It's my weakest stroke." There was no need for me to be defensive, but maybe I was being critical of myself because Ryuu Kimura was at the other end of the pool, doing a really fast butterfly sprint.

"I'll be the judge of that. Ready? Go!"

I swam a butterfly stroke to the end of the pool and back.

"Yes, yes, yes!" Tanya said when I emerged from the water. "We need to work on your explosion off the block, but you knocked off one-point-five seconds on the fly. I'm so stoked you've joined us on the ICS-Sailfish team, Zoellner."

I shamelessly basked in the praise of my swim skills as I grabbed a towel. The pool was heated, but the autumn Tokyo air was getting chilly. The school also had an indoor pool, but it was being cleaned to prepare it for winter use. "What was my time?"

"It's right there," said Tanya, pointing to the electronic

scoreboard behind the diving board, which flashed my time and announced to everyone in sight that Elle Zoellner was now, officially, the fastest female swimmer in her class.

YES! Even without Reggie goading me, my game was strong . . . and swimming was probably the *only* thing I'd be better at than all these overprivileged students. Considering how long it had been since I'd swum on the Y team, I was surprised my performance was so solid. The daily swimming was paying off, probably most especially on my waistline. My body was leaner than it had ever been, despite all the delicious Japanese food I was devouring.

Tanya turned to address the other swimmers, doing drills in the far lanes. "See this girl, everybody? She's the one to beat. Let's go!"

Suddenly, Ryuu Kimura emerged from beneath the water next to me. He didn't wear a swim cap, and his streaks of wet icy-blue hair gave him the appearance of having a halo under the sun's glare.

"Finally," he said, "someone at this school who's almost as good a swimmer as me."

Then he slid underwater again and returned to the other side of the pool.

• • •

"He said *what*?" Imogen exclaimed at lunch.

I repeated Ryuu's declaration, trying to infuse it with the same absurd intensity he'd given it. " 'Finally, someone at this school who's *almost* as good as a swimmer as me.' "

Jhanvi said, "He really needs to get over himself. He's not that great a swimmer."

Ntombi said, "Have you ever actually seen him swim?"

Jhanvi said, "No."

Imogen piped in. "I have, with Arabella. He's great at backstroke, okay at everything else. He shouldn't confuse being top swimmer at ICS-Tokyo with actually being talented. ICS-Taipei killed the Sailfish last year, because he choked on breaststroke."

Ntombi asked, "Why does he wear those boy briefs when he swims? They just show how pale he is."

Oscar said, "He has a *great* body. Lean, muscled, not too tall and not too short. Just right."

Nik said, "Just right for an imbecile."

These snarky people! I pointed out, "For someone who's supposedly iced out, you guys seem to talk about Ryuu Kimura a lot."

Imogen placed her arm over my shoulder affectionately. "We promise to objectify you in a swimsuit when you're iced out, too."

"You're a true pal," I said. My phone beeped with a

text from Akemi, who was sitting a couple tables away and appeared to be studying on her laptop but was obviously listening to my table's conversation.

I read her text: "Nekokaburi." It means to make your face like a kitty, pretend innocent.

I laughed at the message. I would enjoy the Ex-Brat lunches so much more if Akemi joined us, but they didn't want her, and she preferred to be a loner at school. During our morning car rides, when she wasn't napping, she peppered me with questions about the Ex-Brats. But during the actual school day, she seemed to prefer to keep to herself.

"Who are you texting with?" Imogen asked me.

"A friend from home," I said. Not a lie.

I texted back to Akemi. "Curiosity killed the cat." It means being too inquisitive, like a cat with nine lives, can get you into trouble.

Ntombi said, "Guys, my parents are away this weekend, so you know what that means. Let's do something fun!" Ntombi's mom and dad were super strict. They didn't let Ntombi go out on school nights or on weekends until all her schoolwork was done, and even then, only to a limited range of places within the Minato district where they lived and where most of the embassies and consulates were located.

I sent another quick text to Akemi. I was on a roll with

cat phrases. "When the cat's away, the mice will play." It means when there is no supervision, people will be naughty!

"Our field hockey game is the priority this Saturday," said Jhanvi. Then her eyes twinkled mischievously. "But we should go somewhere fun after, to celebrate crushing the British International School." She pulled out the pencil holding up her messy bun of black-red hair, which now fell down her back.

"Shibuya!" Nik called out. Then he asked me, "Have you been to Shibuya yet?"

"Nope." I hung out with the Ex-Brats at lunch, but my surprise inclusion in their group hadn't involved going to cool places outside of school.

Nik said, "Shibuya is probably the most fun part of Tokyo. Everything happens there. I'd only take you to the best places—trust me!"

Imogen rolled her eyes at Nik and then said, "All right, everyone, hand over your PASMO cards."

The group complied—everyone except for me. "I don't understand."

Imogen said, "We're taking up a collection for Ntombi's housekeeper. We give her these. She sells them at a lower cost to the other Filipina housekeepers in exchange for cash. She then lets Ntombi do whatever Ntombi wants over the weekend, and her parents never find out."

"Wow. Way to work it." I reluctantly took my PASMO card from my wallet and handed it to Imogen. "But how will I get around on the subway if I don't have a PASMO card?"

The group laughed but stopped when they realized I was serious. Jhanvi said, like it was obvious, "Just say you lost it and your dad will give you a new one. He's nice, right?"

If Mom was here, she'd never give me a new one. She'd tell me I was a sucker for going along with this bribe scheme just to hang out with the popular crowd. But Kenji would be thrilled to tell his assistant to get me a new one, if my new PASMO card would also give me weekend time with the "right" friends.

A new text from Akemi popped up on my phone. "Kysuuso neko wo kamu." It means a mouse that has been put into a corner will bite the cat.

I typed back: The weak ones can win if they're brave.

Yes! she replied.

I wished Akemi was joining the Ex-Brat adventures. She'd hate it, but I would relax more having someone around that I could just be myself with.

chapter twenty-three

The ICS-Tokyo volleyball and fencing teams, who usually occupied most of the seats on the after-school bus, had been knocked out by the flu. This afternoon, there were only two people on board besides the driver. Me and Ryuu Kimura.

Akemi had violin lessons after school in a neighborhood nowhere near Tak-Luxxe, and I usually stayed after school for study time or for swim team practice and then took the early-evening bus back into the city. ICS's version of a school bus service was a private chartered luxury coach with plush, clean seats, Wi-Fi, and a selection of healthy snacks like nuts, fresh fruit, and a drink refrigerator filled with alkaline water bottles and cold-pressed juices. Like an airport shuttle service, the bus made drop-offs at hotels in different neighborhoods in the city.

Students could either walk home from the closest stop or get rides. Usually I did homework on the bus ride home or tried to take a nap.

Today, Ryuu was sitting one row behind me on the other side of the aisle. "Hey, Elle."

I turned around. His black-blue hair was still wet from swim team practice, and I could practically smell the chlorine wafting from it. I loved that smell. "What?"

"Do you mind if I practice my music? Just asking because you're not wearing headphones."

"I don't care," I snapped, like I was Imogen. But the Ex-Brats weren't on the bus. No bitchy instinct necessary. If a girl was mildly pleasant to a boy who was iced out when there was no one else around, was it like that tree falling down in the forest? With no witnesses, did it actually make a sound? My hands were clean here. I could be as nice as I was curious about Ryuu. Genuinely. There was an instrument in a case on the empty seat next to him. I asked him, "What do you play?"

He opened the case and pulled out . . . a ukulele! "Any requests?" he asked.

"I don't know any songs for a ukulele."

"Sure you do. Any song can work on the uke. What was your favorite song growing up?"

"I dunno. I loved *The Wizard of Oz*. 'Over the Rainbow'?" Grrr! What a corny song choice. I needed more time to think of a clever song. She wasn't even here, but I could totally see Imogen rolling her eyes at me.

"Love it," said Ryuu. He strummed the chords and didn't sing aloud, but I could hear Judy Garland's voice in my head. *Somewhere, over the rainbow, skies are blue.* The melody being played on a ukulele made me feel so safe and happy. *You are a dork, Elle Zoellner.*

"You're pretty good," I told Ryuu. He played with confidence and a slight smile on his face, like he was enjoying himself. "But why'd you pick up the ukulele, of all instruments?"

He changed the chords he strummed and made up a new tune as he sang, "Went on vacation to Hawaii when I was ten. Bought a ukulele in the hotel gift shop. Liked it even better than playing guitar. Kept at it because . . . it really annoys my father. He doesn't think the uke is a manly instrument. So I play it to confront his gender bias." Ryuu stopped playing for a moment and then shredded the ukulele for a finale with flourish. In a heavy metal–style voice, he bellowed, "I am available for weddings and bar mitzvahs. Thank you, after-school bus, you've been a great audience!" He finished and raised his pinky and thumb, twisting his hand.

I had no idea he was so funny. I didn't give him the satisfaction of a laugh because obviously I needed to be too cool, but I did tap my hands together in applause. "Just don't fart this way and I don't care if you practice your ukulele on the bus."

Ryuu resumed his strumming. He sang out, "You will improve your butterfly time if you try to keep your body as close as possible to the surface of the water."

Hey, I didn't need his criticism. "Did I ask for advice?" I should have known Ryuu couldn't go more than a couple minutes without being arrogant and offensive. I pulled my headphones out and opened my chemistry textbook.

Conversation over.

• • •

I returned home to Tak-Luxxe after ignoring Ryuu for the duration of the bus ride. I pressed forty-nine on the elevator and it shot up, stopping at floor forty-six. Kim Takahara stepped into the elevator.

"Oh, hello," Kim said to me. She had a look of surprise whenever she saw me around Tak-Luxxe, as if she'd forgotten I existed and couldn't believe her brother's illegitimate daughter actually lived here now. "How's school going?"

"Fine," I mumbled. I never knew what to say to her. She hadn't made any effort to get to know me, so

I didn't see why I should try with her. I didn't know if her indifference to me meant she was too busy, just plain uninterested, or rude like her mother.

"I love your hair," she commented. She said that every time I saw her in the elevator. It was pretty much all she ever had to say to me.

The elevator door opened on forty-eight and I spied Kenji in the hallway, waiting for Kim at Mrs. Takahara's front door. I was about to step out to ask him about our dinner plans for that night, but Kim stepped in front of me. "Family only," she said.

The elevator door closed in my face.

SO RUDE!

Shake it off, I told myself. I pressed fifty-five to go to the Sky Garden instead of going directly home. I could relax in the hot tub by the pool and decompress from Aunt Rude's subtle slap to my face. I had an extra swimsuit in my gym bag. I went into the women's changing room when I got off the elevator to put on the suit. Then I went out to the pool area.

Ugh, someone was in the hot tub. But it wasn't a stranger. It was Akemi.

"How was your violin lesson today?" I asked her.

"Hard. My elbows hurt from playing the instrument, so I came here to feel better."

"Smart!" I stepped into the hot tub, relishing the

warm, bubbly feel of the water. I sat opposite Akemi and pressed my back against one of the water jets. The pressure massage felt amazing.

"How was your swim team practice?" she asked me.

"Intense. My elbows also hurt!" I moved my arms around until I felt a jet swirl that I could press my elbows against, as Akemi was doing on her side of the hot tub.

Akemi said, "I think I was playing my violin too hard because I was upset. I got a C on my English grammar test."

"What was the test on?"

"The parts of speech. Like noun, adjective, conjunction. English is so different from Japanese. I'll never get it."

I had a flash of inspiration. "Chikusho!" I exclaimed.

Akemi giggled. "Why you say that?"

"I have an idea for how you can remember the different parts of speech. We'll use the English word 'fuck' as our example."

"Fuck," Akemi whispered.

"A noun is a person, place, or thing, right?" Akemi nodded. "So, a person who is rude is a fucker."

"Nik Zhzhonov is rude," said Akemi.

"You think? He strikes me more as arrogant. He's so rich he doesn't know better. But we can use him as an example. That Nik, what a fucker."

"Noun!" said Akemi. "But what's gerund? That confuses me so much."

"A gerund is a verb that acts like a noun and ends in I-N-G." I looked around the pool area to make sure no one had come in to overhear my next example. "Fucking is what makes babies." Akemi blushed. "As a verb, it would be, Mom fucked Dad and now I'm here."

Akemi splashed water at me, and I splashed some back as we fell into fits of laughter. Finally, I said, "Now use our word as an adjective. To describe a noun."

Akemi thought about it and then said, "My elbows hurt fucking bad."

"Yes! I'm so proud."

"So *fucking* proud," Akemi corrected me.

I dipped my head under the water and then came back up for air. "You're my perfect student," I told Akemi.

"Thank you very fucking much," she said. "But what's interjection?"

"It's a transition word that's mostly used to show emotion by the speaker." Seriously, I had no idea I knew grammar this well until now. Someone give me a practice SAT exam, cuz I'd ace it! "Like, *Hmmm*, I don't know what I want for dinner. Or, *Fuck*, I'm late for dinner."

Akemi nodded. "*Â, sô desu ka,*" she said.

"What does that mean? I feel like I hear that phrase here all the time."

"It means, like, 'oh, really?' or 'ah, I see.' It's Japanese interjection. Japanese people like to acknowledge what is being said to them, as a form of politeness. So they have like a transition phrase. They say Â, sô desu ka after someone tells them something."

"Thanks, Akemi! That's really helpful to know."

"You're fucking welcome," she said, and splashed water at me again.

• • •

That night, I had dinner with Kenji in the Ikebana Café. I preferred it over the fancier restaurants at Tak-Luxxe. It was more casual, and it was fun to choose from a buffet rather than commit to a specific menu choice. Also, here the waiter knew my standard drink request.

"One Coca-Cola coming up," Dev Flaherty said before I even asked.

"With—" I started to say.

"Lots of ice. Got it." Drinks never came with ice in Japan. You had to ask. When you got the ice, it was never enough. "Sparkling water for you?" Dev asked Kenji.

"Yes, please," said Kenji. "No ice. I'm not American. I drink mine like a civilized person." He winked at me, teasing. When Dev left our table, Kenji brought up the subject before I had to. "Kim asked me to apologize to you about earlier in the elevator. The elevator closed before she could explain."

"Explain what?" I said, still feeling sulky about the incident.

"When Kim said 'Family Only,' she was referring to a long-standing tradition we have with Mother. Once a week we join her in the late afternoons for a Japanese tea ceremony. It's a very formal tradition, not something a teenager would enjoy."

How could I know if I'd enjoy it if I didn't even know what it was? "What's so formal about it? Isn't it just tea?"

"It's not just tea. It's a particular *matcha* green tea that's prepared in a ceremonial fashion. Mother and Kim wear formal kimonos. It's a Japanese custom that's important to Mother. Kim and I always found it boring."

"It sounds like it could be interesting." I didn't want to say *I'd like to join you* because I didn't want to sound that needy and I also didn't want to invite myself to spend time with Kenji's mother. "I guess it's something expats aren't allowed to do?"

"Certainly, tourists pay a lot of money to attend formal Japanese tea ceremonies here. But the family ceremonies are private."

There it was again. Subtly being told I wasn't one of them. "Sure," I said.

"By private, I mean we discuss business. Kim and I have found that since our father died, presenting ideas and plans to Mother goes better when we do it under the guise of a Japanese tradition."

"Sneaky," I said.

"Thank you," he said. "How was your day today?"

Talking about school was our safe topic. It was so much easier than discussing all the years we never spent together. "I got a B-plus on my Spanish test."

"Well done. Improvement from that last B-minus, right?" I gulped down a sip of pride, with extra ice. Praise was nice, from anybody. From him, it felt a thousand times more magnified. "Did you get your *Great Gatsby* essay back?" He never actually checked my homework or offered to help me with it, but he knew all about it from our nightly dinner conversations.

"Yes. I got a B."

"That's good."

We both knew it wasn't good. It was just okay.

"The teacher said my thesis statement was excellent, but my paper focused too much on description and not enough on persuasion." When I read through the essay after getting it back, I could see the teacher's point, but I also wanted to whine, *I never had to write an essay that long for English class before coming to ICS-Tokyo. Cut me some slack!*

"Should I hire a tutor for you?" A few tables away,

Dev Flaherty delivered beers to a group of diners. Kenji looked at Dev then back at me. "He went to Princeton. I'm sure he knows how to write a good English essay."

"He's busy enough here! I'm surprised you don't also have him fixing the plumbing."

"How do you know I don't?" Kenji joked.

I laughed. "There's a writing tutor available in the school library to help. I'll go there for help with my next essay."

"Good idea. Don't be stupid like your old man. When I was at Andover, I never took the tutoring help that was available. Things would have gone so differently if I had. My father was always angry when he saw my report cards. He'd say, 'I send you halfway around the world for the finest education, and this is the best you can do?'"

"Your father sounds like a bummer," I said.

I didn't mean it as an insult, and he didn't take it as one. Kenji nodded. "He was very smart and hardworking but rigid and impossible to please. At least, for me. Kim could do no wrong to him."

"Because she was his favorite or because she was a girl?"

"Probably both. And she was like him: brilliant. She was the orange of his eye."

"I think you mean 'apple.'"

"Why apple?"

"That's the saying. The apple of someone's eye. Their favorite."

"Yes. Kim was Father's apple. I was his rotting apple. Grades never good enough. Disappointment in business."

Geez. With hypercritical parents like his, I started to understand why Kenji developed a drinking problem.

I said, "I doubt he felt that way about you, or he wouldn't have left his business for you to run." It seemed odd that Kenji could run a company with thousands of employees worldwide, yet so openly question his own ability.

"In Japan, the man runs the business." *Even though Kim has the degrees with honors from Harvard,* he didn't say. Maybe I would be uptight like Kim if I knew that no matter how hard I worked or how smart I was, my brother would get the top job in the family business—even if he wasn't right for it.

My phone lit up with a text message from Nik Z. Shibuya, Saturday! Don't make other plans!

Okay, I texted back.

"Already getting texts from boys?" Kenji asked me. "Anyone I should know about?"

"Nik Zhzhonov wants to show me Shibuya this weekend."

Kenji nodded, pleased. "Excellent," he said, like I'd accomplished something just getting a text from Nik.

chapter twenty-four

Early Saturday afternoon, I stepped out of a taxi with Oscar and Nik, into the world of Shinjuku, the entertainment district of Tokyo, with high-rise buildings and neon signs dotting the upward landscape of bars, restaurants, and shows. The girls would meet up with us later. Jhanvi and Ntombi had a field hockey game while Imogen had karate training. I couldn't believe the boys had invited me to hang out with them on our own ahead of the other girls joining us. I'd had enough lunchtime hangs with them that I no longer felt nervous in their presence, but I was still a bit suspicious about their intentions.

"They call this area 'the pleasure labyrinth,'" Nik told me, chivalrously helping me step out of the cab that he'd just paid for. "Creepy bars, tryst hotels, cabarets. All the good stuff." He looked excited to be here, his deep blue eyes twinkling.

Oscar said, "Nighttime in Shibuya is really where all the action is. But we thought we'd show you Shinjuku first. Because we're that awesome."

"Tell me straight up," I said. "Are you guys hazing me?"

"Like a fraternity haze?" Nik asked.

"Yes."

Oscar and Nik looked at each other and laughed. Nik said, "No. But every hazing should be as fun as what you're about to experience down those stairs."

Nik picked up our tickets from the "will call" window at a venue called Robot Restaurant. We stepped onto a narrow, discreet set of curved stairs with walls of glass, and walked down a few levels into a waiting lounge that looked like a Vegas casino on acid. Every inch of the space was covered in gold, silver, leopard print, and Japanese pop art spectacle furniture and fixtures that would have made Elvis Presley's Graceland designer rage with jealousy. At the corner of the lounge, a jazz band, including a sax and keyboard player dressed as robots, and sexy Japanese girls wearing robot-themed lingerie outfits singing in Japanese, performed on a small stage.

Everywhere I looked there was some sort of glitter,

sparkle, or neon. There was also what I'd found to be a common sight in Tokyo—a glassed-in area for smokers. The coffee shops had glassed-in smoking rooms. Even some 7-Elevens had dedicated smoking areas. But none of the smoking rooms I'd seen in my limited travels so far resembled a bedazzled little palace as closely as the one at Robot Restaurant.

"Is this place for real?" I asked the boys.

"You haven't even seen the main event yet," said Nik.

Oscar looked at a text on his phone. "Middle of the second half and the British International School is ahead of ICS by four goals. The girls are going to be in a bad mood when they get here."

"Sports are, like, your life, huh?" I asked Oscar. I didn't mean the question offensively. Every interaction I'd had with him so far involved him checking sports scores on his phone or discussing the ICS polo team.

"I care about beautiful boys just as much. Too bad there aren't any here." He shoved Nik. There were other gay students at ICS-Tokyo, but Oscar was the only one I'd met so far who was so fully out and fully proud of his sexuality.

Nik placed his arm around my shoulder. "I'm too busy with a beautiful lady to be insulted."

I didn't have time to decide whether I liked Nik's arm around my shoulder or not; we were called for the main show to start, another level down. The main stage area was surprisingly small, with two sets of bleacher seats with video screens covering the walls behind them, and an empty area in between the seats, about the size of a boxing ring. We were given glow lights, and then we sat down on the highest level of seats and waited for the show to begin.

The stage lit up with a dazzle of lasers and LED lights. Suddenly, a giant animatronic Godzilla emerged from the front of the stage, followed by a bevy of hot Japanese girls, burlesque dancers, and drummers. They performed pop tunes while images of African safaris played on wall-size screens behind each set of audience seats, flashing English words like *Wild!* and *Crazy!* Each number was weirder and more awesome than the one before it. The girls danced and fought with Godzilla, then an animatronic dinosaur, then guys in robot suits. Then the robots fought with dinosaurs to a soundtrack of pop music. The girls had laser lightsaber battles while singing and dancing.

Oscar popped some popcorn into his mouth. "This could only be better if they added go-go boys to the dance troupe."

Nik had a huge smile on his face watching the action on the stage. Maybe because he was Slavic and always looked very intense and serious, or because Oscar was so ridiculously handsome, but I hadn't noticed before how handsome Nik was. His buzz cut wasn't as interesting as Ryuu Kimura's black-blue flop of hair, but Nik had amazing high cheekbones, rosy cheeks, and probably the whitest set of teeth I'd ever seen. Either he was a master of teeth-cleaning skills, or he spent his father's money on professional teeth whitening services. Whichever option it was, a smile looked good on him.

"What did you think?" Nik asked me after the show ended.

"I've never been as appalled by bad taste and entertained at the same time in my life," I said.

"Ah," Oscar said, looking at a text on his phone. "That's because you've never seen the Ex-Brat girls after they lose a field hockey game."

• • •

If I died in a freak accident while hurrying through Shibuya's notorious "scramble" intersection, where thousands of pedestrians crossed from all directions at once when the WALK light shifted to green, I hoped whoever performed my funeral service would know I died satisfied. Shibuya felt like being in the center of the vertical world, with tall buildings flashing advertisements, neon lights, and level after level of stores and restaurants visible through glass windows. So many people, so hurried, so much to look at and experience. Fashionista women wearing skinny pants with stiletto pumps riding bikes down crowded sidewalks. Harajuku girls with pink hair and crazy outfits. Loud izakaya bars where men's conversations and laughter spilled onto the street, and women walking by wearing kimonos with white socks tucked into flip-flops. Young people strutting around dressed in *kosupure* ("cosplay," Nik translated) outfits from their favorite anime, like it was Halloween every day here.

TOO MUCH FUN.

I didn't want to die, but if I did, I would tell the souls I met in the afterlife: Don't feel bad about my premature end. I saw it all in my short time down in the upworld of Tokyo.

Meanwhile, Imogen literally stopped in the middle of the chaotic crosswalk while thousands of people scurried past to reach the curb before the light turned red, and cars streamed across from all directions again.

"What the hell are you doing, Im-san? Move!" pleaded Jhanvi, tugging desperately on Imogen's arm.

"He's everywhere," Imogen groaned, gesturing up at one of the tall buildings that was covered in a collage of colors—blues, blacks, reds, whites, yellows. It presented an enormous electronic mural portrait of her father—who I'd learned in the last few days was not just a sculpter, but one of Japan's most prominent pop culture artists. Akira Kato's colorful dreadlocks and naked bod—except for a Sumo wrestler *mawashi* (loincloth)—were certainly . . . interesting. If Mrs. Takahara argued with Kenji in Japanese again about what I was supposed to wear at Destiny Club, I should flash her a photo of Imogen's near-naked father plastered over the scramble, and let Mrs. T reassess what a proper dress code should be then.

Imogen's father really was everywhere. I'd seen that same face displayed on trash cans, subway trains, newspaper advertisements. He might as well be on the Japanese yen, his face (and pudgy, exposed chest and tummy) were so familiar to Tokyoites at this point.

Imogen didn't budge, so Nik and Oscar grabbed Imogen's arms and carried her to the curb, arriving exactly as the pedestrian light turned to red, and cars and trucks and buses took command of the intersection again.

"Don't do that!" Ntombi chided Imogen.

"Sorry," Imogen grumbled, most insincerely. "I'll be so glad when his exhibition is over."

"How much longer?" asked Jhanvi.

"One week," said Imogen, turning her attention to me. "I'm gonna celebrate so hard when it's finally over, okay?"

"We can start celebrating now," said Nik. He pulled out two beers from the inside of his jacket that he'd purchased at the train station. I still hadn't gotten over how easy it was to buy beer here. It was sold in vending machines; no need for ID. Vending machines were everywhere in Japan—in alleyways, in front of konbini stores, on train platforms—selling everything from soft drinks, coffee, tea, cigarettes, candy, soup, and other hot food to sake and beer. "Who wants?"

Imogen raised her hand; the others declined. Nik handed over a can of Asahi to Imogen and opened the other for himself. An older Japanese lady passed them and scolded Imogen in Japanese, probably assuming Imogen didn't speak the language. In fact, Imogen was the one Ex-Brat who did. She yelled back at the lady, who swatted Imogen with her shopping bag, and then hurried away toward the train station.

"What was that all about?" Oscar asked Imogen.

"Naughty, rude, drunk teenagers! The shame!" Imogen said. She clinked cans with Nik, they both chugged their beers, and then tossed the empties into an Akira Kato–plastered trash can. Imogen burped. "That was good."

"Fuck my diet. I need a feast to soothe today's loss," said Jhanvi.

"The hunger situation *is* getting dire," said Ntombi.

"Tokyu Food Show!" Oscar and Nik both said.

I eagerly followed the gang to their favorite local food spot in Shibuya Station, where another Japanese department store with a basement food hall offered dazzling displays of grilled eel, fried pork, fish salad, sushi, seafood-and-rice wraps, dumplings, mochi cakes, chocolates, and jellied confections.

"What'll it be, Elle-san?" Nik asked me as he ate octopus on a stick.

"I like the food better when I see it in plastic first," I joked. Another of my favorite sights in Japan were all the restaurants whose outside windows displayed perfect plastic versions—soups, meats, tempura, noodles—of the foods they served inside.

"Try this," said Nik, offering me a piece of octopus.

I shook my head. "Ew. I think I'll just have some mochi."

Of the many benefits of moving across the world to live with a stranger father who worked all the time was that I had no supervision of my nutritional choices. And Kenji had a sweet tooth like I did; he wasn't going to nag me about protein and eating my greens like Mom used to, before the Beast.

"What time do you have to be home?" Imogen asked Ntombi, knowing that while Ntombi had a bit more free rein with her parents out of town for the weekend, she also had to negotiate a not-too-late curfew with her housekeeper in order to keep the nervous woman from having a worry-related heart attack.

"Ten tonight. How about you?" Ntombi asked me.

I shrugged. The other benefit of no supervision? No supervision.

Imogen said, "Let's follow some *gyaru* and hang out wherever they go. So long as it doesn't suck."

"Gyaru?" I asked.

Jhanvi said, "The Japanese schoolgirls wearing short uniform skirts with street-fashion tops."

Imogen said, "With fake eyelashes to make their eyes look really big, and dyed hair like bronze or pink or whatever."

"With naughty little teddy bear knapsacks on their backs," said Nik.

"I spy gyaru!" I exclaimed, totally in on this fun game. If anyone had told me two months ago that soon I'd have private-school friends, and we'd be tracking Japanese schoolgirls wearing crazy fashions through the streets of Tokyo, I would never have believed them. We followed a group of giggling gyaru up the escalator, back onto the street, and through a winding maze of blocks that led to a tall building where the girls got on the elevator and the Ex-Brats stepped back to decide whether to follow.

"Where do you think they went?" Imogen asked.

The floors were lit on a monitor over the door at the

ground level, which showed the elevator stopping on floor eight. Imogen read the building's directory, which was in Japanese. "Oh, karaoke! Let's go, Ex-Brats."

We took the elevator to the eighth floor, where Imogen handled the transaction with the counter clerk in Japanese. "The Hello Kitty room is the only one available right now. Sorry, Oscar!" she told him, not sorrily. "We all know about your pathological fear of the Sanrio store. Brace yourself." Oscar laughed.

A clerk led us to a small room with a huge video monitor on its far wall, bench seating against the other walls, and a table with a menu for snacks and drinks in the middle. The whole room was plastered in Hello Kitty wallpaper, giving the space a pink, red, white, and bow-tied psychedelic effect, made more awesome by the Hello Kitty dolls on the benches and the Hello Kitty plates on the table. "You get first song choice, rookie," Imogen told me.

I paused. I didn't want to make an uncool pick, but I blurted out the first song that came into my mind. " 'Mr. Roboto'?"

I cringed at my quick, dumb choice. I only knew that Japan-themed song because Mom used to sing her favorite part, *Domo arigato, Mr. Roboto,* to me when I played with a robot toy in the bathtub when I was little.

"Too obvious. Pass," said Imogen, who chose "Hotline Bling" for the group instead.

The song came on with the lyrics spooling across the video screen, and everyone except me sang with joy and abandon. Mostly, I watched and mouthed along, entertained, but not ready to reveal what a terrible off-key singer I was. Imogen ordered popcorn and beer to be delivered to our room. I laughed at their silly song-stylings so hard I thought I was going to pee my pants, which made me finally ready to sing aloud, as I singsong announced, "I have to go to the bathroom!"

I left the karaoke room. Nik followed behind me. "I need the loo, too," he said.

As we progressed down the cramped hallway, another karaoke room door swung open, and two drunk salarymen wandered out and went into the bathrooms ahead of us. Since we had to wait anyway, Nik motioned for me to join him in the drunk men's karaoke room, where three other drunk dudes were sitting on a bench singing "Uptown Funk."

"I'd like to funk *you* up," Nik said into my ear, pulling me onto an empty bench.

I looked into his face. He had a hulky athlete's body, very cut and muscled and on display in his tight polo shirts, with a wickedly cute face accentuated by smiling eyes and pink lips.

The drunk men sang harder and more flamboyantly for our benefit, like they were on *Japanese Idol* and they were in it to win it with their serenade to the gaijin expats. Nik had his own show to offer them. He leaned over to me and just like that, when I didn't expect it at all, it happened.

My first real kiss.

chapter twenty-five

Was there a nice way to say to a guy, *I like you, but kissing you did nothing for me?*

Nik sat next to me at the long, rectangular-shaped table in Marine Science class while our teacher exhibited different samples of seawater and tested for temperature, salinity, transparency, density, and pressure. Nik kept nudging at my side, like we were in on a little secret.

I was trying to take notes on the lecture, but Nik placed his hand over mine and wrote on the open page in my notebook. *This class is so boring!*

I agreed with him, but at this moment, I desperately wanted to focus on the lesson instead of his hulking figure sitting next to me. I removed my hand from under his.

I couldn't believe I'd kissed Nik over the weekend. Or, more specifically, that he'd kissed me. I'm not entirely sure I invited him in for the lip smack. I didn't *not* invite him, so it's not like he forced himself on me, but when it happened, I was taken by surprise. I was flattered and curious, for sure. I was having so much fun, I wanted it to keep going. But I didn't expect the kiss, and I didn't expect the kiss would be so bland, or that his mouth would taste so unpleasantly like beer and garlic.

Did it feel sloppy because I was inexperienced or because it was just a bad kiss? My lips felt no sizzle of attraction. My mind was much more in control, going, *Um, you seem to be kissing a boy right now. Try to act like you're into it. Is that a tongue? Act like you know what you're doing! Ew . . .*

I'd never been attracted to girls, so I didn't think I wasn't into the kiss because of that. I knew the answer, regrettably, was simpler. I just wasn't into Nik in that way. Disappointing. Kenji would be so impressed if I dated Alexei Zhzhonov's son. I would be solidified in the Ex-Brats if Nik was my boyfriend. I'd be more than the new girl Imogen had taken in. I could possibly be the girlfriend of the richest guy in school. But the status wasn't worth it to go out with a guy I wasn't attracted to.

I hadn't told the Ex-Brats that I'd kissed Nik. I didn't want them to make a big deal of it when I already knew I didn't want to go further with him. But I wondered if Nik had told them.

Why couldn't I fake being more into him? Because I

understood the difference between genuine attraction and zero chemistry.

I'd sort of kissed another boy two years earlier, and I'd definitely liked it. The summer before my freshman year of high school, just before Mom's problems started, my swim team at the Y had won our meet. We were on our way to Ledo to celebrate. Reggie and I sat together at the back of the bus, as always. When everyone stood up to get off the bus, Reggie reached for my hand to keep me in my seat. "What's up?" I said.

"You swam great today," he said.

"So did you," I said.

I'd known him for so long, almost like a brother. But suddenly the glance between us was different. Not at all like how siblings were supposed to look at each other. His hand that held mine was sweaty, and mine turned warm. For the first time, I noticed not just how sweet his face was, but how handsome. When his eyes looked into mine, I saw this person I'd known forever, but who suddenly looked different, and my heart pinged, *YES!* Neither of us pounced, as Nik did to me at karaoke. Instead, it was like Reg and I were in perfect sync. Our mouths moved closer and closer until *boom*, they touched. Total electricity. The best half-second of my life. So yeah, maybe that was my first real kiss, but it was so quick, I'd never felt like it counted.

"Has anyone seen my jacket?" Our coach had returned to the bus. Immediately, Reggie and I pulled apart and stood up, guiltily, even though our "kiss" had been more like a quick peck. The coach saw us. "Let's go, Zoellner and Coleman! Pizza time."

Soon after, Reggie was placed in foster care, and then the Beast came into my life. We didn't see each other much after that, and we never spoke about what had happened between us. I think we both knew we were better off as friends because our lives were too complicated for more. There was too much history between us. It would hurt too much to be torn apart if we let our friendship move to the next level and it didn't work out.

Do you want to hang out at my house after school? Nik wrote in my notebook. *We have a private screening room. My dad gets all the latest movies sent to him. We have a karaoke machine there, too.*

I wrote back, *I have too much homework, but thanks.*

He waited a few minutes to answer, like he thought I'd change my mind. Then Nik drew a sad face onto my notebook. Next to it, he wrote, *Got it.*

Phew, I thought. That was easier than I expected. Brutal, but swift.

NOVEMBER

---

chapter twenty-six

Dear Mom,

It's so beautiful here in the fall. The trees look like bouquets of gold, red, green, and yellow lollipops outside the windows, with glitter from the sparkling electronic billboards on the buildings beyond the trees. I'm no longer in that awed stage where I can't believe I live in this exotic place. The forty-ninth floor seems normal now. Walking on streets filled with mostly Japanese people seems normal. You wouldn't believe how there could be so many people everywhere, but everything is so clean and orderly. My favorite thing is when I go to the store to buy food, and the counter clerks bow to me at the end of the transaction and wrap my purchases like they're cherished

Christmas presents instead of, like, a basic container of soba noodles.

I'm obsessed with the apples here. They're so much sweeter and juicier than I remember back home. And I can't stop drinking the apple juice in Japan. It's become a joke on the swim team. Coach Tanya gives me an apple juice bottle whenever I best my times. So guess who has improved her 50M butterfly stroke by a solid four seconds?

School is good but hard. I am finally catching up with the workload. I really like Akemi, the girl who lives in my building and goes to ICS-Tokyo. We exchange English and Japanese phrases with each other. She thinks "Cool as a cucumber" is the silliest expression she ever heard. My new Japanese favorite is tsume no aka wo senjite nomu, *which literally means "brew and drink the dirt from under someone's fingernails." It means you should brew the dirt from under the fingernails of someone smart and worthy of respect and then drink it like a tea so that person's qualities will transfer to you.*

At school, I hang out most with Imogen. Her other two best friends at school, Ntombi and Jhanvi, are okay, but maybe if Imogen didn't hang out with them, I wouldn't either. They're kind of snobs. So is Imogen, but she's a fun snob, LOL. There's this guy named Nik who is also in Imogen's crowd, and he could probably have any girl he wants. He likes me, and I was flattered but honestly not that into him. He keeps texting me and sending me cat memes, and I'm hoping a cute new girl shows up to ICS-Tokyo soon to divert his attention. Kenji thinks I should hang out more with Nik because it would be "good for business," but I said I was too busy with school to have a boyfriend. Kenji laughed at that and said, "When did I say you should have a boyfriend?" Did I tell you in my last letter about the moody boy on the swim team named Ryuu? He's the team's best swimmer. I hang out with him on the after-school bus but don't tell Imogen because she doesn't like him. He's really funny.

Most nights I have dinner with Kenji, but that's pretty much all the time I spend with him. His mother and sister also live in the building. His mother is not very nice and whenever I see her, I duck into a corner so she won't notice me. His sister is okay, but I could never imagine her as an auntie. She's only politely interested in me, so I've decided to be the same to her. When I see her in the elevator, we talk about the weather.

I miss you so much, Mom. I miss my real family. I think about you all the time, and I hope you are surviving okay. Uncle Masa said maybe during my spring break next year we could take a trip to Washington and I could visit you.

Love,

Elle

PS—Remember how on my thirteenth birthday you made me promise I'd tell you when I had my first kiss? Okay, I kissed that guy Nik once and it wasn't all that. He's acting all weird now. Boys are stupid.

chapter twenty-seven

"Are you sick?" Ryuu asked me from his seat on the other side of the aisle on the ICS-Tokyo after-school bus. Unlike back home, most of the boys on this bus were well-behaved. They preferred to play video games on their phones rather than do homework, have IRL conversations, or bully other kids on the bus. The exception to screen time was Ryuu. He was usually either reading an actual book (and never one that was part of the school curriculum—he read for pleasure, what a unicorn) or scribbling in his swim journal. Yes, his swim journal. Ryuu kept a notebook to analyze his swim times in various strokes, measured by time of day and foods eaten that day. No computer spreadsheet or phone app for his analysis. Instead, he wrote in a binder with ruled pages, using different colored pencils to signify different types of data.

The method was so Japanese of him. These people at the forefront of technology *loved* their stationery supplies, so much so that I wouldn't be surprised if I stumbled on a vending machine filled with different kinds of Post-its, notebooks, pens, and pencils next to their infinite supply of beverage vending machines. I secretly loved that Ryuu even kept his colored pencils in a pencil case that he tucked into a hole-punched zippered sleeve at the front of his nerd binder.

"Why would you think I'm sick?" I asked Ryuu.

I moved from the window side of my seat to the aisle side; he did the same. This seating arrangement seemed to happen every time we were both on the after-school bus. As usual, I took a furtive sniff now that he was sitting closer. With his after-swim hair still wet, he smelled like chlorine and intensity, my favorite boy smells. His trusty ukulele was at his side. He said, "You're always drinking apple juice. Do you have a Vitamin C deficiency?"

"The only deficiency I have is the sixteen years I spent on this planet not knowing how good apple juice could be."

"Isn't it the same everywhere?"

"That's what I would have thought, till I tried it here. The apples here are just next-level delicious and perfect. The juice is naturally sweet, refreshing, and satisfying."

"You sound like a commercial." With his flop of

blue-black hair falling in front of his eyes, I saw only his mouth. It was smiling at me. I grinned back. Ryuu looked at his Apple Watch. "The driver's late. We should have left campus five minutes ago."

"Maybe not everyone here operates on Japanese time efficiency?" No American student would notice or care about a driver's tardiness.

"The later the driver leaves, the worse traffic will be." He glanced down at his swim notebook and then back up at me. "Are you ready for the practice meet this weekend? We lost last time to the British International School, but I think we have a chance this year."

"Are they that good?"

"They *were*. But their best swimmers graduated. And now we have you."

I felt a blush on my cheeks. I didn't understand why the Ex-Brats iced him out. Could I get him thawed and back in with the gang? Would I even want to? Maybe I liked not sharing him.

I said, "Does the team go somewhere fun to celebrate if they win? When I was on the Y team back home, Coach took us to Ledo for pizza after a good meet."

"Sometimes. But it's usually some touristy place in Shibuya where everyone acts stupid because sushi comes on a moat, and they think they've had some authentic Japanese experience."

"Sushi on a moat sounds pretty fun to me, actually! What do *you* think would be an authentic Japanese experience?"

"I don't know, but it's not going to Robot Restaurant, where Coach Tanya and her boyfriend took us at the end of last season."

"I liked the Robot Restaurant," I said.

"Yeah, I mean, it's okay," he said quickly. "But there's more interesting Japanese experiences that aren't so touristy."

"Like what?" I asked.

"Well, tourists love to go to Akihabara, the 'Electric City' where all the buildings are lit up with advertisements, and the stores sell all the latest Japanese technology. It's cool and over-the-top. But my favorite place is in the same area, but completely opposite in vibe. It's Book Town in Jimbocho, which is a small neighborhood in Chiyoda. It's where the Tokyo publishing business is. Lots of second-hand bookshops there. It's a great place to browse vintage magazines and find good deals on used books."

"That sounds like a really nice place to escape all the go go go energy of Tokyo."

"It is. I'll take you sometime if you want to go. But most of the books are in Japanese. Maybe that's why there aren't a lot of tourists there."

I really wanted to see Book Town with him, but

Imogen wouldn't approve. It was pretty bold of him to ask me, knowing that I hung out with the Ex-Brats. I liked that he didn't care at all about their hierarchy. But I was too chickenshit to accept his invitation. I only just got elevated social status. I wasn't ready to blow it.

"How come your English is so good?" I asked him. I'd met many Japanese people who spoke excellent English, like Kenji, but their English was usually accented, and sometimes their phrasing was awkward. Ryuu's was confident and without accent.

He said, "I was born in New York. I went to ICS-New York from kindergarten to sixth grade. I only spoke Japanese at home. All other times was English."

"New York! I've always wanted to go there! Did you like it?"

"Loved it. It's a lot like Tokyo, with the crazy energy and lights and tall buildings. We lived in the West Village, where the buildings are old and there aren't skyscrapers and it really did feel like a little village in the middle of a huge city. I hope to go back to Manhattan for university. Maybe Columbia or NYU."

"Really? How come you don't want to go to college here? Tokyo is amazing."

"But my family is suffocating," he said, laughing.

I didn't get a chance to ask him more, because Nik Zhzhonov came barreling down the aisle. "Move over," he said to me. "Make room for Daddy." I never knew with Nik whether he was being flirty or crude or was just a dude who was clueless about how ridiculous he sounded.

The bus finally moved; the driver must have been waiting for Nik.

I didn't budge from my seat. I said, "The row ahead of me is empty. Sit there."

Nik made a sad face but sat down on the seat in front of me. He leaned over and said, "Is that Ryuu guy bothering you?"

Ryuu was sitting right there. Why'd Nik have to be such an a-hole? I said, "No. And it's not really your business if he did."

"You're feisty, Elle-san. That's why there's hope for us."

There wasn't hope for us. I thought he'd said he got it, but clearly he didn't, as evidenced by all the text messages he sent me, and him showing up on the after-school bus when I knew for a fact he had a private driver to shuttle him home. That night at karaoke, when Nik's mouth landed on mine, it was a surprise. I wasn't expecting it, but since the kiss was already happening, I went along with it. I was the new girl in Tokyo making out with a tech billionaire's son in a karaoke bar. I wasn't so new anymore, but I didn't know how to tell Nik to fuck off without jeopardizing my friendships with the other Ex-Brats.

If I was going to make a go of it with a boy, I wanted

romance, not a sudden lurch make-out. I'd been through enough in life already. I didn't want to settle for less than.

Ryuu picked up his ukulele from his seat. He strummed it and sang aloud, "'Cause I want the one I can't have, and it's driving me mad.'" My eyes widened and my heart wanted to burst. Mom's favorite Smiths song!

"Shut up, Kimura," said Nik.

I didn't care if he was iced out.

I liked Ryuu Kimura.

• • •

That night I went up to the Sky Garden to do homework. Kenji wasn't free for dinner, and it had become a habit to take my studying and dinner up there when he wasn't available. Tonight, Akemi joined me. We had sushi delivered up to us from the Ikebana Café as we pored over the books, surrounded by the garden's rosebushes, looking out over the twinkling Tokyo skyline.

I liked these study times with Akemi. She was so much easier to hang out with than the Ex-Brats. She loved gossip, but she was never bitchy. She appreciated my help with her English grammar exercises, and she'd taught me more about the Japanese language than my own Japanese father.

A text flashed on my phone from Nik Z.

What's up, gorgeous?

Should I change my phone number? I didn't answer him, but Akemi saw the text on my screen.

"He likes you," she said.

"I know," I said, and sighed.

"You don't like him?"

"He's annoying."

"Arabella Acosta didn't like him, either. Oscar's sister. She was also part of that group."

Intriguing. "How do you know that?"

"I heard her and Jhanvi arguing about him once. Arabella said Nik acted one way in front of all the friends, like a cool guy, but when he was just with her, he was too intense." Exactly! "Jhanvi said Arabella was being dramatic and Nik was a good guy. She warned Arabella not to spread rumors about Nik, because his father is very powerful."

That was precisely my fear of telling the other Ex-Brats about my own experience with Nik. That they wouldn't believe me or that they would automatically take Nik's side.

Since Akemi seemed to know all the dirt, there was another issue on my mind.

"Can I ask you a question?"

Akemi nodded.

"Promise not to tell anyone I asked you?" Akemi nodded again. "How come Ryuu Kimura really got iced out?"

Akemi placed her hands around her mouth and leaned over to whisper into my ear. "Because he got Arabella Acosta pregnant. Please don't tell my mother I know that word!"

chapter twenty-eight

"She's popular. I never see her. She's always with her school friends," Kenji said that night to Uncle Masa while we were at dinner in Fantasy League. I hadn't seen Uncle Masa outside of FaceTime chats since he'd first delivered me to Tokyo not quite two months earlier, but what felt like a lifetime ago. Now he was in town for a business trip. "The son of Alexei Zhzhonov likes her!"

"We're just friends," I lied. Kenji really knew nothing about how I spent my time when I wasn't at dinner with him. "And I don't hang out with friends after school. I have Sailfish practice." I turned to Uncle Masa and explained, "That's the swim team."

Uncle Masa said, "When's your next meet?" His simple question stung. Kenji had yet to ask me when the team would have a competition, or let me know if I should expect to see him there if I did have one. Kenji lived in a prison of work, and sometimes I felt like I lived in a prison of wishing he would try to be more involved in my life, but not challenging him about that because I didn't want to lose my cushy living situation. Tokyo offered so much opportunity for me. But I felt like a coward living here, enjoying all its privileges but not being the person I wanted to be—someone who had the guts to demand her father *be* a father to her.

"We have a scrimmage next weekend," I said.

Uncle Masa inspected his calendar on his phone. "I'd love to see you compete, but I'll be back in Geneva. When is your next meet after that?"

I told him the date. "But it's in Taipei, Taiwan." Even if I'd gotten comfortable living in a penthouse, it still seemed unreal that I was a member of a school swim team that took international flights to travel to meets against other schools.

"I have a trip to Shanghai a few days before. I'll join you in Taipei that weekend, if you want the company?" Uncle Masa said.

"Great!" I looked at Kenji. His face gave no indication that he was going to jump onto this party bus, so I mustered my courage and asked him, "Will you come, too?"

He looked at the dates on his calendar. "I can probably make it to your competition this weekend, but I have to go to Sydney the weekend you go to Taipei."

That was something! But I couldn't help asking, "Maybe Emiko could reschedule you for another time? It would be so fun to travel somewhere with you and Uncle Masa."

Kenji said, "She could. But we don't reschedule *him*." He looked in the direction of Takeo Kinoshita, Akemi's father, who'd just entered the restaurant with Akemi's mother. He was an old man, probably in his seventies, who walked with a slight hunch and held on to Akemi's mother for balance. "Mr. Kinoshita's company handles the construction loans. We go to Sydney when his schedule says we go."

Akemi's parents stopped at our table to share greetings with Kenji in Japanese. They were a clichéd pairing— a short, old man with wrinkled skin, and his tall, much younger paramour who looked like a fashion model. When the Japanese discussion finished, Mr. Kinoshita said to me, "Akemi got A on her English test. She said you've been helping with her grammar exercises in the car to school. Good job."

Fuck yeah, Akemi! Her father patted my shoulder in a friendly manner, and Kenji beamed brightly. I wonder if he knew about Mr. Kinoshita's other family in Osaka.

But of course Kenji knew. Akemi had once shown me an online article about her father. Mr. Kinoshita was a benefactor of the arts scene in Osaka. The article showed a photo of him at an opera gala with his wife and grandchildren, who were all older than Akemi. His other life wasn't a secret.

When they spoke in Japanese, I wondered what secrets Kenji and Mr. Kinoshita shared. About secret business dealings, and having secret daughters.

· · ·

After dinner, we were granted an audience with Mrs. Takahara in her suite. She wanted to see Uncle Masa, who was her nephew. Of course no mention was made that she wanted to visit with her granddaughter, too, but I was part of the group-visitors package tonight.

I had a hard time imagining being old enough to be a grandmother, but if I was one, I couldn't fathom meeting my own granddaughter that I'd never known and not wanting to suffocate her with attention. I'd want to make up for lost time. I'd want to take her to museums and find out what books she liked and what she felt passionately about. I'd care. I'd *try*.

"You look well," Mrs. Takahara said to me when Kenji, Uncle Masa, and I sat in her living room, along with Kim.

She poured tea for me. I don't really like tea. "Tokyo agrees with you." She sounded disappointed by that admission.

"Thank you," I said politely. I pretended to sip a spot of tea, trying not to squirm in my seat. Was I supposed to cross my legs or my ankles? I looked toward Kim, whose ladylike legs were turned to the side. I did the same.

Kim said, "I had dinner with Chloe Lehrer last night. She said you're doing very well at ICS. She said your teachers appreciate how hard you've been working to catch up." I knew I was being flattered, but I felt like I'd been gently slapped in the face, reminded of the inferior schools I came from. And why was the Upper School dean talking about me to my indifferent aunt? It felt like an invasion of privacy.

Uncle Masa said, "Elle was always an excellent student. Teachers always commented in her report cards that she was eager to learn and a delight to have in class."

I looked toward Kenji, who did not make eye contact with me. He'd never seen a single one of the report cards I brought home as a kid. I knew Uncle Masa was boasting about me for Mrs. Takahara's benefit, and I felt glad to have one longtime connection to my old life here to support me.

"When are you finally returning to Tokyo?" Mrs. Takahara asked Uncle Masa.

"My embassy assignment goes through the end of the year," he said. "Then, maybe."

Kim said, "More importantly, when are you finally coming to work for Takahara Industries?" She turned to me. "Wouldn't it be lovely if he lived and worked here?"

Now I realized why I'd been invited to tea. The family wanted me to sell Uncle Masa on moving home and working for the family business. Damn right I'd play along. I'd love it if he lived here.

"Yes, yes, yes!" I said to Uncle Masa. "Please move back to Tokyo!"

Kenji said, "We have a suite available on the forty-sixth floor we are holding for you." So the idea of Uncle Masa living and working in Tokyo wasn't just a pipe dream. It was something the Takahara family was actively pursuing as a serious option for him. Was it because they knew how happy I would be to have him here?

Nah.

Mrs. Takahara said, "We need someone we trust who has good connection to government."

Then she and the rest of the group started speaking animatedly in Japanese, and I was locked out once again.

• • •

"Is it really a possibility you'll move back here soon?" I asked Uncle Masa. He'd accompanied me back to the penthouse after our meeting with Mrs. Takahara and Kim

Takahara. Kenji had returned to work, as always.

"I probably will," said Uncle Masa. "It's the right thing to do for the family."

That was an interesting response. It had nothing to do with what Uncle Masa thought was the right thing to do for himself. "Why's that?"

I sat down on the living room sofa, and he sat down in a chair at the sofa's side. "Your father probably wouldn't want me telling you this, but I am only telling you so you have some understanding of why he works so often. There's a government audit going on of the construction loans used to finance this building." He paused. "It's fine. It will all get resolved."

Why didn't I feel convinced? "Should I be worried?"

"Of course not!"

"I mean, whatever is going on won't cause me to lose my home here, will it?" After living through the Beast, Mom's jail sentence, and then three foster homes, I knew I wasn't wrong to catastrophize the worst-case scenario for me.

Uncle Masa smiled at me. "Stay on Mrs. Takahara's good side and you will always have a home here."

That answer didn't make me feel better *at all*. I'd gotten a makeover, I was working my ass off at school, I'd made friends with the "right" people, and hadn't caused any trouble since my arrival. What more could I possibly do to stay on Mrs. Takahara's good side?

I preferred a conversation topic that didn't give me anxiety. "Maybe you'll meet a nice Japanese lady here," I teased Uncle Masa.

He laughed. "That would be nice, actually! It's been hard to settle down with all the travel I do. I'd like to be rooted to one place."

It occurred to me that Kim and Kenji were rooted to one place, but they didn't seem to date. I knew Kenji's girlfriend had moved away, but what about Kim? "How come Kim's not married?" I asked Uncle Masa. "She's so beautiful and smart. I would think she could have her pick of any guy."

"She *was* married, to a banker at one of the most prestigious Japanese firms. But she got divorced soon after my uncle died. I think the marriage had been more to please her father than herself."

I tried to picture Kim as a traditional Japanese wife and I couldn't see it. I knew divorce was far less common in Japan than in America, so I had an even harder time picturing Kim breaking that news to her mother. "Mrs. Takahara must have been *pissed* she got divorced!"

"She certainly wasn't happy about it."

I wanted to hear so much more of the Takahara family

gossip, but my phone buzzed with a FaceTime call from Reg. It was so hard for Reg and me to connect with the time difference, and I didn't want to lose the opportunity. I'd been unsettled since finding out what happened between Ryuu Kimura and Arabella Acosta, and I really wanted screen time with my oldest friend; the comfort of a familiar face. "Do you mind if I take this?" I asked Uncle Masa.

"Go," he said.

I ran into my bedroom and answered the call. "Coleman!" I said.

"Zoellner!" he replied.

"What's up?"

"All good. Just passed my GED. I'm free and clear to join the army."

"Congrats! Did you do anything to celebrate?"

"Carmen treated me to crab cakes at our favorite restaurant."

What? They had a favorite restaurant?

"Cool," I said, thinking: Gross. "So you guys are officially a thing now?"

I hated to say it, but his face glowed with a new happiness. "Yup. We're even talking about getting married."

"WHAT?" That was insane. "You're not even eighteen yet! You've only been going out for, like, a month!"

"When you know, you know," he said. "I'm going to have a good job. Some stability for the first time in my life. We could make a life."

So often I had to take care of myself like I was an adult, but I was nowhere near thinking about adult decisions like having a good job and getting married. It sucked that Reggie thought he should make those choices now. I wanted more for him than being tied down so young. But I totally understood how after the life he'd had, he would want the security he thought he could get by having his life so decided.

"Are you sure?" I asked, knowing he was making a big mistake and also knowing I was powerless to stop it.

"I'm sure. And I have something to tell you." The expression on his face had turned uncomfortable.

"Oh shit, is she pregnant?"

"No, no, not like that. The thing is . . ." Even over a FaceTime call where the image blurred as the connection dipped in and out, I could see him squirm. "I don't know how to say this, so I'm just gonna say it. Carmen doesn't want me talking to you anymore."

"Please tell me you're kidding." I knew he wasn't. I could feel the Maryland girl in me bursting out of my posh Tokyo clothes. I wanted to fight this girl, and take her down.

"Yeah, she just wants us to, you know, have a clean slate. She gets jealous even though I told her nothing is going on between us. I mean, you live across the world."

Even worse than this girl's ridiculous request of Reggie was that he apparently was going along with it. What did that say about him? "After all those years of us knowing each other, you're just going to turn me off like that?"

"We'll stay in touch. Email and whatever. She'll settle down. She just needs time to feel more secure."

"That's bullshit," I said.

"That's how it is," Reggie said.

I hung up on him.

I couldn't believe it. I was so hurt and angry.

Reg was my only real connection to my old life, and now he was gone from my new one. By choice.

I returned to the living room, where Uncle Masa was watching TV. "I need cake," I said.

"Room service!" he said enthusiastically. He would never start dating a woman and then cut out people in his life who loved him because she was an insecure bitch.

I dropped down next to him on the couch, and in very informal, un-Japanese fashion put my head on his shoulder. "Please move here."

Uncle Masa put his arm around me while his other arm reached for the phone to dial for cake.

chapter twenty-nine

I woke up on Saturday excited for the swim meet at the British International School, and even more excited that Kenji would be going. At 8 a.m., I went to the kitchen to get some lucky apple juice but found Kim sitting in the living room with Kenji's assistant.

"Hi?" I said, not pleasantly surprised by their company.

Emiko said, "We're waiting for Takahara-san to finish dressing. Business meetings."

"He's supposed to come to my swim meet this morning!" I couldn't believe the first time he'd said he would come to a school activity of mine, he was bailing.

Kim said, "Unfortunately, he won't be able to go."

"But it's a Saturday!" I said.

"The meeting wasn't expected," said Emiko.

Kenji dashed into the hallway. "Sorry, Elle!" he said. "I

really wanted to go to your swim competition, but something important came up. I look forward to hearing about your win later this evening." He buttoned his suit jacket. The expression on his face was distracted.

"What's so important?" I rarely asked him about his business because he didn't seem to want to talk about it. Anytime I did, he changed the subject.

"Government auditors are here," he said.

"Why?" I dared to ask.

"That's not your worry," he said. And with that, he left the apartment with Kim and Emiko.

But it *was* my worry.

A text from Imogen arrived on my phone.

No field hockey or karate today. J n N n moi have decided to take an expedition. Join us for a girls' day outside the city?

I typed, Busy. Swim meet. Then I thought about it before hitting SEND. I was tired of being the good, responsible girl. The swim team could do without me. It wasn't even a real meet today. The last thing I felt like doing now was swimming. Between Reg expelling me from his life and my new father not letting me into his, I could use a time-out from my scheduled life. I deleted my first response to Imogen and sent another instead:

I'm in.

I texted Coach Tanya.

Sorry Coach T, I can't make the swim meet today. Girl problems, bad cramps, achy.

Liar.

. . .

Immediately upon greeting the Ex-Brat girls at the train station, I knew I'd made a mistake. The boys were at a polo tournament in Miami, so at least I didn't have to deal with Nik. That was some consolation. But I was upset about Reg and Kenji, confused about Ryuu—and a day away with the Ex-Brats while skipping out on my swim teammates was the wrong way to deal. The whole time we stood on the train platform, I kept imagining how the competition was going. *Now it's the 100M relay. Now Ryuu is killing it on the butterfly. Now the team is talking about what a shit teammate I am for not showing up.* I felt queasy with anxiety, which only felt worse when the girls told me where we were going—to their favorite amusement park outside the city, Fuji-Q Highlands. Great. What could be better for my uncomfortable stomach than roller coaster rides?

"Girls' trip!" Jhanvi loudly squealed as we stepped onto the JR train at Shinjuku. Sometimes I was embarrassed when the Ex-Brats were so loud and obnoxious in public places. From the stoic looks being shot our way from the neighboring seats, the native people clearly did not appreciate their noise. But they were too gracious to complain aloud.

We sat down in assigned seats, two seats facing forward opposite two seats facing backward. I sat down on the aisle of the front-facing seat, but Imogen pulled me back up and said, "I get nauseated going backward. You sit in the other seat."

I moved to the backward seat. Joushi was in one of her moods, too. This wasn't the day to ask her what really happened between Arabella Acosta and Ryuu Kimura. Now that I knew part of the story from Akemi, I was dying to hear the rest. Had Ryuu dumped Arabella when she found out she was pregnant? Pressured her to get an abortion? What was so bad that Arabella took off for Bolivia to recover from the stress?

"Parents out of town again this weekend?" I asked Ntombi.

Ntombi nodded, and her cornrow beads click-clacked. "Seoul. They didn't take me because they don't want me to spend all my time with Luke. I hate them. They're ruining my life."

"At least your parents give a shit what you do," said Imogen. "Not like ours, right, Elle?" She lifted her fist for me to bump. I kept my hand on my lap. The truth hurt.

What the hell could be happening that the government showed up on a weekend to audit Tak-Luxxe?

I was dying to know more about Ryuu. Didn't his businessman dad also get in trouble with the Japanese government? "Can hafus be yakuza?" I asked Imogen.

"What does that have to do with anything?" Imogen demanded.

"Just curious in case I decide to join." I yawned so it would seem like a silly, casual question I didn't care about.

Imogen said, "Yaks are often hafu. But they're not women. The group started from Koreans working in Japan who turned to crime for more opportunity when they got shut out of businesses for not being Japanese. Now yakuza are Japanese and Korean Japanese."

"I'm not sure that's true," said Ntombi. "At the embassy, they say—"

"Google it, brainiac," Imogen interrupted. "I'm right."

Jhanvi said, "Let's just agree that yakuza are bad guys."

Good and bad was never that simple. Mom was in jail, a criminal, but that didn't mean she was a bad person. More like a lost one.

I knew better than to go there, but curiosity was killing me. "Didn't you say Ryuu Kimura's father was yakuza?"

Imogen said, "I knew it. You like Ryuu Kimura."

"I don't!" I protested. "But I see him at the pool like every day. Can't I be curious about him?"

"Curious," said Jhanvi. "Not like-like."

"Off-limits," said Ntombi.

"Iced out," said Imogen. She took a swig of beer she had hidden in a paper bag and finally smiled in satisfaction. "Ryuu's dad was the chief financial officer for a big Japanese corporation. He was indicted for cooking the books and cheating shareholders."

Jhanvi said, "I thought he was indicted for insider trading?"

"Same thing!" said Imogen.

"Again, pretty sure you're wrong," said Ntombi.

"Did he go to jail?" I asked. I shouldn't be excited by this information, but knowing that Ryuu also had a parent who'd faced criminal charges was oddly comforting to me in this world where everyone's parents seemed to be ridiculous overachievers.

Ntombi said, "No. He just had to pay huge fines."

Imogen said, "Don't worry about the Kimuras. They had plenty of money left over, according to Arabella."

Jhanvi said, "His dad got sent to the other kind of Japanese jail. The shame jail. Where you still live your life, but it's like you're invisible to proper Japanese society. Unwanted."

I said, "I thought yakuza were, like, gangsters. I hardly think someone's dad with a big corporate job would be in organized crime."

Jhanvi said, "Where do you think the money he was swindling was going to? Yakuza!"

Imogen burped. "Your Tak-Luxxe dad is probably in bed with the yakuza, too. Most everybody in the construction and entertainment businesses is."

"He's in the hotel business!" I seriously was about to kick the shit out of Imogen.

But in the back of my mind, I was thinking about Kenji's late-night meetings, his monitoring of the mahjongg games in the gaming parlor, the private men's club. Could he be involved in criminal activity?

• • •

When I returned to Tak-Luxxe that evening, I found Kenji at the end of the main driveway, smoking a cigarette by the bushes.

"You smoke?" I said.

He blew smoke through his lips. "I try not to. Today, I do. How was your swim meet?"

"I didn't go."

"Why not?" he asked, surprised.

"Just didn't feel like it."

"You shouldn't let your teammates down like that."

Oh, like how you let me down on a daily basis? I thought. But I said, "That time of the month."

His face reddened and I knew he wouldn't give me more grief about bailing on the meet.

"Then where have you been all day?" What, my own father was curious about my whereabouts in this city of thirty million where anything could happen? That was a first.

"I went to Fuji-Q with Imogen and her friends." I'd been hanging out with them since I arrived at ICS-Tokyo, but I still thought of Jhanvi and Ntombi as Imogen's friends, not mine.

He nodded, pleased with this information. "Good." Then he added, "I'm going to ICS-Tokyo Parents' Night." He sounded almost defensive, like he knew he should have attended my event today, but he wanted me to know he wasn't a completely lost cause as a parent. "I hope to meet Shar Kato in person then." Of course there was a business angle to his attendance. "I can't wait to tell her our daughters are friends. How'd you like Fuji-Q?"

Though the girls had told me it was an "amusement park," Fuji-Q would be more correctly called a "horror park," in my opinion. It included an infamous haunted hospital, with a maze of operating tables, weird organs in jars, torture chambers with bloodied walls, dark corners and hallways, mangled "patients" in cages, and guests being chased and screamed at by ghosts and maniacal hospital "staff."

The Ex-Brats had given me no warning what to expect. I felt pranked.

I shrugged to Kenji's question. "It was fine."

"I remember going there in my twenties. Terrifying!"

"Kind of." I laughed. At least we shared that.

He stubbed his cigarette out on the pavement and then picked it back up and tossed it into a waste bin. "Shall we have dinner? I could use a good steak after today."

"Was it bad?" I asked. I followed him toward the building entrance. *Should I be worried?*

"It wasn't great."

"Are the auditors there because it's, like, tax stuff, or . . . I mean, the company's not, like, doing anything wrong, is it?"

"Why would you ask that? Of course there's no criminal activity."

"I just want to know what's happening with you," I said, finally being honest with him. "If you're my family, I want to be there for you."

"You don't need to be here for me," he said.

He might as well have pushed me off a cliff to certain death, the blow felt that bad.

I said, "So maybe you should have just sent me to boarding school."

I turned around to go inside, alone. "Wait! Elle!" he called to me. But I got into the elevator as he stood there looking confused and stunned.

chapter thirty

"It's just parents. It's not that bad," I called to Ryuu, who was sitting at the farthest corner high up in the bleachers in the basketball gymnasium, hunched over a book. Between the horror show of the Fuji-Q trip, and then that horrible conversation with Kenji afterward, I didn't care if the Ex-Brats saw me talking to iced-out Ryuu at school.

Parents mingled in the center of the room, eating hors d'oeuvres from trays brought around by waiters, drinking wine, and looking at their kids' school projects—dioramas, paintings, science experiments—placed throughout the large room. It was a few days after the Fuji-Q debacle, at an evening party for Parents' Night, with the ICS-Tokyo parents getting tours of the classrooms, talking with their kids' teachers, and seeing their precious progeny's projects.

As promised, Kenji Takahara was in attendance. Despite being in a room teeming with expats, some basic Japanese instinct had kicked in for me. Kenji acted like our tiff never happened; and I did the same. Courteous and nonconfrontational. We were back to being polite roommates.

"It's that bad," Ryuu said.

I said, "Your artwork is amazing. I had no idea you were an illustrator." On the wall behind the basketball hoop hung a framed work of Ryuu's, drawn to resemble a comic book cover. The manga-style illustration pictured a superhero-looking gopher dressed as a golfer, swinging a club on a parkland overlooking the Tokyo skyline, with the title *Golpher*.

His brown eyes peeked from under his tousle of blue-black hair. "What happened this weekend? How come you weren't at the swim meet?"

"Because I'm a jerk," I answered honestly. Despite what the Ex-Brats said, in my heart I felt confident that Ryuu Kimura didn't suck as a human being. In fact, I thought exactly the opposite. I mean, I thought I knew Reggie Coleman. I thought he was my best friend until he dumped me, totally out of the blue, for a lazy, whiner swimmer who complained when her hair got wet . . . *in a pool!* So if my first impression of Ryuu was bad—and the Ex-Brats only tried to reinforce that impression—that didn't mean Ryuu wasn't a good person. I knew better. It's impossible to really know someone until they truly let you in.

"No, no, no," came a familiar voice from behind. Imogen. "This is not a swim meet. Leave the moody loner *alone*, Elle. That's why he's all the way up here—he likes it that way. Come on. My folks want to meet you."

"Sayonara, Joushi," said Ryuu, not looking up from his book.

I let myself be led away. I almost said, *I'll come when I'm ready and don't tell me not to talk to Ryuu.* But with Kenji in attendance, I wanted to be on best behavior and avoid confrontation.

Imogen broke through the swarm of people surrounding her parents, who held court at the center of the room. Her mom looked smaller than she appeared in magazines, and not nearly as couture fashion as I expected, more like boho chic yoga mom. Shar Kato wore simple leggings with cowboy boots, a white knit sweater, and a large diamond pendant necklace, with her brunette hair in a high ponytail and a minimum of makeup—just lip gloss and mascara. She had the same blue eyes as Imogen and a confident demeanor. She let her husband, Akira Kato, be the fashion plate of the event. He wore crimson-colored plaid cargo pants, with a proper white shirt and suit coat, and had a red top hat on his head. "You must be

Elle," Mrs. Kato said to me in a British accent, extending her hand. "I've heard a lot about you!" She had?

"I haven't heard *anything* about you," teased Mr. Kato. "Should I have?"

"Yes you have, Dad. You just weren't paying attention," said Imogen.

"That sounds like me," her dad agreed amiably.

"Elle, you'll have to come over one weekend so we can get to know you," said Mrs. Kato. I was honored. Socializing at other people's houses wasn't common in Japan the way it is in America.

"She'd love to!" said a new member to our group. No less than Kim Takahara. She introduced herself to the group as my aunt. I was shocked enough that Kenji was here tonight and hadn't bailed for whatever was happening at Tak-Luxxe. But I almost passed out when Kim joined us. I was confused, until I realized she was working the parent crowd like a pro. She let Nik Zhzhonov's mother explain an app on her phone that I knew Kim was perfectly proficient in already. I had never once seen Kim laugh, but when Jhanvi's engineer dad told the worst joke ever, Kim responded like he was a professional comedian. She'd invited Ntombi's mother to host an embassy reception at Destiny Club.

Chloe Lehrer joined the group, sliding in alongside Kim and Kenji. "I'm needing parent chaperones for the junior-class trip to Kyoto this spring. Any volunteers here?"

Radio silence from the Katos and Kenji. "I'd love to!" said Kim.

"I could go," Akira Kato pronounced, eyeing stunning Kim with blatant admiration. Awkward!

"Please don't," Imogen said.

Chloe said, "I see you're all getting to know our new star swimmer! Elle, did you know Kim was also an excellent swimmer at Harvard?"

Kim smiled. "I swam. But not on the school team."

Chloe said, "She could have swum on the team, but she chose not to. She was too busy taking extra language classes so she could complain about her housemates' dirty laundry in their native tongues."

Kim said, "Thinking back, I suppose I should have joined. It's not like I wasn't up early enough for their practices." Kim and Chloe laughed.

"We were roommates as freshmen and I rowed crew," said Chloe, even though no one had asked for an explanation. "I was always up at five a.m."

"No consideration," teased Kim.

"Dawn wake-up calls. That's what friends are for," Chloe sang.

A school dean sang at Parents' Night?

Kim legit had friends?

They were *roomies* at Harvard five hundred years ago? Gross.

Kenji looked at his phone with concern. "There's an emergency back at Tak-Luxxe. I'm afraid I need to return to the property immediately." He leaned over and whispered into Kim's ear. She nodded.

I was disappointed but not surprised. I still couldn't believe he'd shown up to begin with. I glanced at Kim, hoping she'd volunteer to go back to Tak-Luxxe in Kenji's place and deal with the situation herself.

"Go," said Kim to Kenji. "I can handle things here."

"I'll go with you," I said to Kenji. "I don't need to be here if you're not here."

Kim said, "You can't leave, Elle. Stay so you can show me around your school." But Kim's eyes were honing in on Shar Kato a few feet away. *Stay so you can help me schmooze your friend's mom, Elle* seemed to be the implicit message.

Ryuu Kimura had finally been extracted from his bleacher seat and walked toward me with his parents on either side of him. They stuck out—the most Japanese people in this room of expats, both parents wearing navy suits. Ryuu approached our group like he was about to introduce me to them, Imogen be damned, and I started to smile.

But Kim's radar must have dinged an alarm, because she latched on to my arm and said, "I'd love to meet your teachers." I stood firm, not about to be led away again.

But Ryuu did not bring his parents to me. They walked on by, like they'd expected not to be introduced.

I seriously wanted to mangle Kim's beautiful face with a good old-fashioned punch to the nose.

Nik Zhzhonov and his father—who looked like an older version of Nik—joined the group. Nik said, "Dad, this is my friend Elle. She moved here from Washington, DC, recently."

His dad looked me up and down in that same appraising way Nik had when we first met. "Lovely," he opined, and extended his hand to shake mine. I weakly shook his, wishing I'd thought to bring some hand sanitizer.

"She's my niece!" Kim chirped. Oh, so "Aunt" Kim was finally acknowledging me as her niece? What a phony.

"I see where she gets her good looks," said Nik.

I wanted to be anywhere the Zhzhonovs weren't. I said, "Oh, Auntie Kim, my Marine Science teacher, Jim, is over there. Let's go say hi to him." I said the word *auntie* with full sarcastic intent, then felt sad. I would love to have a true auntie—not someone only interested in her niece as a meaningful business connection at an elite private school.

"Let me know if you want me to email you a list of

those Tokyo restaurant recommendations," Kim said to Nik's father, holding up his business card. "And please, everyone—come to Destiny Club as my guest."

She handed out a few business cards of her own and bowed.

. . .

On the way home, Kim only made my annoying night worse by chattering about everything she'd "accomplished at the party." She'd gotten Akira Kato to consider designing a scuplture to be placed in Tak-Luxxe's Sky Garden. She'd gotten Jhanvi Kapoor's dad to agree to take a meeting to discuss job possibilities in the Tak-Luxxe empire. Nik Zhzhonov's father said he was going to check out Destiny Club as a potential board meeting space. It hadn't been Parents' Night after all. It had been Kim's Night. She'd totally stolen my chance to show Kenji the school and meet my teachers. Whatever "emergency" had happened, surely Kim could have handled it in Kenji's place. But clearly seeing my school life in action was not Kenji's priority.

"Chloe never told me that Satoshi Kimura's son went to ICS-Tokyo," Kim said, referring to Ryuu's father. "That was a surprise."

"Who cares where they send their son to school?" I asked.

"That's exactly right," Kim said, completely misunderstanding me. "Kimura-san's children can't go to a proper Japanese school because of what he did. I hope you know Ryuu Kimura is not the sort of person you should be friends with at ICS."

"That's absurd!" I protested, knowing I was a hypocrite because if it weren't for the Ex-Brats not liking him, I would probably try to be better friends with Ryuu. But I did point out to Kim, "Whatever his father did isn't his son's fault." She wasn't listening, her attention lost to the business document she was reading. If whatever was happening with the government investigation of Tak-Luxxe caused a scandal, would Kim still be so dismissive of where Ryuu went to school? Would she worry about how the Takaharas' business problems would tarnish me?

My phone lit up on the car seat and I picked it up to read the message, not realizing it was actually Kim's phone that buzzed. She hadn't noticed it because she was busy typing on her laptop. The message was from Chloe Lehrer. See you later tonight. I'll have the champagne and bathtub ready! I love you.

What?!

Kim was a lesbian? And Chloe Lehrer was her girlfriend. Of course! That's why Chloe was always talking about Kim. I'd bet it was also the reason Kim divorced her husband as soon as her father died.

Whatever Kim was reading on her laptop caused her to chew on her pinky cuticle anxiously. My annoyance with her dissipated. I felt sorry for her. Why be closeted in this day and age? It was so not necessary. Then again, if I had traditional Mrs. Takahara for a mother, I might not be so keen to come out, either.

I told Kim, "I think your phone is going off."

Kim picked up her phone. "Probably my banker friend. Having drinks with him after I drop you back at Tak-Luxxe."

Riiiight. Sure.

I wanted to tell her she didn't need to lie to me, because I would only applaud her for having a girlfriend, but I didn't. We weren't close like that. Like family.

• • •

I thought Kenji and I had an unspoken agreement to avoid confrontation after our little tiff in the driveway. Then came Parents' Night.

The next morning, I scarfed down a quick bowl of cereal in the kitchen before heading down to meet Akemi for our ride to school. Kenji wandered in, already dressed in a suit for work. It was unusual to see him before I left for school in the mornings. Usually he didn't return from Destiny Club until about 2 a.m., and then he usually

277

slept until 7 or 8 a.m. before returning to work again. He looked very, very tired. If I wasn't still sore that he left the Parents' Night prematurely, I might have offered to make him breakfast or coffee, like a good daughter.

"Good morning."

He didn't greet me. Instead, he reached into the fridge and grabbed an apple. He glanced at me and said, "I saw you talking to Satoshi Kimura's son last night."

"So?" I said, wanting to add, *And I saw you leave the only event you've ever attended for me after less than an hour there.*

Kenji said, "Imogen Kato and Nik Zhzhonov are the kinds of people you should be friends with. Not Kimura-san's son."

Outrageous. No. Unacceptable. I didn't care that the Ex-Brats made the same demand. As a principle, it wasn't something I was going to accept from the father who'd abandoned me for the first sixteen years of my life.

I scoffed. "He has a name. It's Ryuu. He's his own person. Whatever his father did wrong should not be a reflection on him."

Kenji shook his head as he retrieved a water bottle from the kitchen cabinet (drinking cold water from the fridge was a particularly American habit, I'd learned) and then walked toward the foyer.

"Of course it is," Kenji said. "Just as you are a reflection on the Takaharas. You live here. We send you to school at ICS."

I followed him to the foyer, where he was putting on his work shoes to leave the apartment. "That makes no sense at all. Whatever I do is about me. Just like whatever you do is about you."

"You are thinking like an American. You must learn to think like a Japanese person if you are going to live here."

"*Should* I live here?" I couldn't believe I'd spoken my fear aloud. "I'm not sure I like your value system."

He didn't seem at all concerned by my deepest anxiety, like it didn't register with him at all. To him, we were having no more than a quick, awkward talk on an issue he felt the need to address to me. No more, no less. "If you plan to stay, you'd better learn it," he said matter-of-factly. His phone buzzed with a call. He started to walk out the front door. Before he left, he looked at me with exasperation, like he was trying to make me understand something for which there was no actual logic. "Just don't associate with that Ryuu Kimura. That's all I'm saying. Don't make it a big deal."

He answered his phone call, and the front door closed behind him.

It was a big deal. To me.

chapter thirty-one

Uncle Masa couldn't care less about the politics of who I should be friends with at ICS. He just wanted to hang out with me. We started our weekend in Taipei with a lovely walk. Then came the champagne.

On Saturday morning, he'd chosen his favorite place in Taipei to show me, Chung-shan Park. We wandered on a beautiful walking path around a lake with spraying fountains, surrounded by trees, and under the shadow of Taipei's iconic skyscraper, which was called Taipei 101. It was a great place for people-watching, with young couples on romantic walks, parents pushing babies in strollers, older people practicing tai chi, kids riding bikes, and nature lovers snapping photos of flowers. Best of all were the *baobing*—delicious shaved ices with a super-thin texture and condensed milk that added an extra sweet flavor. I topped my baobing with mango chunks, while Uncle Masa chose sweet potato chunks on his, an addition I never imagined could be delicious until I sampled his for myself.

The swim meet wasn't until the late afternoon, so the early part of our day was free for sightseeing. And, as it turned out, drunken revelations.

We returned to the hotel for lunch, where I tried my first sip of champagne, sneaking a taste from Uncle Masa's glass. It was tasty, but I didn't dare drink more. Coach Tanya was sitting nearby with her boyfriend, watching over the team players who lounged in the rooftop hotel swimming pool before the big meet in a few hours.

"So have you decided if you'll move back to Tokyo when your Geneva assignment ends?" I asked Uncle Masa.

He laughed. I didn't realize I'd made a joke. Maybe he was feeling extra jovial. Uncle Masa was on his fourth glass of champagne, enjoying a rare day without work. "Family and work are better separate." He took another sip and then added, "Working for Kenji is very risky."

"Risky how? He says you're like a brother to him. I'm sure you'd be fine if you worked together."

"Kenji doesn't need another brother."

That made no sense. "I know you're just cousins—"

"No, I mean, he had a brother who died. Kenji is at risk the same way."

"Wait. I had an uncle? How old was he when he died?"

"Masaru was the oldest son, three years older than Kenji, their mother's favorite. He died in a boating accident when he was nineteen. Drinking too much and lost control of the boat."

"I had no idea." I felt a pang of sympathy for Mrs. Takahara. I couldn't imagine how devastating it would feel to lose your child. Not like it was okay to be mean and bitter, but I could understand how a tragedy like that could turn a person that way.

"Masaru was like a prince. Kenji worshipped him. And then Kenji became like him."

"Kenji *is* like a prince of the family," I agreed.

"No. A drunk."

"But he doesn't drink anymore!"

Uncle Masa was too tipsy to care about discretion. "But when he did, it was a huge problem. He drank too much, partied too much, made business deals with bad people. If I went to work with him, I'd have to clean up the messes he created."

My instinct was to believe Uncle Masa, but the logic didn't add up. "Why would Kenji be put in charge of the family business if he wasn't sober? His mother would never allow that. She's too smart."

"She had no other choice. CEOs in Japan are not women. Kim was still left doing the hard work that Kenji got all the credit for. Until Kim and Noriko got him to stop."

"Stop what? Drinking?"

"Yes. In exchange for their support to bring you to live with him in Tokyo, he agreed to stop drinking. And he did. For you."

I hadn't realized the extent of the sacrifice Kenji made to bring me to Tokyo to live with him. Still, I was skeptical. "Did he ever go to rehab?"

Uncle Masa vehemently shook his head. "No rehab, no AA. Rehab is not a big business like in America. In Japanese culture, once someone becomes an addict, he or she is looked down on. It's very hard for that person to regain their previous status after recovery. They must go cold chicken—"

"Turkey. Cold turkey."

"Yes. They must go cold meat or be considered weak. It's a common struggle in Japan, between *giri-ninjo*, social duty, and *ninjo*, personal inclination."

"If he can't go to AA, then his mother should support him more," I said. "She's always bickering with Kenji in Japanese when I see them together."

"Or, she's trying to keep him on track with sobriety so he can have his daughter near him."

I was too stunned to respond. That possibility had never occurred to me. Mrs. Takahara had a heart?

My mom had nearly destroyed her life and mine with substance abuse. Kenji got clean to make a life for me.

With Uncle Masa good and tipsy, I could really get some answers from him. I poured the remainder of the bottle into his glass. He happily sipped it.

I confessed, "Kenji doesn't seem that interested in being a father. To be honest."

Uncle Masa said, "He wants to be your father. He wouldn't have gone to all the trouble to bring you to Japan if he didn't. But it's going to take some time for him to figure out how to be a parent. His own father was very stern and always treated Kenji like he was a disappointment. You've seen how challenging his mother is. Try to be more patient and understanding."

I was the kid. I didn't want to be understanding. I wanted to be *understood*.

chapter thirty-two

Ryuu killed the 200M backstroke heat, winning easily, clocking in at 2 minutes and 31.25 seconds. I was almost hoarse from screaming so loud to cheer him on. From the bench, Coach Tanya called to him, "Your best time yet, Kimura! Way to go!" She turned to me, sitting behind her. "I notice he swims his best times when you're around."

I looked down so she wouldn't see, in case I was blushing. "He says he swims best in indoor pools," I said. The ICS-Taipei pool wasn't as nice as the ICS-Tokyo outdoor pool, because it wasn't surrounded by lush green landscaping, but it did have the advantage of a stable temperature and a more intimate environment, where swimmers on the sidelines could cheer on their teammates and really be heard (to the dismay of the ICS-Taipei parents in the stands, many of whom put their hands over their ears at Tokyo's unofficial cheer squad led by me).

Ryuu came and sat down beside me while the next heat prepared to start. I high-fived him. "Great swim!" If Kenji just took time to get to know Ryuu, he'd never tell me not to associate with this awesome guy. But then, Kenji couldn't be bothered to take the time to get to know his own daughter.

"Thanks," Ryuu said. "Felt good." But his uncharacteristically happy face quickly turned to a scowl as unexpected team support arrived in the stands and sat behind us: the Ex-Brat crew of Nik Zhzhonov and Oscar Acosta.

"What are you guys doing here?" I asked them.

"Supporting the team," said Oscar, like it was obvious.

"In *Taipei*?" I asked. What the fuck?

Nik said, "We had a polo match yesterday in Brunei. I directed Zhzhonov Air to stop here on the way home to see your first meet." He looked like he expected me to be flattered. I felt stalked. I said nothing, so finally Nik added, "You're welcome."

I could feel my swim mojo disappearing, and mine was the next heat, the 100M butterfly. From the top row of bleacher seats, Uncle Masa looked down at me and gave me an enthusiastic thumbs-up. It would be the first time he'd seen me swim since I was a kid. I wanted to impress him. I didn't need my mental preparation ruined by unexpected company who'd "stopped off" on their way back from a polo match in a place I'd never heard of.

Nik told me, "We can give you a lift back to Tokyo if you want." He directed his gaze at Ryuu and then back at me. "But only you."

"I'll stay with Ryuu and the team," I said. I was pretty sure I saw the sides of Ryuu's mouth curl up into an almost-smile.

"You don't know what you're missing," said Oscar.

Actually, I did. And no thank you. I couldn't believe I'd ever kissed Nik. I looked at him now, all arrogant and creepy, and thought: Never again.

• • •

"Go, Zoellner!" I heard Nik shout right before my swim relay. I looked up into the stands. He blew me a kiss.

The starting gun rang and I dove in. And promptly choked on the fly. My 100M time usually averaged around one minute and ten seconds. My time in Taipei was one minute twenty-five. *Terrible.* I should have used my anger to power my arms and legs. Instead, my body flailed. My concentration was on the uninvited Ex-Brats in the stands, not in the water. What was that air kiss supposed to mean? From someone who just randomly showed up, uninvited, to a meet in a foreign country? Should I just tell Nik to back the fuck off, or let a restraining order give him the message?

"You were amazing!" Uncle Masa lied as he came to say good-bye before leaving to catch his flight back to Geneva.

"I came in last," I reminded him.

"You were clearly the most powerful swimmer in your race. But you seemed distracted."

"Focus, focus, focus," I muttered, remembering Reggie's constant reminder before a race. Too bad I was remembering it *after* the race.

In very un-Japanese fashion, Uncle Masa gave me an American hug.

I needed it.

I headed to the locker room to change before getting onto the chartered bus that would take the team back to the Taipei airport. It was pretty deserted, since most of the team had been through there while I was talking with Uncle Masa. I took a shower and put on my clothes, stuffing my loser's swimsuit into my gym bag, then found my way back outside. Like the ICS-Tokyo campus, the Taipei campus was large, and it was dark, and I had to use my phone as a flashlight to find my way back to the central driveway where the bus was waiting.

I passed the side of the main building, about to round the corner to the central quad, when a guy jumped out from behind a tree and scared the bejesus out of me. "Boo!" said Nik.

"Don't do that!" I said, shoving him.

Before I could tell him I was possibly about to have a heart attack from the sudden fright in the dark, he pulled me to him. "You're such a tease," he murmured, and then his mouth descended on mine.

"Get off!" I stammered, turning my face so his lips couldn't touch mine.

"You wanna play rough?" Before I knew what was happening, he pushed me down to the ground and tried to kiss me again. Was this actually happening?

Focus, focus, focus, I heard Reggie's voice say, overruling the panic and revulsion I was feeling while I . . .

"OW!" Nik screeched, falling off me and onto his side. He hunched over, his hands over his crotch, where I had finally found my swimmer's power and kneed him as hard as I could. "You fucking bitch, that hurt like shit! I was just playing with you."

"Don't *ever* play with me like that again." I stood up. Someone's phone flashlight glared onto us.

Ryuu. He looked at me and said, "Let's go, Elle," his eyes reassuring me that I was safe. Then Ryuu looked down at Nik. Ryuu told him, "If you ever try that again, I'll kill you."

chapter thirty-three

"It's not a big deal."

This was Jhanvi Kapoor's reaction on Monday when I told the girls what Nik had done over the weekend. We were on a class field trip to the Meiji Shrine, a Shinto shrine dedicated to the spirits of a former Japanese emperor and his wife. It was an incredibly peaceful, evergreen forest of towering trees smack in the middle of the city, with an enormous cedar gate called a *torii*, leading to a path featuring stunning temples, a treasure museum, walls of white sake barrels stacked in neat rows, and Shinto priests and maidens wearing traditional clothing. The serenity of the setting felt at odds with the pounding of my heart—my body's reaction to the crazy nonresponse of the Ex-Brat girls to my revelation.

Ntombi said, "He was probably drinking too much. He gets like that."

"Date-rapey?" I asked, shocked by their indifference.

"Inappropriate," said Imogen. "He was just horsing around. He wasn't going to hurt you."

Jhanvi said, "He's a good guy that gets dumb when he drinks."

I said, "He must have known it was wrong! Look who was conspicuously absent from school today."

Jhanvi said, "Thanksgiving is this week. Half the school is out visiting their families in America."

"Nik's not American," I pointed out. My guess was Nik was probably absent because Ryuu had threatened to kill him; I didn't tell the Ex-Brats that part. Ryuu never had a lot to say, but when he did speak up, it counted. I wished he was on this class trip now so I could hang out with him instead of these so-called friends. I thought back to the night before, when Ryuu sat beside me on the flight home to Tokyo from Taipei. He barely spoke a word to me. His silence said everything: *I'm here for you.* Under the cover of the darkened plane in the nighttime sky, I put my head on his shoulder and he put his hand on my knee, and I hadn't felt so safe and cared for since coming to Japan.

Imogen pulled ahead, then turned around and directed

us to stop walking. "Girl-talk time," she said, directing her gaze at me. "Elle, Nik's our friend. You can't have it both ways."

"What ways?" I asked, confused.

Jhanvi said, "You can't say he's date-rapey and still expect to be part of our group."

I gasped. Was this conversation actually happening? Weren't girls supposed to be supportive of one another? I was too disgusted to respond.

Ntombi said, "We've known him awhile. We hardly know you."

I couldn't take it anymore. I said, "Then get to know me now. Know why I moved to Tokyo? I was in foster care before I came here because I had no family to live with when my mom went to jail. All my clothes came from Target or Old Navy, and I'd never even been on an airplane. I might not have come from all your privilege, but at least I know the difference between right and wrong. At least I know a guy jumping from behind a tree and then pushing a girl to the ground is not a good guy."

No one had a retort until Imogen clapped her hands and announced, "Well said, Meryl Streep."

Ntombi said, "I'm sorry things have been hard for you. But Nik's still our friend."

Imogen latched on to my arm and resumed our

walking. "Don't be sore, Elle. I'll have a talk with Nik and smooth it over."

"I didn't ask you to smooth it over," I said.

"That's what a Joushi does," Imogen said.

I was even more confused. Did we have an argument or was everything okay? Did I even want it to be okay?

. . .

Three days later, I was still confused. But I was trapped. Since none of the Ex-Brats were American and their families didn't celebrate Thanksgiving, they had wanted to celebrate the holiday at Ikebana Café. Their original queen was in town and Imogen wanted to take her to Destiny Club. Imogen had promised me she wouldn't invite Nik to join us.

Arabella Acosta had an angular face featuring intense brown eyes, thick eyebrows, a perfectly imperfect hooked nose, and a regal air. Her wavy, dark brown hair looked as if there was an invisible fairy hovering over her head to keep it casually tousled at all times. I didn't hate her on sight because she was beautiful. I hated her because Ryuu Kimura once dated her.

"So let me understand this," Arabella said to me with an aristrocratic accent that bugged the hell out of me.

"You didn't even know who your father was until the day you came to Tokyo?"

"So?" I said. Did Imogen have to blab everything?

Kenji had requested that Ikebana Café have a Thanksgiving menu for dinner that night. It was a nice gesture in my honor, but what he didn't seem to understand was that Thanksgiving was supposed to be about a meal a family shared together, and not one where a father casually said he would drop in "if I find the time." (So far, he hadn't.) Even though most of the clientele was not American and probably couldn't care less, the food options featured a turkey carving station, mashed potatoes, creamed spinach, and an array of pies—apple, pecan, lemon meringue, sweet potato, and pumpkin. It was certainly a more sumptuous offering of food than my Thanksgiving last year, just before Mom was arrested. She was passed out on the sofa and I microwaved a frozen meat loaf dinner for the holiday. For dessert, some stranger off the Internet showed up to buy pills off Mom and mistakenly left behind a McDonald's apple pie. I threw it out but woke up the next morning to see that Mom had dug it out of the trash and eaten it.

Interestingly, with Arabella back in town, Imogen seemed to be temporarily displaced as Ex-Brat boss to Ntombi and Jhanvi.

Jhanvi eagerly told Arabella, "We came in second in the field hockey league this season!"

"Should have been first," Arabella sniped. But then she gave Jhanvi a consoling expression. "I'm sure you tried."

"How come Oscar's not here with you?" Ntombi asked Arabella.

"He and Nik are working with a polo trainer in England this week. Imogen, stop fidgeting. You keep bumping my leg."

I honestly could not understand what Ryuu ever saw in this girl. Besides her beautiful face and body.

Akemi Kinoshita appeared in the dining room and looked mortified to see a meeting of the Ex-Brat girls sitting at a table by the dessert buffet station.

"Hi, Akemi!" I called out. "Want to join us?" I knew she'd never accept, to the Ex-Brats' relief, but I wanted her to know she was welcome.

"No, thank you," she said meekly, not making eye contact with the other girls. "My mother asked me to bring a piece of pumpkin pie up to her. She loves American pie."

"How cute," said Arabella. "Bye-bye, now."

Akemi scurried away. I'd had it. "Please don't be rude to my friend," I said to Arabella.

Arabella said, "Oh, that nobody is your *friend*?"

Jhanvi told me, "Elle, quit with the charity cases."

Ntombi said, "Nik says you're, like, friendly with you-know-who Kimura, even though he's iced out."

"Really." Arabella raised an eyebrow at me. "I guess that makes sense. I heard your new father is yakuza, too." She gestured around to the lavish Ikebana Café setting. Like it was so obvious, she added, "You don't build a palace like this in Japan otherwise."

I was done with these girls. I told Arabella, "Well, I heard you got knocked up by a guy who dumped you."

Loud gasps ringed around the table.

Already, I knew. Now it was my turn to be iced out.

DECEMBER

---

chapter thirty-four

Dear Mom,

Guess whose grade in Spanish went up to an A? Sí, sí, sí—me!

Good result, bad reason. The popular girls I was hanging out with at school when I first arrived in Tokyo dumped me. Muy bien—now I have more time to study and less reasons to be distracted. You know how sometimes when your fears come true, you realize the fear was harder than the actual circumstance? (Maybe Jessup Correctional Institute is like that? I hope?) Don't worry, I'm fine. (Thanks for your last letter and letting me know you are, too.)

*It doesn't make sense, but no one at my school seems to
actually like the popular people. Students follow their
lead, but otherwise dread them. Now that I'm not walled
in with the popular kids, I've been getting to know other
students who are more normal and not so snobby. There
is this girl in my Spanish class who I never talked to
before and it turns out she is from Maryland, not far
from where we lived! She is originally from Bethesda but
moved to Tokyo when her mom got a job at the American
Embassy here. She's been telling me interesting things
about the holidays in Japan, like how people here don't
celebrate Christmas as a religious holiday, but it's a big
deal for dating. People order buckets of Kentucky Fried
Chicken way in advance (because it sells out!), and then
on Christmas day, couples wait in line to pick up their
order where guys dressed up as Santa Claus versions of
Colonel Sanders keep the crowds entertained. And people
eat a special treat for dessert that's a lot like strawberry
shortcake. KFC and strawberry shortcake—sounds more
like a July Fourth meal, right? At New Year's, there's
a five-day work holiday so employees can go home to
their prefectures to see family and honor their ancestors
and bring them mandarin oranges. They welcome their
ancestors home and then say good-bye to them again at
the end of the holiday. I like the idea of that tradition. If*

I was dead, I would be so happy and honored if someone welcomed me back for visits from the afterlife and brought me mandarin oranges.

It's beautiful here right now. Japanese people don't have Christmas trees in their homes or exchange gifts on December 25, but the streets have white lights in the trees shining bright at nighttime, and the stores are all decorated, and Tak-Luxxe even has a super-tall Christmas tree set up in the hotel lobby decorated with giant gold balls and sparkly Christmas lights. The weather is cold and there's even been snow flurries a few times. It really feels like Christmas! I love it. Except for how much it makes me miss you. I miss making Christmas cookies with you and planning the fun things we will do together over Christmas vacation like when we lived at the old house. I can't imagine Christmas with Kenji and not you.

I love you,

Elle

chapter thirty-five

Ryuu no longer sat alone at lunch. Now he had company. Me and Akemi Kinoshita.

It was too cold to eat outside, so the table dynamics had moved to the indoor cafeteria, where the Ex-Brats took the center round table, and everyone else ate at satellite tables outside of their exclusive orbit.

"Do you think they talk about you?" Akemi asked me as she bit into her favorite cafeteria food, a classic American PB&J sammie.

"Maybe." I shrugged, trying not to care. I stole a furtive glance in their direction, but none of them were looking at me, so it was impossible to say if their bitchy conversation included trashing me. I wanted to think they didn't talk about me, but I knew how many lunches I'd spent with them where they couldn't gossip enough about

Ryuu Kimura, and I doubted they were silent where I was concerned. As if to confirm my suspicions, Nik Zhzhonov caught my glance, flashed me his middle finger, and then the rest of the Ex-Brats broke out into laughter.

"Let's talk about *them*," said Akemi.

"Let's not," said Ryuu. "The benefit of being iced out should mean being invisible. It should work both ways." A blue-streaked piece of his hair fell over part of his eye, and I wanted to put my hand on it and tuck it behind his ear so badly.

"These chicken nuggets are *good*," I said, biting into the cafeteria food that I was enjoying for the first time. No more cool girl konbini bento boxes from 7-Eleven for me. What a relief to eat normal student food again.

"I want to try the nuggets," said Akemi. "I love American food. I'll be right back." She got up and returned to the serving area.

"You like fried chicken?" Ryuu asked me.

"Sure. Who doesn't?"

"Vegans." I laughed.

Then Ryuu asked me, "Do you have plans on Christmas Day?"

"Doubt it. My father said the hotel and Destiny Club will be extra busy at Christmas even though it's technically not a day off here. Expats having parties and stuff, and Japanese people who like to celebrate the holiday."

Ryuu looked to the ground. He seemed uncharacteristically nervous. Finally, he asked me, "Want to go to KFC with me that day? It's, like, a tradition here."

OMFG! Ryuu Kimura had just asked me on a date! Seriously!

"I'd love to," I said, like it was no big deal even though my heart was about to explode with happiness. Ryuu grinned, looking both pleased and relieved.

I could feel a stare coming at me from the center of the cafeteria, and I couldn't help but look over to the Ex-Brat table again, where Nik Zhzhonov was giving me the evil eye. This time, *I* flipped *him* the bird.

· · ·

"So what really happened between you and Arabella Acosta?" I asked Ryuu that afternoon on our post-swim practice bus ride back home to Minato. Apparently, setting up a KFC date had gotten me to the point where I felt comfortable asking him this intimate question.

We no longer sat separated by the bus aisle. Lately, I always sat next to him, and we huddled together at the back of the bus, rows away from the other kids, creating a private sanctuary for ourselves.

"You really want to know?" Ryuu asked.

"Yes."

"You might not like it."

Oh no. It probably wasn't just a rumor that he'd gotten her pregnant. Was it a terrible idea to go out with a guy with that kind of baggage, even though I really wanted to?

"I can handle it."

"Why do you want to know?"

"I guess I'm asking because I'm surprised you went out with someone like her. You're so quiet and independent. Arabella struck me as . . ." I was about to say how she was really arrogant and mean, then decided I shouldn't trash his ex to him. "She struck me as not like that," I said as diplomatically as I could.

He looked right at me and spoke genuinely. "Arabella's not that bad. She just has a really messed-up family. Too much money and no one looking out for her."

Like you? I wondered. "Did you love her?" I asked quietly.

There wasn't anyone sitting anywhere near us, but he still whispered. "We were never really a couple. We, you know, explored things but realized we liked each other more as friends."

"Really? Then why'd she leave Tokyo? Imogen said you broke her heart."

"Imogen makes up stories to fit her un-reality. She needs a villain. But the rumor that Arabella went home to Bolivia because she was pregnant was true. Only I wasn't the father."

"Then who was?"

"Nik Zhzhonov. She suspected he put a roofie in her drink. There was a party at his house when his parents were away. She woke up in his bed with him but didn't remember how she got there."

"Holy shit." I never thought I'd feel sympathy for Arabella Acosta. I wanted to violently choke Nik Zhzhonov. I hated the Ex-Brat girls even more for not believing me—and my bad experience with Nik wasn't even that bad in comparison to what Arabella went through. I didn't like Arabella, but I seriously wanted to hug her and tell her she was going to be okay. Jesus. "She didn't want to press charges against him?"

"She had no proof it was forced, and her loyalty was torn. Her brother Oscar is Nik's best friend. She was too embarrassed to tell Imogen and the other girls. So she went home to Bolivia to take care of it privately."

"And you took the blame."

"I don't care what anyone thinks of me or what they say," said Ryuu.

I couldn't believe my boldness, but I reached my hand closer to his, and let our pinky fingers touch. My hand never felt so warm. "I like that about you," I confessed. "I want to be more like that."

He turned his head to look at me. He latched his fingers into mine. I waited, hoping.

My hope was not in vain. It lingered in the air for maybe half a minute, filling me with anticipation, knowing by the look he gave me that everything was about to change between us.

Finally, Ryuu leaned over and kissed me, his lips soft but firm, and sweet, so fucking sweet.

This was the real first kiss I'd waited a lifetime for. The one with fireworks and a true prince.

chapter thirty-six

I wasn't ready to let him go. He felt the same.

"Come with?" Ryuu asked me just before the bus stop where he usually got off.

"For sure." I didn't care where we'd go. So long as I got there with him.

We stepped out of the bus near an entrance to Shiba Park. "I want to show you my favorite place in the park," said Ryuu, and I couldn't contain my smile, giddy that he wanted to share his spot with me. With red-and-white Tokyo Tower looming over the green grass, the air chilly and crisp, and trees offering vibrant displays of late autumn leaves in reds and yellows, it was a perfect day for a walk with gorgeous views (and an amazing boy who asked me to KFC and who just kissed me!).

We stopped at the park entrance, where there was a

beautiful gate that looked more like a temple, a red four-sided structure with lacquered pillars and gold trim on the domed roof. Ryuu said, "This used to be the gate to a mausoleum for one of the ancient shogun rulers. There were more, but this was the one that survived the bombing during World War Two."

"Who are those guys?" I asked, gesturing toward two statues nestled in the gate. The burgundy statues made me think of samurai monsters; one held up a hand as if to say "stop" and the other held up a gold knife, ready to strike. "They look like fierce warriors."

"They're guardians. They represent strength."

Ryuu took my hand, and I clasped on. With him, I felt protected, but also independent—my own best version of strength. We walked, surrounded by trees and gardens, as other couples strolled by holding hands, and I felt a part of some secret society of sweethearts.

"How far do you live from here?" I asked Ryuu.

"About a fifteen-minute walk. I usually come here after school. If the weather's good, I sit on a bench or in a café and do homework."

"I notice you don't hang out with friends at school."

"I like being on my own." He paused, then clenched softly on my hand. "Till now." Swoon.

"You're not like other boys who just want to get home and play video games?"

"I am like that. But it's better if I can get home with my homework mostly already done. Then I can be ready to show my father my work is complete when he yells at me for being online when really I'm just trying to avoid him."

"Why do you avoid him?"

"He hates everything I do. My ukulele. My drawings. He says there's no future in anything I'm interested in."

"That sucks. I'm so sorry." Kenji's indifference to me seemed so benign in comparison to Ryuu's dad's unkind nature.

"Don't be. I'm used to him. Two more years and then I can go to college in America and not deal with him."

"What about your mom?"

"She's okay, but she never stands up for herself. My father is a bully about what she should wear and how she should look and behave, and she goes along with it."

"Maybe she's scared not to."

"That's exactly what she is. Since his business scandal, they hardly go out. Our house is like a private prison, but with maid service and excellent meals."

"Sounds like Tak-Luxxe."

"Is it okay if I ask about your mom?" I'd never told him about her, but he must have heard gossip about where I came from.

"Yeah."

"How much longer is she in jail?"

"She was sentenced to five years. She'll be eligible for parole next year."

"Then what?"

"I have no idea honestly. It scares me to think about that just as much as it scares me to think about her being there."

"Why?"

"Because I don't know where I would go if I had to make a choice. Do I go home and be with her, or—"

"This is your home now."

"Is it? Sometimes it doesn't feel real. I've been here two months and . . ." I hesitated to say what I really felt, then realized Ryuu had just confessed to me about his father and I shouldn't shy away in return. "I still hardly know my father. And the Ex-Brats seem to think . . ." I hesitated again. Could I speak the word that had brought Ryuu's father and their family down? I looked into Ryuu's trusting eyes. I knew I could. I said, "They think that my father might be yakuza. I don't know what I would do if he went to jail, too."

It was amazing how much lighter I felt just speaking my fears aloud to someone who cared.

"If he's anything like my dad, he'll have good lawyers to make sure his prison stays private, at home."

I stopped walking. "Do *you* think Kenji Takahara could be yakuza?"

Ryuu must have seen the concern on my face because he rubbed his hand against my cheek. "I have no idea. But you should know, yakuza is just part of business here. Being yakuza doesn't mean your father's a criminal. It means he's . . . doing business like many Japanese businessmen."

Ryuu made it all sound so normal. No big deal. Maybe for him, it wasn't. His father was indicted and let go. Ryuu's privileged life went on, despite the Japanese "shame jail" the family existed in. But if my father went to jail, then I'd never get to know Kenji at all. Plus, I would have two jailbird parents who were also addicts, and oh yeah, I'd be left homeless again. Or would Kim and Mrs. Takahara allow me to stay? Would I even want them to?

Ryuu must have sensed my anxiety. He took my hand again, silent and content just to keep walking. I had all these fears, but I didn't necessarily want to talk them out. I wanted someone to be there for and with me while I let all these scary thoughts settle.

A few minutes later, we reached a café in the center of the park. At the same time, we both cried out, "Hot chocolate!"

We ordered two hot chocolates. While we waited for the order to be prepared, I admired a gorgeous Shiba Inu puppy sitting on the ground next to her human. The dog had a collar with a nametag in English that said "Kicho."

"Is it okay to pet Kicho?" I asked Kicho's human, who looked American.

"Sure," she said. "She's very friendly. Loves everyone."

I crouched to the ground and Kicho immediately rolled over to allow me to rub her tummy. When Kicho had decided she was finished with the belly rub, she got up, and trotted off with her owner. "Bye, Kicho!" She barked an enthusiastic good-bye as her human waved at us.

"Do you like animals a lot?" Ryuu asked me. We returned to our walk on the footpath with our supremely delicious hot chocolates.

"I love animals. I used to have a cat back in Maryland who was pretty much my best friend." Ryuu draped his arm over my shoulder, like he knew without my telling him that my cat story did not have a happy ending. "I've asked Kenji for one, but he said no."

"Have you—"

"Been to a cat café?"

Ryuu smiled at me. That smile! I'd never seen the expression of his face turn so bright. My heart flip-flopped. "Yes, that's what I was going to say."

"I went to one. It creeped me out. The cats seemed like zombies."

"Do you know about the Japanese cat islands?"

I stopped walking. "Are you kidding me?"

"I'm not. There are a couple remote Japanese islands with cat colonies roaming freely. The fishermen feed them. The cats basically rule these places." He also stopped walking and googled some photos on his phone. "Look."

"Whoa," I said to the images of the packs of island cats wandering, playing, fighting, eating, and of course, sleeping, pressed up against one another for warmth and obscene cuteness. "Now that would be *my* kind of desert island."

We resumed walking. Our hands immediately latched together again, like magnets.

"Right here is my favorite sanctuary in Tokyo," said Ryuu. "It's called Momijidani. It means 'autumn leaf valley.'"

We'd reached an artificial ravine with a waterfall tumbling down from a high rock formation about three stories tall, surrounded by a variety of rocks, and maple trees with red autumn leaves. A stream ran below the waterfall, with a picturesque bridge path over it. The effect was spectacular, like being deep in a valley surrounded by mountains—serene, private, magical—but with Tokyo Tower looming over it, a reminder of the bustling city just beyond.

We sat down on a bench, the only people there at this moment. "Can I kiss you again?" Ryuu asked me.

"Please do," I whispered back.

His lips met mine. This time the kiss was longer and deeper, without that tension of wondering if the other person would be into it, and the excitement of knowing there would be so many more kisses in our future. Instinctively, I knew. *This* was the life I wanted. With Ryuu. Simple. Easy. Joyful. I wanted to build this life in Tokyo with him. Suddenly, I felt less angry with Reggie. I totally understood how, after everything he'd been through, he'd want to dive deep, and quickly, into a relationship with his girlfriend even though she was a bad swimmer. When I kissed Ryuu, I felt flooded with a sense of pride that he chose me, and delirious with happiness.

Please don't let this be a dream, I thought.

chapter thirty-seven

No way, no how was I going to stay away from Ryuu Kimura.

It wasn't hard to keep our new relationship secret from Kenji. He might have passed down an edict for me not to associate with Ryuu, but he was never around and took no active interest in my life. When I first arrived, that was frustrating. Now, it was beneficial.

I could share secret kisses at the back of the after-school bus with Ryuu. I could hold hands with him under the water in the ICS hot tub after swim practice. When Ryuu and I weren't physically together, I could spend every waking moment texting with him. Kenji would never know.

I enjoyed this private little bubble Ryuu and I had

fallen into since our first kiss two weeks earlier. Having a boyfriend I adored was amazing. Having a boyfriend who was all mine because we'd mutually decided to keep our relationship to ourselves for the time being was surprisingly sexy. Every shared glance, every text exchange, every secret kiss felt like a delicious bond—us against the world, only the world didn't know.

Ryuu and I ate lunch together every day at school, but we didn't walk around ICS like we were a couple. We didn't want to flaunt it. Not because we were scared of the Ex-Brats, but because we loved the illicitness of keeping our relationship to ourselves, without the chatter of school gossip.

"I want to take you somewhere besides Tokyo once school is on holiday," Ryuu told me as we rode the Ginza line train through central Tokyo, on our way to Ueno Park. It was a half-day at school with no sports practices in the afternoon because of teacher meetings, so Ryuu was taking me sightseeing. The train wasn't that crowded, but I still pressed up close against his side as I sat next to him.

"Like where?" I asked him. I traced my thumb over the inside of his palm.

"Kyoto is one of the most beautiful cities in Japan. We could start there. Then we could go somewhere far from the city where it's quiet, like an *onsen ryokan*—that's like a Japanese-style inn where there are hot springs. There's so much more to Japan than what you see as an expat in Tokyo. There are mountains and lakes and—"

I pressed a kiss against the top of his arm. "And lions and tigers and . . ."

"Oh my!" we both said, and then laughed.

It was an awesome fantasy, to go away somewhere with Ryuu, but we both knew it was just that—a fantasy.

We exited the train at Ueno station and began walking toward the park, holding hands. It was a brisk day with the feel of early winter. Buildings were adorned with Christmas decorations, the leaves on the trees were mostly gone, and the air was chilly but not yet so cold that I could see my breath. The weather was just right for wearing my boyfriend's jacket over my school uniform, and loving that public showcase of mine-ness here where no one knew us, but all the people strolling the park would also have no doubt Ryuu and I were a couple.

"How come you know your way around so well?" I asked Ryuu as he expertly navigated us across a big street and then through the park entrance and on to a path across which I could see a pond at the end. "You never look at a map."

"I had to learn to be independent when all the bad stuff started happening with my dad. My parents were totally checked out. I was always on my own. I decided to explore, rather than sit in the house and wait for the news to get worse and worse."

I had noticed that young kids took public transit alone when they were still elementary school age. "It's nice that Tokyo feels like such a safe city. My mom never let me take DC Metro alone until I was fourteen. Of course, by then she was so checked out, I could have taken the train to New York City and she wouldn't have noticed. And Kenji couldn't care less where I go now."

"Sucks that we share that in common," said Ryuu.

"Agreed," I said. "Not all Japanese parents are like yours and Kenji, though, right?" I was also thinking about Akemi's nontraditional parents.

"Ours are definitely the exception to the rule. Japanese people are very traditional and family-oriented. You get a skewed perception at a school like ICS-Tokyo, where people are so wealthy and privileged."

"It doesn't feel like real life there," I admitted.

"Exactly," said Ryuu.

We reached the entrance to the pond area. Ryuu said, "This is Shinobazu Pond. In the summer, the water is covered in green plants with lotus blooms. It's pretty spectacular."

I clenched his hand. "You are a nerd. You know that?"

He smiled down at me, a flop of blue-black hair

covering the side of his face. "Aw, stop flattering me. Want to go on a boat ride?"

"I sure do!"

I thought he meant we'd take a city cruise along the river. Instead, we went through a turnstile in the park where small boats were lined up at a dock, available for rent.

"No!" I said. The boats were shaped like swans, with little cabins to climb into that looked like kids' covered wagons. So cheesy, so amazing.

"Yes!" he said.

He paid for our rental, and we stepped inside a pink swan pedal boat. "Do you have a license to operate this?" I teased.

"Only a license for . . . danger," he joked. He made a *VROOOM* sound, and then we both pressed onto the pedals. We zoomed away from the dock and out into the water at what felt like a turtle's pace. Leisurely, we swan-boated across the pond, surrounded by the park's trees and the city's tall buildings in the distance.

"You're kind of perfect," I said to him when we reached the middle of the pond and stopped our pedaling.

He leaned over to kiss me. "No, you are," he whispered.

I still hadn't told Ryuu that Kenji said I shouldn't associate with him.

And I never would.

Because I would never, ever let Kenji forbid me from seeing this magical boy.

. . .

"I don't want to go home," I told Ryuu as he walked me across the driveway to the entrance of Tak-Luxxe. I was so wrapped up in him, I didn't care how close we were to my building, where Lord Skyscraper, somewhere up in the clouds, would be displeased if he saw me bringing Ryuu home.

"Me neither."

"Want to hang out tomorrow?" I asked. The next day was Saturday. We could spend the whole day together.

"I wish. We're going to visit my grandmother in the countryside tomorrow. Maybe Sunday."

"Sunday Funday! Yes!"

We'd reached the end of the walkway. "Text me when you get upstairs," said Ryuu.

"I'll text you when I'm in the elevator."

"I'll text you when I'm back on the main street."

We both laughed, our hands still clasped together. I wasn't ready to kiss him good-bye here, in front of all the Tak-Luxxe employees. Instead, I gave Ryuu a friendly nudge on the shoulder and said, "Bye. Text you in five minutes."

Ryuu swept away a blue streak of hair that had fallen in front of his beautiful face. "See you," he said. He turned around and headed in the opposite direction, away from my fluttering heart.

When I looked up, Kim Takahara was standing at the taxi area. I'd been so enamored of Ryuu that I hadn't noticed her there. A bellhop blew a whistle and called out *"Takushi!"*

Kim asked me, "Was that Satoshi Kimura's son dropping you off?"

"Yup!" I said, giddy about Ryuu, and double giddy that it would piss off Kim. This thing between me and Ryuu was real. It was amazing. I hadn't intended to flaunt it at Tak-Luxxe, but I wasn't going to hide it either.

• • •

I was shocked when I reached the penthouse to find Kenji at home, at five o'clock in the evening. I'd never seen him home on a school day until after dinnertime, and then usually just to quickly drop me off after our meals together.

He didn't bother with hi. Instead, he said, "Satoshi Kimura's family cannot be seen here. My sister just messaged me to tell you not to bring that boy home from school. Is he your boyfriend?"

I came into the living room after changing my shoes, and when I sat down, I saw that there was a bottle of scotch on the side table next to where Kenji sat, a glass in his hand.

Fuck.

Okay, I'd try to react calmly and not blow up the way I wanted to.

I answered truthfully. "We're good friends. I like him a lot."

"He's dangerous to have as a friend. I told you not to associate with him."

Even though I wanted to explode with anger at Kenji, I managed to keep my voice steady and firm as I stated my case. "You can't tell me who I can and can't hang out with. I'll be friends with and date whomever I want, whether you like them or not. And you shouldn't hold Ryuu accountable for the sins of his father. That's ridiculous."

Kenji took a gulp from his glass.

Double fuck. Triple fuck. A million trillion fucks.

I was so angry at Kenji and Kim for saying Ryuu wasn't welcome here, but I restrained from further challenging Kenji. The drink in his hand was so much bigger a problem. I knew a Beast returning from the dark when I saw it.

Kenji said, "Why can't you go out with a boy like Nik

Zhzhonov? I saw how he looked at you at Parents' Night."
Oh, you mean before you left the event early? "It was obvious
he likes you."

"Well, I don't like him. In fact, he and Imogen and
their crowd have shut me out. We're not friends anymore."

Kenji shook his head. "That's very disappointing," he
said, without asking *why*, implying I was at fault.

What a fucking outrage. "I did kiss Nik once," I admitted. "But it turned out Nik thought it meant more than it
did. Did you know Alexei Zhzhonov's overprivileged son
is also into little date-rape games?"

"Don't say such terrible things!" Kenji slobbered. It
didn't seem to occur to him to ask, *Did he try to hurt you?* I
couldn't believe it. If I'd told Mom about this, even if she'd
been high out of her mind, she would have immediately
called the cops and had Nik arrested. Even when she was
wasted, her protective instinct was intact. Kenji had none.
I didn't have a chance to sputter an answer before he
added, "Maybe you living here isn't a good idea."

I didn't know if I was more upset that he was drunk
and defending Nik fucking Zhzhonov, or that I knew for
sure in this moment that Kenji would *never* be the knight
in shining armor I wanted him to be. His wealth and cha-
risma only masked his true self: a coward.

But he was a drunk coward I desperately didn't want
to leave. I'd only just started to feel settled. I was doing

well in school, even if I'd been excommunicated by the Ex-Brats. I had a good friend in Akemi, the official swim team competition would start in early spring, and Ryuu was here. Ryuu, Ryuu, Ryuu.

And, I wasn't prepared to be abandoned. Again. Even if I wasn't surprised by the possibility.

"I don't want to go," I stated plainly. I was tired of holding back what I really felt. "Even if you are a lousy father who cares more about working and appearances than getting to know the daughter you left behind, who so pathetically wants to be part of your life." It hurt so much to say it, but it also felt liberating. The truth was out there now, even if Kenji was so drunk he probably wouldn't even remember what I said.

He took another drink of his scotch. His face reddened, absorbing the impact of the booze or what I'd said, or both. His phone buzzed. He looked at the message and then stood up. "I have to return to work. We'll discuss your options tomorrow."

Kenji left the apartment.

Hell no.

I wasn't leaving Japan. I refused to be a disposable daughter.

chapter thirty-eight

I returned to my room to text Ryuu, but I had several messages on my phone from Akemi, asking me to meet her in Ikebana Café immediately. I went up to the restaurant, which was humming with dinner patrons. I found Akemi sitting at the bench that circled the giant ikebana tree in the center of the room. She had a stack of takeout food containers sitting next to her.

"What's going on?" I asked her. She looked both sad and agitated.

"I'm so glad you saw my messages. I came down here to get some food for the plane. My mother will be here any second. We're leaving."

"Where are you going?"

"We're leaving Tokyo." She could barely get the words out. She looked like she was about to cry.

"For the weekend?"

"No. We're going to Brazil. To stay with my mother's brother there."

No way! "You're leaving, like, this minute? How come you didn't say anything before?"

"I only just found out. I came home from school today and Mother said we're leaving. Father has business trouble. His money has been frozen by the banks. The police are going to arrest him."

Holy shit! "For what?" Akemi took an English-language newspaper from her backpack and handed it to me. It was folded open to an article about the Japanese government's case against crime lord Takeo Kinoshita for money laundering and drug trafficking.

Oh my God.

The few times I'd seen him, Akemi's father seemed like a nice enough old guy—at least for a man who kept families in different cities. I thought having two unreliable addicts for parents was tough. Poor Akemi. "I'm so sorry, Akemi. Did you know?"

She shrugged. "It was like I knew but pretended I didn't." I totally understood. That was exactly how I felt when the Beast took over Mom's life, and mine by extension. I knew it was going to end badly, but I pretended as long as I could that we would be okay. Just like I was probably doing with Kenji right now.

Akemi's mother arrived, carrying a travel bag. I saw the bellhop waiting in the lobby behind her with four large suitcases. She spoke to Akemi in Japanese and smiled at me for the first time. I didn't know she was capable of a smile—and now, of all times.

I couldn't help myself. Japanese people weren't huggers, but I grabbed Akemi into a hug anyway, and squeezed hard. "Text me when you get there. Okay? We'll stay in touch. Always."

Tears streamed down Akemi's cheeks. She nodded. "Let's be friends forever."

"You can't get rid of me," I said, feeling myself choking up.

Her mother extended her hand, and Akemi stood up and took it. "Bye, Elle," she said. They followed the bellhop to the elevator, and Akemi was gone.

Everything in my life the last few years had prepared me for this sudden shock, but that didn't make the sadness any less powerful. I knew better than to think anything good, like a privileged life in Tokyo, could last. Today should have been one of the brightest days of my life. I liked a cute boy. He liked me back. I had *just* been daydreaming about our future together. Now it felt like everything was crashing down around me. That sinking feeling was made worse when Tak Luxxe's jack-of-all-trades employee Dev Flaherty approached me. His face appeared grim as he saw the newspaper article Akemi had left behind on the bench. "Crazy stuff, eh?" he said.

"Basically," I said. Crazy and wrong and unfair that whatever crimes her father had committed, Akemi's life had to be totally upended.

As if I didn't feel bad enough, Dev said, "Kim Takahara just called the concierge desk. She's looking for you. I said I spotted you up here. She asked if you'd meet her in Mrs. Takahara's suite."

Great. Just what I needed right now. But everything was shit anyway. I stood up, knowing it was about to get worse. The storm had turned to a cyclone.

• • •

When I arrived at Mrs. Takahara's apartment, tea service had been set up in the living room, with fine china and beautiful little cookies arranged on a tray. It was like they were having a tea party for the girl I suspected they were about to throw to the lions.

Mrs. Takahara sat regally in her side chair, with Kim sitting on a chair opposite her, and me in the middle, on the sofa. I didn't dare touch the tea or cookies. I was so nervous I was sure I'd spill the tea or barf up the cookies.

Kim said, "Thank you for coming, Elle. I think it's time we speak frankly."

I gulped and nodded. Mrs. Takahara sipped from her teacup and let Kim do the talking.

"I presume you saw Kenji this evening?"

"Yes," I said.

"Then I presume you could see he was drinking. Unfortunately, this isn't an isolated incident."

"I know he's had alcohol problems in the past," I said. "I'm sure it's just a onetime lapse. He'll be fine!" How fucked-up that I was trying to defend him, when he was doing nothing to protect me.

Kim shook her head. "It's more than a temporary lapse. He's been drinking privately for the past few weeks."

"How do you know that?" I said.

Mrs. Takahara spoke up. "I pay employees to watch him and tell me." That made total sense. She seemed like exactly the kind of person who would do something like that to her own son.

Kim said, "As you may have noticed, the environment at Tak-Luxxe has been tense with the government audit. The pressure is too much for my brother, in my opinion."

Since we were speaking frankly, it seemed like the best time to ask what I really wanted to know. "Is he yakuza?"

Mrs. Takahara's eyes could have burned a hole in me. She and Kim started speaking rapidly in Japanese. The conversation sounded heated. Finally, Kim said to me, "While Mother doesn't consider that a polite question to ask, the answer is no. However, Kenji did make some improper financial deals with Mr. Kinoshita, which are having a ripple effect on Tak-Luxxe now that Mr. Kinoshita is being indicted."

"Whoa" was all I could say. Did that make Kenji a criminal? Or an accessory to a crime?

Kim said, "Kenji is going to need to take a leave of absence from the company to address the improprieties. And sort out his own life." She looked to Mrs. Takahara and nodded.

Mrs. Takahara reached for a binder on the table next to her. She picked it up and handed it to me. "Options in America for you," she said.

I took the binder and opened it. It was filled with laminated brochures for boarding schools in America.

So, Kenji was a crook and a drunk, and because of that, I was going to have no home.

I decided to go for broke and say what I really felt. What did I have to lose? I looked at Mrs. Takahara and addressed her in a manner I thought she'd possibly appreciate. It killed me to speak so openly and without anger to this person I didn't like, when my heart and mind both felt like exploding from stress. "I would like to respectfully ask to stay. I like my school and I like my life here, but it's not about the privileges you've so kindly given me. It's about wanting to connect more with my Japanese heritage. I admire the work ethic here, the order and the sense of duty, the kindness of the people." *Except for you,* I didn't add to Mrs. Takahara. "I promise I won't be any trouble." *Except that I will never accept your unfair dismissal of Ryuu Kimura. You just need to get to know him!* "I'd like the opportunity to know my own culture better. I'd like to know *you* better, and be part of your lives."

I knew I sounded like a pathetic suck-up, but I actually meant what I said.

Mrs. Takahara and Kim spoke in Japanese again. Damn it, I needed to learn this language already. Then Kim said to me, "We appreciate your wanting to be connected with your Japanese heritage and family. That's very admirable. It's unfortunate that the timing of you being here is so bad. We are too focused on the crisis at the business. We can't be the family that you'd want us to be right now. If you look through the brochures, you'll see we found some nice schools in Maryland and Pennsylvania so you could be near to your mother. Of course we will pay for your education and make sure you are able to visit with her."

We all knew that was a guilt payoff on their part. But I didn't get a chance to tell them that, because Kenji came through the front door and then hustled into the living room without even changing his shoes. I could smell the alcohol on his breath before he was even close to me. His hair was disheveled, his shirt and tie loose, his eyes bloodshot. He looked like hell. If he was at a level-five drunk when I saw him an hour or so ago, now he was at an eight or nine.

"Oh, so now you're all meeting without me!" he said in English.

Mrs. Takahara stood up and started berating him in Japanese.

He didn't answer her but turned to me when his mother was finished. He said, "She's right. I missed too many years with you. Maybe now it's too late."

"It's not!" I cried out.

I'd never felt more betrayed. Not when the Beast consumed my mother and she lost our house and her negligence caused Hufflepuff to die, or when she was arrested and sent to jail, and I was the collateral damage sent to foster care. I wanted to die of shame—for *him*.

In English, Mrs. Takahara said, "Kenji, your daughter should not be here. You are no good for her."

Kim said, "I'm afraid I have to agree. I regret encouraging Kenji to try this experiment. I know he wanted to be part of your life, but Kenji's clearly not able to be a father."

"I'm not *an experiment!*" I said.

Kenji sank down onto the couch and put his head in his hands. Then he looked back up at me and said, "They're right, Elle. You should go back to America."

chapter thirty-nine

Absolutely not.

I wasn't ready to leave Japan.

I *refused* to leave Ryuu.

My deadbeat father and his family who appeared out of nowhere after sixteen years didn't get to decide where I was going. Nobody but me should be allowed to be the architect of my destiny. *I* decided where I was going, and that place was: I didn't know, long term. But short term: anywhere away from Tak-Luxxe.

I texted Ryuu. I have to get out of here. Everything is falling apart. He texted back, Where do you want to go? I said, Anywhere quiet and far from Tokyo. Fifteen minutes later he texted me that he had a plan and I should meet him at Tokyo Station.

"So we're runaways?" Ryuu asked when I found him on the train platform.

"I guess," I said.

He pulled me to him and held me close. "What happened?"

We boarded the train and I told him what had happened with Akemi and Kenji. I didn't know where we were going, and I didn't care.

Once we were settled on the train, I texted Uncle Masa:

I just want you to know I'm okay. I don't know where I'm going, but I'm with a friend and we are safe.

Kenji didn't deserve the courtesy of knowing how or what I was doing, but I knew Uncle Masa would be upset when they told him I was gone, and I wanted him to be reassured, even if I myself was anything but assured I would ultimately be okay. But for now, with Ryuu at my side, at least I was with someone who cared about me.

As the train traveled away from Tokyo, I fell asleep with my head on Ryuu's shoulder. I don't know how many hours I slept, but it was early morning when Ryuu woke me. "Time to get off," he said.

We exited the train in a city called Ishinomaki. "Where to now?" I asked him.

"A taxi to the ferry," he said.

It was a quick taxi ride to the ferry terminal, where we boarded a boat with a mermaid painted on it. "Where exactly are we going?" I asked Ryuu.

"To a small island called Tashirojima. I didn't know where to take you, and then I had this sudden impulse about where we could go to *really* get away. Cat Island."

"I don't believe you."

"You will when there are hundreds of cats prowling all around you."

It was exactly the distraction I needed. Frivolous and simple. A world away from Tokyo. There was too much to think about and I wanted to think about none of it. The sea breeze on the morning ferry now felt cold and welcome—an excellent wake-up. After a forty-minute ride from Ishinomaki, we got off the boat at Nitoda Port. Ryuu said, "I read about this place on my phone while you were asleep. It's one of two tiny villages on Tashirojima. The islanders take care of the cats, who outnumber the people about six to one. There aren't schools or restaurants here. Just old people and lots of kitties."

"I already love this place."

As we walked off the plank, we were greeted by a swarm of felines that clearly knew the boat's arrival time. There were cats stretched out on the dock, cats lounging in the morning sun, cats playing and fighting one another, and cats cleaning themselves. Calicos, tabbies, tuxedoes, ginger, and black cats. At the end of the dock were crates that had been converted into blanket-covered little cat apartments. Tails stuck out from inside the shelters. The few buildings on the street were adorned with graffiti of cats.

A Japanese tourist couple also getting off the boat were more prepared than us—they had bonito flake treats to dole out to the felines. But the local fishermen sorting their wares in sheds by the road were the real treat-givers. They threw out small fish to the cats. The lucky cats on the receiving end pranced by us with fish heads and tails sticking out from either side of their mouths.

I crouched down and held my hand out for any kitties who wanted to smell my fingers. A friendly calico came to me, sniffed, decided he or she liked the smell, and rubbed against my leg. "Sorry I don't have treats for you!" I told it as it let me rub its head.

"Are you hungry?" Ryuu asked.

"God, yes." After all the stress and upheaval last night, I thought I wouldn't have an appetite, but I was surprised to find I was starving.

"Me too. There's only vending machines and one store, so let's stock up now before we walk across the island."

There were more cats gathered on the steps of the island's lone store, Kamabutsu Shoten, where we bought waters, chips, and candy, and *onigiri,* which are rice balls. We lounged on the steps with the kitties, fortifying with snacks, then set off to see the island. Was Kenji wondering where I was? Did he care?

Narrow roads and walking trails crisscrossed the forested island's interior. Under the canopy of so many trees, with few humans to be seen and cats darting in and out between trees, I felt calmed. And happy. All hell had broken loose back in Tokyo, but I was wandering Cat Island with the awesomest guy, who held my hand as we walked and didn't break the calm with idle chatter. Like me, he appreciated a good silence. That was the way to hear the birds chirping, the trees swishing, the cats meowing—the perfect sounds to drown the anxieties in my head about what was happening back at Tak-Luxxe.

The main path led uphill, where we saw houses built at the higher altitude. Around midday, we found Nekokamisama—an actual cat shrine. It was a small out-door area about the size of a large bedroom, partitioned by a red fence, with a proper torii gate leading into it, and red flags with Japanese lettering on them heralding the entrance. Through the gate were several boulders sur-rounding two-tiered surfaces, on which people had left offerings—rocks with cat faces painted on them, little maneki-neko statues, and of course, Hello Kitty dolls.

Ryuu translated a placard explaining the cat shrine.

"It says this shrine was a resting place for an island cat who was killed by a falling rock. The fishermen built it to honor the cats."

"Let's get married here," I joked. The site was legit enchanted.

Ryuu said, "We can serve our guests tuna from cans and bowls of milk." My knees nearly buckled.

"And catnip-flavored wedding cake." We both made horrified faces. "Too gross. Sorry."

We hit the trail again. When we'd reached the top of the island, we had a clear view to the ocean surrounding it. The best sighting, though, was the cat-shaped buildings overlooking the prime ocean view. They were small cottages painted in red-and-white stripes, with ear-shaped roofs, and window holes for eyes, and doors painted with noses and mouths, with whiskers painted on the sides of the doors.

"These cottages are the only lodging on the island," said Ryuu. "They have tatami mats for beds, and bathrooms, and that's pretty much it."

"Can we stay here tonight?"

"They're closed this time of the year."

"You mean we have to go back to the real world?"

"Yes." He clenched my hand. "But we can come back in a few years when they're open, for our honeymoon," Ryuu joked.

· · ·

"When did you know you liked me?" I asked Ryuu. We were back on the mermaid boat, returning to Ishinomaki, where we'd find a youth hostel to spend the night. I had decided not to turn my phone back on to see messages until we got off the boat, to put off the reality check as long as possible. I wondered if the Takaharas had even noticed I was gone yet.

We sat outside on the rear of the boat, wind whipping around us, huddled against each other for warmth.

"When you practically killed me with the car door getting out of the Bentley on your first day at ICS. What about you?"

"When you came up from the water in the lane next to mine on my first day swimming at ICS, and said finally there was someone at school who was as good a swimmer as you."

"I said that?"

"You did!"

"And you still liked me?"

I kissed him as my answer. For everything wrong and tragic about my life back in Tokyo, so much of what was right about it was here in Ryuu Kimura.

When our lips let go, he turned serious. "What will

you do if your father really tries to send you back to America?"

"I don't know. I need to talk to Uncle Masa. He'll help me, I'm pretty sure. I can't go back to the life I had before I came to Japan."

"Was it bad?"

"It wasn't good. I mean, when my mom was at her worst, I used to have to steal money from her wallet to buy food, otherwise neither of us would have eaten. But foster care was worse. Living with strangers who resented me. Dirty places, mean people. I'm sure the Takaharas would send me to a good boarding school in America, but I don't want that life, either. It would be so lonely."

"I won't let that happen."

"I can take care of myself." I appreciated him wanting to protect me, but in the end, as always, I knew only I could protect myself. That's how it had been my whole teenage life.

"I know you can. But I'm here for you."

We shared another kiss as night started to fall and the boat docked back in Ishinomaki.

When we got off the boat, Uncle Masa was waiting for us at the ferry terminal landing.

chapter forty

"I was in Osaka on business when Kim called me and told me what was going on."

"How'd you find us?" I asked Uncle Masa. He looked perfectly businesslike in a navy suit, but exhausted, like he hadn't slept in two days.

"The police tracked you here through your credit card. Kim chartered a private flight for me to come retrieve you."

I'd used my Amex card to buy my ferry tickets. It didn't occur to me that I could be so easily traced through it. It also never occurred to me that the Takaharas would care enough to look so hard for me. I wasn't sure whether I was relieved or pissed.

"Where's Kenji?" I asked.

"Sobering up to welcome you home."

"Really? I have a home?"

"Your home is in Tokyo."

. . .

"Will you be okay?" I asked Ryuu.

We were standing in the driveway at Tak-Luxxe, where a taxi waited to return Ryuu to his own home.

He smiled and my heart melted. "I'll be fine," he said unconvincingly. "My parents will be mad, then go back to ignoring me and being miserable."

I kissed him. In plain view, for anyone at Tak-Luxxe to see. He was here, he was mine, and I would *never* accept him being anything less than warmly welcomed on this property. "Thank you," I whispered into his ear.

After Ryuu left, I returned to Kenji's penthouse. There was a family meeting taking place in the living room, with Uncle Masa, Kim, and Mrs. Takahara waiting for me there. There were no cries of "Thank God you're safe, Elle!" or "We're so sorry you felt the need to run away!"

No. There was tea and a nice assortment of Japanese confections beautifully arranged on a tray and a quiet acknowledgment that everything was different, but somehow, I'd made my point.

"Where's Kenji?" I asked.

"Meeting with a doctor to discuss a treatment plan,"

said Kim. She looked pointedly at me, and for the first time—from the gentleness in her voice and the concern expressed in her eyes—I felt she looked at me as a niece and not a stranger. "He is genuinely sorry about what he said to you before he left. He doesn't really want you to return to America. But he is very aware that he does not know how to be a father."

"I don't know how to be his daughter," I admitted. "But I want to try."

"He does, too," said Mrs. Takahara, to my surprise. "We had a family talk after you left to decide how to proceed. We know we *all* need to try."

Like a therapist or just someone very experienced with diplomacy, Uncle Masa served us all tea and said, "We're happy you're home, Elle. We all have amends to make. Who would like to start?"

No one said anything.

So Uncle Masa said, "I'll start. I should have tried to be here more often when you came to Tokyo, for consistency and transition. I've fixed that now. I'm coming to work for Takahara Industries. I'll be taking over Kim's old job and living in a suite on the forty-sixth floor. My home will always be your home, too." The prospect of having Uncle Masa so close was beyond comforting.

"You may call me *obaasan*," Mrs. Takahara said. I

knew from Imogen once talking about her own Japanese grandmother that Mrs. Takahara was asking me to call her the formal Japanese word for someone else's grandmother and not *sobo* for someone's own grandmother, but it was a start. I appreciated that she was trying.

Kim said, "Mother and I would like you to start joining our weekly matcha tea ceremony."

I was secretly pleased but didn't want to give her that satisfaction, so I didn't let it show. I said, "I'd like for you to be who you are."

"What does that mean?" Kim asked.

"Be out and be proud" was all I said.

Kim looked surprised, and Uncle Masa and Obaasan looked clueless. Kim answered me in Japanese.

"What's that supposed to mean?" I said, feeling wary.

Kim said, "You'll know soon enough. We've arranged for you to start taking Japanese lessons with a tutor after the New Year. If you're going to be one of us, you should speak our language."

"I'm proud of *you*," said Obaasan out of nowhere. "You are a strong girl. You talk back too much, but you're smart."

I said, "Thank you, Obaasan. If I'm strong and smart, maybe I got some of that from you."

She nodded, as if to say, *Well, duh.*

Suddenly, Tak-Luxxe seemed so much less like a castle prison. It felt like a home, with all the glory and awkwardness of a flawed family.

For the first time here, it felt like a true fresh start for me.

* * *

Uncle Masa had brokered some kind of peace in the Takahara family. I would never be privy to what he'd said and how he'd fought for me to stay, but he'd persevered and won. He arranged for Kenji to start an outpatient alcohol recovery program during his leave of absence from work. Kenji would go there during the day and be home with me at night. Uncle Masa had convinced Mrs. Takahara and Kim that the potential "shame" of people knowing of Kenji's addiction would be better than all of us living with the consequences of not dealing with it. Kim would be stepping into Kenji's job permanently. She'd be the first female CEO of Takahara Industries. Kenji would support *her* when he returned to work, and not the other way around. Maybe the company would survive the government audit and Kinoshita scandal; maybe it wouldn't. Certainly with Kim leading it, Takahara Industries had a better chance not to go directly into bankruptcy.

My job in the family would be to resume my life at Tak-Luxxe and ICS-Tokyo. I liked that offer.

When I returned to my bedroom after the family meeting, I finally turned my phone back on. There was a message on it from Imogen Kato.

Hey. I heard what happened with Akemi. Fuuuuck! And I heard you ran off with Ryuu Kimura? I hope all this scandal doesn't mean my favorite expat is returning to America, because things are only just starting to get interesting. Arabella finally told us (and her family) why she really left for Bolivia. I guess what I want to say is: I'm sorry. I was a jerk. PS— Nik's been iced out and Arabella's family has hired a lawyer to press charges against him.

I rolled my eyes in Imogen style. The Ex-Brats were so shallow and stupid, but I couldn't deny I liked Imogen. And I was proud of Arabella for speaking up.

I sat down at my computer to write a letter to Mom, when a knock came at my door. I opened it and saw Kenji standing in the hallway, next to a box on the floor that was covered in a blanket with a bow on top.

"For you," he said. He looked sober but tired. The devil I knew. "I ask for your forgiveness. I never wanted you to feel like you were an experiment here. You are my daughter. I will learn to be a father. I want to do better."

"I want to do better, too," I said. I was still sore but also hugely relieved. I wanted to stay and try for us to build a life as a family. I wanted to be honest with him and I wanted to support him through his troubles. "What's in the box?"

"Open it."

I removed the blanket. There was a cage beneath it.

With a cat inside.

I opened the cage and the sweetest black kitten emerged, meowing. I picked up the soft, furry angel and snuggled it under my chin.

"What should we call him?" Kenji asked.

"Ravenclaw," I answered.

I remembered a Japanese expression that Akemi had taught me. *Neko no uojitai*, to describe a cat refusing fish. She said it was a phrase used to describe someone pretending they didn't want something they'd eventually break down and just take.

I didn't want to deny what I'd hoped for my whole life.

For the first time, I hugged Kenji. After the slightest hesitation, he hugged me back.

My imperfect, alcoholic, charming, generous father.